THE JAM MAKER

ALSO BY JEN GASH

The Last Drop

Bored

Coaching Creativity

Enabling Positive Change (Co-author)

THE JAM MAKER

J E GASH

The Jam Maker

ISBN: 978-1-0684419-0-5

Jen Gash is a writer, life-long artist and occupational therapist. She started to paint large scale oil paintings at 15 years old but opted for a 'safer' career as an occupational therapist. Jen continued to paint alongside her day job and raising a family until she won Sky Arts Landscape Artist of the Year in 2018. Since then, she has been a professional artist but found that painting more also made her write more. So here we are!

For Peter M.

You never doubted my creativity. Thank you for everything.

ACKNOWLEDGMENTS

Ten years ago I published my first book. It was an academic text about creativity and the process was so painful, I vowed never to write another book. But here I am, having finished book four and shortly finishing book five.

I still don't think of myself as a writer though. I always have been and always will be an artist. Writing that first book on creativity taught me an important lesson – we all have our own brand of creativity and mine is not content with being pigeonholed. Over the years I have also learnt that I need to be completely immersed in whatever creative activity my ridiculous soul has chosen, so whilst writing The Jam Maker my cavasses, brushes and paints have been neglected.

The lack of painting has made me grumpy, so my first acknowledgement is for my long-suffering husband Jeff. He was also worried about his safety after reading The Jam Maker, so I also apologise for the stress this may have caused him. Jeff also deserves huge thanks as he was the reason I continued writing The Jam Maker. He never reads books but took the first few chapters on holiday and insisted I carry on. It was such an endorsement from a man who has only read three books in his lifetime - how could I not finish it?

Thanks also for the huge encouragement from my early readers Rachel Knowles, Chris Hill, Angie Shipp and Jillie Gash. You are all angels. And Janey, I know you will get round to reading it one day!

Two other people need acknowledging. About twelve years ago I meet Peter Mayes, a fantastic coach who quickly became a great friend. We worked on several ideas together, including a project called The Artist and The Engineer, which blossomed from our joint love of creativity and fun approaches to coaching. Peter was also a great writer, mostly of coaching and work-related texts but was super proud of his wife Christine's successful second career as an author. 'There's nothing Chris doesn't know about writing and publishing' he told me, and he was right.

Pete sadly passed away at the end of 2023 and it was around this time that I started writing The Jam Maker. Anxious to have some feedback, I sent a draft to Christine who, much to my relief, liked it and agreed to edit it. Christine, you had your work cut out - I can't thank you enough. In his absence Peter played a role too, as he never wavered in his belief in my creativity. I owe you both so much.

WARNING: Unsurprisingly this book contains some sensitive issues including suicide, physical and emotional abuse and just a tiny bit of murder…

ONE

Verity had not had a good night. She had been invited to be the guest speaker at a large organisation known for its dubious reputation regarding its female employees. She guessed that was the exact reason she was invited to speak, as if her presence might somehow demonstrate a commitment to equality and that they valued their female workforce. In Verity's opinion it hadn't worked, and she had squirmed throughout the evening, too frequently finding she had to keep her mouth shut during conversations of all kinds.

Thankfully tonight's activity was a rare downside to her job of the past twenty-five years with The Women's League. There were many environments where she could speak freely, often vociferously, but this was not one of them. If she had been at *Sisters for Change* or *Women in Business* it would have been a different matter, but the evening had left her bubbling with anger. All the years she had spent speaking, writing, and advocating for women and yet it sometimes felt she was back in a 1970s sitcom – the sort of sitcom that the BBC no longer dared to air. Most of the men tonight had given her a wide berth, but the ones that did speak to her were clearly guarding their words. As soon as they moved on, Verity could see the change in their posture and speech and even heard one of them call a waitress sweetheart.

Verity had been told that the dress code for the evening was black tie, meaning men would be sporting tuxedos and women would mostly be in long dresses. Well, that was never going to happen, so she chose to wear a tuxedo herself, with a cummerbund of bright green silk. She had worn her auburn hair short for many years, but this evening she had dyed her now greying hair a bright orange to offset her outfit and topped it off with large, dangling peacock earrings. She looked stunning and, to many probably a little scary; if she couldn't say what she wanted, her appearance would have to speak for her. Thankfully she had only been asked to talk for five or six minutes and then give out the awards. She could manage such a short speech and had carefully crafted some brief paragraphs which, to those in the know, spoke to the continued lack of women in senior positions, the gender pay gap, and the passive emotional abuse that still happened in most workplaces. She reckoned that ninety percent of the audience wouldn't get it. Her references were intelligent, and she spoke with a humorous lilt that covered over the furious underlying bite.

She was a master craftsman, well, craftswoman.

Back in the taxi now, Verity felt exhausted and more than a bit irritated. She took off her cummerbund, ruffled her auburn hair and took a long breath. The show she had put on for the evening was over and she wanted to scream. She hated not being herself and hated that whatever she did or said as a powerful woman would be judged. She hated the comments that had been jokily made about her outfit. She hated the gammon who proliferated these types of organisations. She loved this new use of the word gammon, which referred to men who had a ruddy, pudgy, sweaty appearance, whose sentences started with things like 'back in my day, we wouldn't have stood for this…' or 'all this woke nonsense, in the good old days…' or 'if I was in charge, I would line them all up and …'.

What never ceased to amaze her was that without exception, these men always had incredibly beautiful women by their side. Women who, without fail, were much better looking than their husbands, and clearly much better at hiding their opinions than Verity could ever be. Verity would often make a beeline to chat to these women and encourage them to join The Women's League. She hoped that spending time with women who had their own income, their own business or at least lives that didn't revolve around their pudgy-faced husbands, might empower them. That these beautiful, intelligent women would up and leave their gammon-faced men or at least stop pandering to them quite as much.

At least tonight, most of the men seemed harmless, but you never knew what happened behind closed doors. In her opinion, feminism had changed very little in the world, so over the last fifteen years she had resorted to different tactics.

Her pocket vibrated and she took out an old mobile phone. She glanced down to read the text message, smiled, then turned off the phone.

TWO

Living in a suburb of anywhere, let alone Swindon, had never been part of Bridget Sullivan's life plan. In fact, when she thought about Swindon for too long, she started to scratch the skin on her hands which were constantly dry from using turpentine and oil paint every day. Bridget Sullivan was an artist. A middle-aged, middle-class artist and just like many female artists throughout history, Bridget felt invisible and being stuck in Little Bampton didn't help.

Little Bampton was once a village in the rambling Wiltshire countryside but these days it struggled to hold on to its village identity. For the past thirty years, new housing had gobbled up farmland and Little Bampton was no longer little and now attached to Swindon by rows of badly built, identical houses.

However she felt about the place, Bridget had a lovely studio at the end of her cottage garden and had made Little Bampton her home for over twenty-five years, raising her children who had now flown the nest. It was never intended to be a forever home, she had never believed in such things, but as so often happens, the longer they had stayed the harder it was to up sticks and move. Now they were firmly embedded in suburbia with Bridget wriggling like a worm trapped on a fisherman's hook. She desperately wanted to move but her husband seemed dead set on staying put until he retired.

Bridget survived by squirrelling money away for small adventures. These adventures included various painting trips, artist residences and courses, which Bridget hoped would break her out of suburban Swindon regularly enough to stop her from going completely mad. And if she were to be completely honest, Bridget Sullivan was no stranger to madness.

Just as Bridget had to compromise about where she lived, once in her studio she continued to make compromises. Despite her love of landscapes, she spent much of her time painting portraits of egotistical, wealthy people and it seemed that the only landscape paintings that sold, were ones that suited magnolia walls.

This pissed her off no end.

In Bridget's opinion, her husband earned more than enough money for her to turn down work that she didn't enjoy or value. However, her husband didn't agree and would make frequent, pointed comments about the lack of luxuries in his life. Bridget didn't really understand this at all. To her, finding a pair of trousers without paint stains on them was a luxury and if she made it through the day without breaking or spilling something, she considered the day a success. So, it was with an ongoing feeling of resignation tinged with resentment, that Bridget accepted the occasional portrait commission. Luckily the dreaded commissions were well paid, more so than she ever told her husband. This meant she only needed to accept two or three a year, spreading the income over the intervening period, allowing her to focus on her true love of landscape painting.

It was sitting with this unfulfilled yearning for the land and the sea, that she was counting down the days until she finished the portrait of Professor Micheal Donahue, her current commission. She'd been working on it for the past two months, not enjoyed much of the portrait process and it had taken quite a push to get it finished. Now she had declared it complete, in her opinion at least, she quickly put it in the store cupboard in her studio and firmly shut the door. This was the only way to stop her tinkering with it and arguing with the person's painted image. This arguing was imaginary and mostly happened inside her head but sometimes, especially if the conversation got excitable or heated, she would talk out loud.

No one knew that she talked to the portraits, well she didn't think anyone knew and if they did, no one ever said anything to her.

The conversations she had with the paintings varied massively depending on who was sitting for the portrait in question. Some people were more interesting than others, some listened better than others and some had far too much to say for Bridget's liking. If the person in the painting had a helpful voice, offered useful suggestions or was supportive, they were allowed to hang on the studio wall in between times. However, if they were too noisy or just too annoying, the portrait would be put out of sight. This particular quirk was just one of many things about herself that Bridget kept hidden from others, including her husband. Talking to yourself was one thing, but talking, often arguing with a painting was quite another.

Professor Donahue's portrait had always needed to be locked way in the cupboard between painting sessions. He was a loudly spoken and over-opinionated dean of a local university, with a background in chemistry, who seemed to think Bridget wouldn't understand anything to do with science. He also had some questionable relationships with various large chemical companies around the world and despite stating unequivocally that they were ethical and environmentally friendly, Bridget wasn't stupid. Although she tried to have some sort of criteria about who she would and would not paint, Donahue had been a bit of a borderline case. She had said yes mostly because she was short on money and had her eye on a painting residency later in the year, so perhaps she wasn't as principled as she liked to think.

Outside of random conversations about the state of further education, far too much time and energy during the sittings were spent discussing the large, hairy mole on side of Donahue's face. He had wanted to take the opportunity of the portrait, to have it *removed* as such, saying, 'Oh, let's leave it out, shall we?' as he gave Bridget an unpleasant smile which seemed to say, 'You are getting paid a lot, so please do as you're told.'

Bridget had tried to explain, far too many times, that it

was a hugely recognisable feature, and it wouldn't be a good portrait if she just ignored it. She would paint the mole back in and, without fail at the end of every sitting, Donahue would walk over, pick up a rag and rub it out, right in front of her. During the final sitting, she decided to let him think he had won and didn't paint it back in, but once he had left, the mole returned, albeit a little less prominent than it really was. What did the silly man think? If he had been from a different part of the world, the mole might have been considered a sign of beauty and no one in their right mind would think to exclude it from a painting or edit it out of a photograph.

With Donahue safely in the cupboard, she breathed a sigh of relief and relished the immediate silence in her studio. She had the whole afternoon to get out into the countryside before preparing for her weekly art group, another concession she had made to bringing in some regular money. Packing a rucksack with a flask, some materials and grabbing a sketch book, she looked out of the window, dismayed to see it had just started to rain – not just any rain but the sort that had come out of nowhere and darkened the sky so much that people had turned on their car headlights. Ten years ago, she might have still gone out and put up with the weather, but right now she felt tired. The Donahue portrait had taken a lot of energy to finish, and she decided to be kind to herself. She put the kettle on, watched a painting programme on the telly before working on something else in the studio.

THREE

Formed just a year earlier than the Women's Institute and not to be confused with the American Woman's League, or the Women's Football Super League, The Women's League of Great Britain and Ireland to give it its full name, had been established early in 1914. Just six months before the outbreak of the First World War. Perhaps its founders had somehow known what was coming and that the lives of women, and of course men, would never be the same again. During that hideous war, women lost their husbands, sons, fathers, nephews, uncles, and friends and they came together to support each other. It was also a time of change in other ways too, with the suffragette movement gaining ground, women in the UK were starting to be seen and heard.

Although a year older than the Women's Institute, the League was not so well known amongst ordinary women. They had far more money than the Women's Institute with

League members including wealthy businesswomen, peers and the occasional politician. This of course, was after women had finally made it into politics. They were also more secretive than the Women's Institute. Not as secretive as the Free Masons with their funny handshakes, The Women's League had and still have, many fingers in many pies, and many secrets.

Today, with over fifty branches in the UK, slightly fewer than the Women's Institute but no one likes to admit it, the League welcomes women from all walks of life. To its regular members it is a source of friendship, support, and learning. If you join The Women's League these days, it's doubtful there would be much singing and certainly no hymns. Cakes are sometimes still baked and preserves and pickles might be made to raise funds. More likely there would be investment clubs, business support, and political, environmental or philosophical debates. And of course, gin and coffee has mostly replaced tea and biscuits.

Just like its weekly activities, leadership of the League had changed over the years too. These days the organisation was led by a highly paid executive, supported by a well-paid and dedicated team, based in their London headquarters. The head of the league would hold the post for maybe ten or twelve years, perhaps leaving with a golden handshake and later receive acknowledgement from the King in his New Year's Honours list.

But the last twenty-five years had been quite different. The formidable Verity Scanlan has successfully held the top job at The Women's League, taking it from strength to strength around the globe and increased its profile without resorting to making a wall calendar of nearly topless women.

FOUR

It was still raining. It had been raining solidly for four days now. In fact, when Bridget thought about it, it felt like it had been raining since her birthday which was months ago. The birthday barbeque in September, with friends and family, seemed so long ago. It had been a pleasant afternoon which her husband managed to turn into a boozy party stretching into the early hours of the next day. When she thought about it, most of the friends at her birthday barbecue were his friends, not hers. This was nothing new. He loved living in Little Bampton and had lots of friends. Some he met at the pub, some at the sailing club and some as part of a men's club – not the one with funny handshake, a less secretive one which still only admitted men.

When they first moved to the village as it was back then, Bridget had quickly made a good clutch of friends, mostly mums in the school playground who met for coffee after the morning drop off. Those friendships had faded as the kids grew up and the mums didn't have to walk them to school. More friendships dwindled as mums returned to work and had little time for a coffee and catch up. These days she only had a couple of good friends and there was a reluctant understanding that they might only see each other once or twice a year. Most of the conversations circled around the varying stages of the menopause, how busy and exhausted they all were, how frustrated that not only were they now working full-time but still did most of the housework and now were supporting elderly parents. Whenever these same old topics bubbled up, Bridget wondered what the early feminists would think of this unintended outcome which saw women now doing twice as much work as before, and still not being paid as much as men.

In some ways, not having a lot of friends suited Bridget. Since becoming a professional artist, she had realised that you couldn't paint and have a busy social life. For years she had resisted becoming a full-time artist, not wanting to risk becoming the mad, penniless, recluse that society seemed to think artists were. The *mad artist* myth had been debunked but similar to other creative pursuits, painting was essentially a solitary and rather isolating activity. Sometimes days or weeks alone in the studio were needed to produce half decent work that could confidently sit alongside other professional artists' works. Perhaps that's why she talked to her paintings so often. Yes, only having a couple of friends suited her just fine.

Running a weekly painting group for aspiring artists was one way of ensuring Bridget didn't become a total recluse and it also gave her a regular income which, as any artist will tell you, was always needed. In recent years she was selling more work, but people never understood why paintings needed to sell for thousands. They didn't realise that if you took off the cost of materials, framing and other expenses, then divided the remaining amount by the number of hours taken to paint said painting, it often worked out that you were earning about sixty-seven pence per hour, significantly less than the minimum wage.

She had given the Wednesday painting group the snappy title 'Exploring modern painting'. Okay, maybe not that snappy but it was better than some she had seen, such as 'Beginner's painting group', or 'Oil painting class'. The group had a steady core of people in their early fifties through to their seventies with people coming and going sometimes for months, sometimes for years. She ran it from her own studio which meant that she didn't need to travel anywhere or pay out for a room, and she had everything to hand. As the years had rolled on, she had to admit that it was rather nice seeing them all turn up, happily chatting as they caught up with each other's news. Many of them felt like old friends now, so perhaps she did have more friends than she thought.

In the winter months, where the rain seemed endless and she couldn't get out into the countryside to paint *en plein air*, much of her studio time was spent working on larger landscape projects or, if she absolutely had to, painting commissioned portraits. She much preferred painting landscapes and had a deep love of nature and the endless painting possibilities that it presented. She could be freer with landscapes – it didn't matter if grass was not exactly right, and she could omit the odd tree if it suited the composition better. Not like portraits – she couldn't exactly omit a facial feature, although some, like Professor Donahue, thought otherwise.

As Bridget squirrelled away any spare money, she wished the art world was different. She often wondered what it would be like if people commissioned landscapes in the same way they commissioned portraits, as it would suit her much better, but they were very different beasts.

It was rare for someone to say, 'Here is ten thousand pounds – please paint my back garden or my favourite tree.'

Sometimes there was an historical garden, castle or fancy country house owned by a large organisation with money, but it was rare for ordinary people to commission a landscape. Few people had houses or gardens that would translate well into paint, especially not your average three bed 1980s semi, although Bridget reckoned she would find a way to make it work! Portraits were easier to understand. Outside of the egotism of having your own portrait painted, portraiture had helped to benchmark history, social movements or important events. People also wanted to remember themselves or their families, and organisations used them to celebrate prominent people.

Over the years, accepting portrait commissions had become a no-brainer for Bridget, so she had found all sorts of ways of making the process interesting. Sometimes she might hide something in the portrait such as a laughing dog or hidden word that only she could see. It was a bit like film makers or video game designers who hide *Easter eggs* in their movies – like a joke or hidden puzzle. Once she had managed to paint some long, curly hair in such a way that she'd hidden a couple having sex behind a lock of hair! That one really made her chuckle and given that it had been ten years ago and still hadn't been spotted, Bridget reckoned she had got away with it.

FIVE

Eddie was feeling a bit lacklustre. He had moved house and changed jobs recently and was now working on the Murder Investigation Team in South Gloucestershire. It was a promotion of sorts, but it was not working out as he had hoped. In fact, several areas of his life were not working out as planned. The new job was slow, his boss didn't seem to like him much, and murders in South Gloucestershire were few and far between.

In accepting the new job, he had promised his husband Graham that he would spend more time at home and find a new hobby. His last job had seen him constantly over-worked and left little time for leisure pursuits. Between the London traffic which meant that a ten-mile commute often took him over an hour and the boredom of working in the traffic division, his old job had taken its strain on his relationship. The couple, who had met and quickly fallen for each other over their mutual love of Harlen Coben novels, quickly found themselves spending all their evenings watching TV as Eddie was too tired to do anything else.

Despite the move and new job Eddie was tetchy and irritable, which was made worse by knowing that it wasn't Graham's fault. Graham was a little older, had been married before and had a local job that didn't involve shift work or unsociable hours. Graham also had hobbies. He played the clarinet and read books – lots of them and seemed able to fill his leisure time without resorting to binge watching Netflix dramas. Graham also had friends who too had hobbies and when they socialised together, Eddie found himself having to be very creative when answering the dreaded question, 'What do you do in your spare time?'

This question was even worse than asking him what job he did for a living. At least for a moment when he said he was policeman, people thought he was interesting. However once they learned that he worked in volume crime, they usually slid away at the earliest opportunity as no one knew what it was, but it sounded boring. When Eddie was offered the new job in South Gloucestershire, they had made the decision to leave London jointly. Graham would have to make sacrifices, but he knew it was the right thing to do, and he knew he could adapt to a different pace of life.

Eddie had only been in his new job for two months and despite not finding the job as exciting as he had hoped, some things were improving. He had more energy, meaning that if he found a new hobby, he might be able to avoid becoming a boring person. In recent months he had tried lots of clubs and activities. First, he had joined something called 'The Circle of Men' recommended to him by a colleague at work, but he quickly realised that as a gay man with a husband, he stuck out like a sore thumb. Although they were a good group of men, he didn't have a wife to moan about or photos of his children or pet dogs on his phone. And when he learned that the initiation ceremony involved ten hours of drinking and challenges involving nudity, he realised it wasn't for him.

Next, he had tried Salsa dancing. Yes, it was bit of cliché for a gay man, but after being hit on by several middle-aged, divorced women, that too had to go. Under Graham's encouragement he also tried a book club but quickly realised two things. Firstly, he didn't read quickly enough and secondly, he didn't really find much to say about the books which seemed to disappoint the other members. He did enjoy the biscuits though, and the occasional bit of celebrity gossip.

Feeling thwarted, Eddie's second to last attempt at finding the elusive hobby ended up being a lucky escape, he'd reflected afterwards. He'd wondered if a more active hobby might suit him, given the previous failures, so he had contacted a local cycling group who were very friendly and encouraging on the phone. He dug out some shorts, made sure his bicycle tyres were pumped up and met the group in a local car park one Sunday morning. It was a bit too early for his liking, but he didn't want to admit that. As people arrived, he started to realise his mistake.

He had rammed his bike in the back of his car and driven to the meeting point, but he was in the minority. Most had already cycled five or ten miles just to get to the meeting point. All of them were wearing Lycra and not the ten quid, black jersey shorts from Primark that Eddie wore. They all had branded shorts and cycle tops from long distance events they had previously taken part in. They all looked like professionals, despite the man on the phone having said they were a *fun* group made up of all kinds of people – well that wasn't true.

They were all slightly older than Eddie, but very fit and trim. They all had modern bicycles too. Eddie looked at his trusty mountain bike that had served him well at university ten years ago, but he could now see that this particular cycle ride was not going to go well. He decided to make the most of it and they reassured him that they would set a manageable pace, but after about twenty painful minutes of busting his guts just to keep up with them, he indicated to the chap who had clearly been allocated to look after him at the rear, that he was going to head back. He peeled off into the nearest layby and once they were round the corner and out of sight collapsed on the floor and couldn't move for half an hour.

Eddie hadn't realised that finding a new pastime was going to be so difficult, so when one of Graham's friends suggested an art class, he jumped at the idea. He made enquires and joined a local painting group run by a woman who ran it from her home, about thirty minutes from where he and Graham lived. The artist who ran the group had seemed pleasant enough, if not a little quiet for his liking, but it would be a start; he could always find another art class once his confidence improved. The art class was called 'Exploring Modern Painting' and Eddie had visions of himself splashing paint around like those modern artists who painted on the floor using big brushes and buckets of paint. However, modern did not reflect the age of the other members. At thirty-two he was by far the youngest person there, neither were there any big buckets of paint anywhere. Bridget, the artist who ran the group, had greeted him warmly and explained how the group worked. Some people had ongoing projects they liked to work on continuously, but Bridget also set a task each week for those who wanted to experiment more and try something different.

At his first group, Eddie sat next to Ralph, who was painting an owl. It soon became clear that Ralph had been painting the same owl for many weeks. Ralph, in his early sixties, explained to Eddie that he was forced to retire from his career in the bank due to stress. To placate his wife, he had taken up painting as she said it would be relaxing and help lower his blood pressure. Ralph didn't seem very relaxed and swore under his breath as he repainted the 'bloody owl's claws' every week. Eddie doubted that attendance at the class was lowering Ralph's blood pressure in the slightest.

The seat on Eddie's other side was occupied by Sylvie, a likeable woman who was, Eddie guessed, also in her sixties. Sylvie was easy to talk to and before the first tea break, Eddie knew most of her life history. He was surprised to hear that Sylvie had given up a promising career in chemistry to raise her children and never returned to her research position. It transpired that her first husband was a traditionalist, which was being polite, and insisted that Sylvie continue maintaining the home, long after the children had started school. At that point, she had decided it was time for a new husband and was now on number three. These days when she wasn't drinking cocktails, she filled her time with the painting class and various activities with her local Women's League.

Sylvie always took part in Bridget's activities rather than working on her own projects and encouraged Eddie to do so saying, 'I'm not in this to paint animals or cottages or flowers…given my choice I would paint naked men.' Sylvie tittered as she said this, saying she was only joking but there was an unmistakable glint in her eye which told Eddie she was telling the truth.

Eddie would also like to draw and paint naked men.

SIX

Bridget had woken up early, on yet another grey winter's day, following a particularly difficult conversation with her husband the night before, regarding money. It was boring. Every couple of months it would raise its ugly head again. She tried to question why they needed more money, which he couldn't adequately explain, and she would end up promising she would cut back on certain things. He would then say he didn't want to cut back on things and just wanted there to be more money. She could almost write this argument down, word for word. It was like a repeating script she knew so well. They always made up before going to sleep, with Bridget making various promises that she had no intention of keeping.

The following morning, Bridget finally opened her laptop and turned it on. In light of last night's argument, she knew she couldn't put off reading an email she had received a week ago, enquiring about a new portrait commission. A new commission would mean a decent chunk of money and would quieten her husband down for the next couple of months. It was still raining anyway, so the hopes she had of getting out in the countryside to paint outdoors were still a long way off. January had proven to be as wet as it could possibly be. She wished she was more committed to sitting in a field, in the mud, drawing muddy shapes and clouds, but she just wasn't.

The email was curt with few pleasantries.

From: Anthea Clearwater
To: Bridget Sullivan
Subject: Portrait Commission?

To mark 25 years of Verity Scanlan being our CEO and shortly to become our honorary president, The Women's League has decided to commission a portrait. Verity has been the face and voice of the UK's first, if only by a year, and foremost women's group. Clearly, finding a female portrait artist is essential and your name had been suggested by a league member who knows you personally.

Are you up for this undertaking?

I look forward to your reply.

Anthea Clearwater, Personal Assistant to Verity Scanlan, Chief Executive Officer of The Women's League.

Bridget noticed a warm feeling inside as she read this email and wondered who had recommended her.

Despite portrait painting not being her favourite way to work, there was no denying that this was both an honour and a financial necessity, and Bridget found herself both relieved and a bit chuffed to be asked. She replied to the email straight away and apologised for the delay in responding. Luckily most people seemed to accept that artists were a little disorganised and replying to emails might be slow. This was a much better explanation than the truth, which was that Bridget monitored her emails every day and was just avoiding them until she was in the right mood, which also meant having a glass of wine in her hand.

Bridget duly telephoned Anthea Clearwater later that day and explained the process, the fees involved and the expected timescales. Verity would have to travel to her studio in Little Bampton for sittings every two or three weeks, for a couple of months with another sitting taking place in Verity's office or home. Anthea asked Bridget to send through a formal contract for the commission and at the word contract Bridget quietly died inside. She didn't do contracts, she hated the formality and the legal bullshit that really held no value for her, but she knew she couldn't avoid it.

'Of course, I'll email over a contract shortly,' she fluffed down the phone, vowing never to accept another portrait commission again. Hanging up she googled the phrase 'readymade painting portrait contract simple free' and downloaded the first one that looked vaguely understandable.

'That's enough admin for one day,' she said aloud and turned back to the sticky, dark brown substance she had been playing with before the phone call. As she smoothed some of the brown substance onto the cardboard in front of her, she smiled, knowing at least that the paid commission would get her husband off her back for a couple of months. She was also relieved that she could just about stomach the business side of being an artist, but only if she limited it to sending one email and no more than two and a half minutes on the laptop each day.

SEVEN

Frank Tisbury scoffed at the news headline on his phone. The Daily Trumpet headline read, 'Same sex couple outraged…' Frank didn't bother to read the rest of the story. He didn't care. He knew that men who were apparently married to other men were always outraged about something or other.

'Bloody gays,' he said putting out his cigarette after squeezing the last possible drag and slightly singeing his lips. 'If I was one of those men,' he said putting the word 'men' in air speech marks using his fingers, 'I would have to just put up with it, wouldn't I?' Frank ladled the quince marmalade onto his toast and took a large bite, managing to fit almost the whole slice into his mouth in one go.

Sarah noticed that a dribble of marmalade had escaped the corner of his mouth and now sat like a tiny island on his chin. She smiled sweetly but did not alert him to the dollop of marmalade. Frank, noticing her smile, was pleased that he had an audience and continued his rant with an increase in both volume and pace.

'If they brought back conscription that would sort them out and I don't know why they stopped doing that thing with hormones – you know, where they give them injections that shrink their dicks.'

Sarah gasped as Frank further increased his pace, seemingly fuelled by the look of shock on his wife's face. Their son's face remained unchanged. Frank would have to do better next time. He would find something to get a response from Rory, something that would shake him up a little, something, anything. Rory was so wet and seemed to have no opinions on these things.

But Frank was wrong.

Rory had many opinions.

Rory felt his body stiffen the moment his father's rant started, but the last comment had been especially disgusting. He wanted to shout back at his father something like, 'You don't need an injection to shrink your dick, you fuckwit,' but as usual he swallowed his upset down. He was well practiced at concealing his discomfort, but it was taking its toll on him. Any sort of comment from Frank would quickly result in him losing his temper and that would make him more like his father. That thought made it easy for Rory to keep quiet. He was nothing like his father. In fact he didn't understand how he could be related to this shameful human being. His mother was so kind, so gentle, possibly too gentle to stand up against this man. Rory finished his muesli and black coffee and left the kitchen table quietly, going back to his bedroom, letting go of a sob as he closed the door.

Rory had moved back home after finishing university the previous year and was trying to save enough money to rent a flat in Bristol, but the rents were huge, and his job paid nowhere near enough. He had scraped through his final exams and left university with a degree in engineering, which he really didn't want. Unbeknown to his parents, he had been so unhappy during his course that he had suffered from depression and developed problems with eating, leaving him thin and weak, which his father also mocked him about. His mother knew that he had been struggling, and she had done all she could to support him and keep his spirits up. She had visited him whenever she could, without raising too much suspicion from Frank who already thought that she was mollycoddling him.

'He will never become a man if you keep mothering him,' Frank often said, but Rory was Sarah's only child, and she loved him more than Frank could ever know.

After Rory was born, Sarah knew she would not have any more children with Frank. Frank was an arse – that summed it up, but she stayed with him because she needed to. She had married Frank when she was eighteen, before she had established a career or life of her own. Frank was considerably older than her and she was seduced by the fact that he seemed to know himself and the world. Initially she had loved his confidence and strong opinions, but as the years wore on, she realised that he was a weak and rather nasty man who knew very little of the world outside his own narrow, insecure views.

Sarah knew that her son had only agreed to take the engineering course to placate his father, and Rory hadn't known what he wanted to do instead. She knew it needed to be creative and equally she knew that his father wouldn't tolerate anything other than a *proper course* and would withdraw all financial support.

Unlike Frank, Sarah also knew that her son was gay and being at university had given him some freedom away from his father. There Rory had been able to explore different relationships and build some fledgling confidence that had been completely lacking under his father's influence at home. In some ways, that made up for the fact that he didn't want to be an engineer – at least he was finding himself, but that had all stopped now he was back at home.

Rory couldn't find a job in engineering as it was difficult to perform well at an interview when he hated the job he was applying for. He couldn't afford to leave home, he couldn't afford to go out, he didn't have any friends and he was becoming increasingly depressed. He had taken a job as a care assistant in a residential home on minimum wage, and in his spare time, Rory would stay in his bedroom, sketching the family dog and attempting to write poetry. Sometimes he passed a lovely clean blade across his thigh, in a place that couldn't be seen, in an attempt to relieve some of the acidic pain that built up inside him. But lately things had escalated, and his thighs were now criss-crossed with angry red lines and the cutting had started to become less effective. His mind was slipping away from him.

The memories of the freedom that he had started to gain

at university were fading and he could feel himself fading away too.

EIGHT

As Verity sat down on the chair in the middle of the studio, Bridget didn't know what to make of her. It had already been quite a palaver securing an appointment slot in Verity's busy diary. Now she was in front of her, sitting in the chair she would always sit in during her studio visits, Bridget felt an all too familiar feeling.

Dread.

Mixed always with initial dislike which thankfully softened to mere irritation as the process drew to a close. It was rare that Bridget genuinely liked anyone she painted. It was one of the reasons she didn't like portraiture – it was like being forced to be friends with someone you didn't want to. She often wondered if this said more about her than she liked to admit.

It was no surprise that she didn't immediately warm to Verity, but Bridget knew she had to put those initial feelings aside. Getting to know her sitter properly was crucial to a good portrait, and it took time. The first session was always a bit uncomfortable. They would both be nervous and there would be more chatting than was ideal for Bridget, but she knew that further down the line, she would have to chat less. Right now though, the person sitting in the portrait chair needed to relax enough so they would show Bridget their true self, warts and all (and that had included Professor Donahue who couldn't exactly hide his).

Bridget's usual questions would surface early on including, 'How long have you been a professor/chief executive/barrister?', as these were the only types of people who had their portrait painted.

'Do you live close to where you work?' Bridget asked.

'No,' Verity responded without even looking at her.

'Do you have pets?' Bridget tried again.

'No.'

'How long have you been with The Women's League?'

'A long time.'

Bridget wasn't getting much from Verity. However, what might appear to an outsider as idle chatting, was more like a game – a strategic game that Bridget knew very well and could control all the moves which were designed to get to know her sitter whilst reducing the huge amounts of anxiety she always felt.

These moves included: being over friendly and supportive during their first session; complimenting the new sitter about their lovely hair or good skin or some other feature. She was self-effacing so that the sitter felt at ease but reassured them at the end of the sitting by showing them the best of her sketches and studies, so they still had confidence in her. She under promised at the start knowing that she would over deliver. She made the sitter feel like they were making all the choices about the pose, backgrounds, clothing, etc without them realising she was giving them limited choices, all of which she would be happy with, regardless of what they chose.

Lastly, and only if she was really feeling insecure, Bridget imagined the sitter on the toilet – a low-level toilet which made their knees high, and their posture silly. Although she saw this as the last resort, this image would often pop into her mind and resurface all too frequently.

She would make one excellent sketch of Verity during the sitting, seemingly spending the whole two hours on it, so that this slow pace would set the pace for future encounters. It also meant Bridget had fidgeted, tested things out in secret and let her mind wander. This last move was a surefire way of covering up Bridget's need to mull things over and buy some time.

Verity, in turn, did not warm to Bridget. In her opinion Bridget encompassed way too many things about women that she disliked. She was bumbling, overweight (in Verity's opinion, although only really a size 14, well perhaps a 16, which was probably considered normal now) and untidy. The only redeemable feature about this woman was that she could paint a decent picture. She had agreed to the idea of a portrait reluctantly. She had no real liking for art and believed that artists were weird at best and at worst they were messy, borderline alcoholics, mostly unsuccessful and undoubtedly poor. However, Verity was aware that her team at The Women's League were loyal, hardworking and she didn't want to let them down, so she agreed to the portrait and, deep down, part of her warmed to the idea.

Flung together like two unlikely friends, they sat in Bridget's studio on a dreary January afternoon, both on edge. Bridget set her game plan into action and Verity reluctantly put on her *nice girl* demeanour. Bridget too tried to be friendly and offered Verity a coffee and, less willingly, a piece of her favourite fudge. It was handmade, clotted cream fudge from a farm in Devon who delivered. Verity initially chose the smallest piece, which pleased Bridget, but then reached for a second piece exclaiming how lovely the handmade fudge was.

'Do you visit the Southwest much, Bridget?' Verity politely asked plopping a third piece into her mouth, much to Bridget's horror – she would have to order another box. Verity didn't wait for an answer, adding that she was partial to a Devon cream tea.

Bridget doubted this very much as the woman was very trim, but the chat broke the ice a little.

Verity had been instructed to bring along three different outfits – one plain, one mostly white and one colourful and patterned. Verity dismissed this idea and brought three suits with her, one dark grey, one black and one emerald green. The emerald green was her one concession to something more colourful, but being a suit meant it still spoke volumes about who she really was. She was also told to bring some special belongings, things that she valued or that suggested her personality or identity. She had struggled with that one. She didn't like ornaments and had little use for nik-naks at home. She liked functional things, clean lines, and things that didn't need dusting. She had opted to bring her mobile phone, a book which she had been meaning to read but hadn't got round to, and a cafetière. She loved strong, black coffee – it kept her sharp and she savoured the bitter taste.

Bridget wasn't surprised at the outfits Verity had brought with her. She had already Googled the woman sitting before her to try and get some idea of what she would be dealing with. Using her strict, daily allocation of two and a half minutes on Google, she had seen image after image of this woman wearing suits, power suits, and the occasional green suit. Never a skirt or dress and never any accessories. The only thing about this woman's personality she gleaned from these images was that Verity didn't need to spend much time in the morning, choosing outfits. Admittedly, these were both things she could relate to, but in Bridget's case, this resulted in her wearing the same grey, paint splattered joggers which she changed for clean grey joggers when she needed to go out.

The outfit Bridget felt would work best was a no-brainer so she persuaded Verity that the emerald green suit would work well in paint and give her complexion a lovely glow, as black or grey always deadened a person's skin tone. As for the personal items, well that was a bit harder. None of those items were particularly personal. Everyone had a mobile phone these days and lots of people use a cafetiere. Put together, it felt like a bit of a cliché. All it would say was that the person in the portrait was driven at work, needed coffee to feel on top of her game, and that her mobile phone ruled her life. So be it, but what about the book. The book felt incongruous, but Bridget jotted down the title nevertheless. This woman didn't seem the sort to read books, let alone a historical book like this. Bridget decided she would outline the book in the portrait initially but decide later whether to include the title or not.

As the first sitting progressed, Bridget used her well-practiced strategy, complementing Verity and making her feel relaxed. She tried to ignore the image of the green-suited woman on the toilet that kept popping into her mind, but given how cold and standoffish Verity was, Bridget knew that she would need to use this strategy at some point.

Two hours later and with a couple of coffee breaks and a visit to the toilet, for Bridget that was, the first session had finished. As per her game plan, Bridget showed Verity the well-executed charcoal drawing, which Bridget had only spent twenty minutes on but looked like it took at least an hour.

'Good likeness,' Verity said without much enthusiasm.

Both women breathed a sigh of relief and Verity left.

Pouring a much-needed glass of wine, Bridget plonked herself down on the sofa in the studio and started to unwind a little. She realised quite quickly that the portrait would be good as Verity had striking features, good bone structure, and the emerald suit would give her lots of options for using colour creatively. She would drag the portrait out longer than necessary, that way she could placate her husband and delay the inevitable question about when she would be paid.

She would weave an unnecessarily complex story for her husband: the portrait had started, the portrait was going well, the portrait wasn't going well, there had been problems with the paint drying, Verity was busy, Verity had cancelled, etc, etc. Eventually she would say it had been delivered and now she had to wait twenty-eight days for the invoice to be paid.

She had this all down to a fine art, and it all delayed her having to accept another portrait.

NINE

Mothers always seem to know, don't they?

Sarah knew that something was different the moment she woke up. She had not slept well and woken in the night with a hot, menopausal sweat and its associated anxiety. As she got out of bed, the house seemed different somehow. It was quiet but not the sort of usual quiet of early morning – the sort of quiet when your stomach tells you something is wrong. As she knocked on Rory's bedroom door, she knew deep down that life would never be the same again.

'Rory,' she called, waiting for his groggy morning hello in response.

Her mind filled with dread when he didn't reply. As she opened the door, she saw something no mother should ever see – her son's lifeless body lying on the floor surrounded by empty packets of tablets.

TEN

Although Eddie was pleased with his job change, he still had to drive half an hour to work every day from his home in Wiltshire to reach the headquarters of South Gloucestershire police, which were located on the outskirts of Bristol. The large offices looked more like the headquarters of a technology company than a police station, and were completely at odds with the rather small and low-key murder investigation team that Eddie was part of. His team was part of CID who which also included the non-suspicious deaths team, or NSD's as they were catchily known. As Eddie walked through the office, NSD were having their regular morning report meeting over a box of Krispy Kreme doughnuts. Eddie wished his boss brought in Krispy Kreme doughnuts, but when she *was* feeling generous, she opted for Tesco's own iced buns, five for 99p.

Eddie looked over to the NSD whiteboard and saw a couple of names of people who had died in the past twenty-four hours, and he wondered what the stories behind them might be. One of the names had an age written next to it. Twenty-two years old and the letters SUI. Eddie knew what that meant. A young person had committed suicide. How tragic, what a waste, the poor family – all the usual things that run around people's head when they hear about a suicide.

Eddie's eyes dropped down, thankfully distracted by the Krispy Kreme doughnuts. Looking at the team surrounding the grubby white board, he thought they looked even more bored than he was, even with their superior doughnuts in hand. He found himself hoping, only slightly, that one of those non-suspicious deaths might become slightly suspicious and the case would be transferred to his team.

South Gloucestershire was turning out to be more than a little boring. In fact, he hadn't known that South Gloucestershire even existed until he had been offered this job. South Glos, as it was shortened to, wasn't Bristol, lovely Bristol with its funky culture, history and great night life, and it wasn't proper Gloucestershire with its Cotswold character and rolling countryside. South Glos was sandwiched in between the two places and consisted of sprawling housing developments and towns which had little character. It was a bit of a non-place and since starting here, Eddie's murder team had been deadly quiet.

The most exciting thing to happen was the death of an accountant over some fraudulent family money problems. That summed South Glos up – the most exciting crime had been a murdered accountant and as it turned out, his wife had done it. Very little investigation had been required as she confessed as soon as she realised that she had left rather an obvious trail of evidence.

She had tried to electrocute him with a toaster in the bath which didn't completely work and when he had stumbled out of the bathroom confused, she had panicked and hit him several times with a ceramic toilet brush, shaped like a duck. The coroner couldn't say for certain whether the electric shock induced the heart attack or whether it was the shock of being hit repeatedly on the head by a duck that did for him. At the time they had all wondered how a toilet brush, even a ceramic one, could have been heavy enough to kill someone, but his wife later clarified that she had needed to use the brush holder as well.

Although this murder had sent much needed excitement through the police community in Filton, it quickly faded as the investigation fizzled out after the confession.

ELEVEN

It wasn't that Frank didn't show any emotion about his son's suicide, it was that even after the tragic story behind Rory's death unfolded over the coming weeks, it didn't change Frank's attitude at all. In fact, finding out that his son had been gay seemed to make Frank's reaction worse.

Sarah now had to listen to Frank's usual homophobic tirade, but it now included more vicious words which stung Sarah's heart every time they spat from his mouth. Every morning, she continued to make Frank's breakfast and watched him eat while he said vile things, but she could no longer hear his words. All she could see was her perfect, gentle son, sitting at the table, fading away with every profanity Frank uttered. Sarah was no longer sad – she was completely empty. She was unable to cry but deep down something had started to prickle. It was stirring inside her, something new, something that was growing into a power and resolve that she had never felt before. Although she doubted its motives, she knew it was deadly and had decided to listen to it.

Attempting to support her, Sarah's friends at The Women's League started to message and call her more regularly. It wasn't the first time a member had lost a close relative and they all knew what they needed to do. They made sure that someone collected Sarah and brought her to their weekly meeting, so she knew she was not alone. Her friends at The Women's League had known what Frank was like and had spent years trying to get Sarah to apply for a job and become more independent, but they knew Frank held too much power over her. It would take something big to change how Sarah felt.

That something had, indeed, happened. Of course it had. Sarah had lost her only child – no mother recovers from that and they had noticed something else, something other than normal grief, if there is such a thing. Following Rory's death there was a hollowness to her eyes but at the same time, when she spoke it was with a new certainty that hadn't existed before.

It was during this time that Sarah developed a friendship with a new member at The Women's League. She met this woman for coffee initially and then after a few weeks, they ended up in a quiet bar, drinking gin cocktails. This new friend seemed interested in what had happened, what Frank was like, how Sarah felt about him and of course, the loss of Rory. It didn't take long for the rage of twenty-five years of marriage to Frank to start tumbling out during these chats, and of course the gin had worked its magic too.

After a couple of weeks of meeting and talking, the rage

started to turn into something else. It was like a horrible taste in her mouth that Sarah knew wasn't really there. It numbed her mouth, her brain, and trickled all the way to her chest. When it reached her heart, she felt like she could start screaming and never stop.

During one of these late-night, gin-fuelled chats, she described this feeling to her new friend who didn't seem surprised.

'How much do you hate Frank?' the friend asked.

'I haven't loved him since Rory was little – in fact, I now loathe him and blame him for my son's death.' It felt good to say it out loud.

'What would you do to get rid of him?'

'If I could get rid of him easily without being found out, I wouldn't hesitate.'

The friend smiled.

TWELVE

The second sitting for the portrait took place in Verity's London office at the headquarters of The Women's League. It was also an opportunity for Bridget to explore possible settings for the portrait, perhaps the river Thames in the background, or the London skyline, or an interesting wall within the building. It would also help Bridget build a portrait of Verity's character by seeing how she related to her work colleagues, how they communicated with her and what they generally felt about her.

The train journey had been unremarkable. It took only an hour from Swindon to Paddington and the tube was so fast that Bridget found the whole journey took less than two hours. She used the time on the train wisely though, thinking up ideas for activities in the art group, researching new and up and coming artists. She also researched the current work of The Women's League; they had branches all over the country, in fact all over the world now, but she knew very little else.

Taking advantage of the free train WiFi, and definitely exceeding her self-imposed Google allowance, she connected her phone and clicked on their website. Thankfully it displayed nicely on her phone, not all websites did, Bridget noted to herself.

The Women's League website was one of those where you were initially presented with a full screen image which you had to click on, which boldly said, 'Enter the world that women have been waiting for'. Bridget wasn't sure what that really meant, musing that it could mean a world of unlimited chocolate, decent art and versions of Poldark. Disappointed to find none of those things, the homepage greeted her with images of women doing all sorts of interesting things. There was a woman sitting at the head of boardroom table, a woman driving a battleship or whatever you did to steer a ship, a woman in a laboratory, a woman on an oil rig, a woman surgeon and right down the bottom of the page, a woman was holding a glass of prosecco laughing with her friends and another picking up her kids from school.

Bridget wasn't sure where she fitted into this world that women had apparently been waiting for. There was not a flabby tummy or crumpled blouse between them and all she remembered from her school careers lessons was the choice between becoming a nurse, teacher, secretary or housewife. It was strange when she thought about it as she had attended a girls' grammar school which was often assumed to be the first stepping stone towards a successful career. However there had been no suggestion of becoming a brain surgeon or nuclear physicist, no pointers as to how to become an investment banker, and most definitely no encouragement to become a professional artist.

Bridget wondered what things were really like these days for young women wanting to carve out an interesting career. Her eldest daughter had pursued a career in photography which, two years after graduating, had fizzled out and she had signed up to do a PGCE and become a teacher. Her youngest daughter had wanted to be a doctor but didn't quite get the grades at A level, so instead did some sort of biology degree and was still figuring out what do with it. Bridget hoped she wouldn't end up as a nurse, but it seemed to be heading that way. Given that forty years had passed since she was presented with rather limited career options herself, her own daughters were now heading for teaching and nursing, making her feel that the world really hadn't changed that much.

The Women's League headquarters were housed in a large Edwardian villa just off Bond Street. The building had strong, clean lines on the exterior, softened at the front door by some climbing roses which managed to survive in the London air. It seemed fitting for an organisation which was over a hundred years old, who had done so much good for women in general and clearly produced generations of surgeons, barristers, and astronauts, if you believed their website. Clearly the League deserved a headquarters with history and a welcoming exterior, however Verity's office was completely different to the warm exterior. Black furniture, dark laminate flooring, chrome edges and plain accessories, with the only colour coming from the dark green walls.

'What a stunning office you have, Verity, just stunning.' Bridget smiled and nodded around the room thinking it was just plain yuk.

Verity seemed pleased with this response, and they discussed whether it would make a good background for the portrait or perhaps outside with the rooftop view from the headquarters. Bridget looked at the dominance of grey and the complete lack of colour in both views. Even one tree which she could have moved or enlarged somehow might have swung it, but she persuaded Verity that the dark green walls offered a great compliment to the emerald suit Verity would be wearing in the portrait. Bridget was also pleased that this interior would easily allude to the strong, stark, secretive, perhaps dark side of this woman.

It wasn't only her office that was in stark contrast to its surroundings, but the staff of The Women's League were very different to Verity too. Anthea, her PA, was a similar age to Verity, but smiley, round faced and wore colourful clothes, almost too colourful. She oozed confidence but in a much friendlier way than Verity. However, Anthea wasn't up for chatting much which suited her as Bridget needed to get crack on, sketching the interior and trying to find some different poses with Verity. She could see that despite her friendliness, Anthea was a loyal and fierce right-hand woman and although she had softer edges than her boss, she was not at all weak and let nothing get past her.

Bridget could see that they made a powerful partnership and wondered if Anthea was the planner, brains and strategist, with Verity being the face and voice that people listened to. It didn't matter to Bridget as she wouldn't have much to do with her, but it was interesting and showed a different side to Verity who clearly needed Anthea.

Having managed to settle Verity down in her office with the door closed, Bridget started to arrange her into a comfortable pose. She sketched for twenty minutes or so but was constantly interrupted by Verity's mobile phone which seemed to beep, vibrate and chirp every ten seconds.

'I hope you don't mind, Verity,' said Bridget cautiously, 'but could you switch off your phone for a bit. I'm finding it difficult to concentrate and I want to make the most of this sitting.'

Verity looked annoyed, almost confused at this request as if it had been the first time anyone had asked her to do such a thing, but she obliged and duly retrieved not one, but two mobile phones from her jacket pocket. Bridget assumed she had turned both phones off completely, but it transpired that one phone was merely put on mute and still received the occasional message. Verity placed both phones on the coffee table which Bridget thought had the potential be part of the final composition. Every time it vibrated, Verity's eyes would dart toward the smaller, older phone. This still irritated Bridget but at least Verity wasn't picking it up and scrolling. As well as being a little intrigued why she had two phones, Bridget wondered whether instead of stopping Verity's distractibility, she could somehow capture it in her portrait.

After thirty minutes or so, Verity requested a comfort break which made Bridget chuckle inside. Most people these days said they just need a wee, or to use the toilet. Bridget advised her that she needed to mark the position of her hands and feet before she moved, which took a few minutes and resulted in Verity rushing out of the room in a bit of a hurry. While she was gone, the older of the two mobile phones vibrated again and Bridget found herself glancing at the screen. The message that popped up was very strange.

It read, '6lbsQMreg@BS32urgent'.

Intrigued, Bridget mindlessly jotted the message down on the side of a sketch. She liked the idea of figuring out what it meant, but she promptly forgot about it as soon as Verity returned. Once back, Verity noticed the old phone and hurriedly put it in her pocket. Perhaps Verity was having an affair or something similar, but Bridget doubted this woman would feel the need to hide anything like that. Whatever it was, Verity made very sure she didn't leave the phone on the coffee table again.

Bridget made some more compositional sketches and some brief colour studies. Later in the session she completed a more comprehensive charcoal drawing which captured Verity superbly, but on reflection there was something about her eyes which disturbed Bridget. Skimming the photographs she had taken; she noticed that they didn't capture the same look in her eyes as her drawing had. Bridget knew that contrary to popular opinion, the camera did lie, well not so much lie as fail to capture things that only real-life observation could.

Her drawings had captured something about Verity that Bridget couldn't easily name.

Was it a certain smugness or perhaps cunning? Whatever it was, it wasn't there at the start of the sitting. It only appeared in her eyes after she had read that text message and hidden that old phone. Bridget made a mental note to look at the weird message from Verity's phone when she got home but promptly forgot for the second time.

THIRTEEN

Frank had not been feeling himself lately. He put it down to the stress of losing his son which, despite what people thought, had affected him. Not in the way most people might imagine, no. It made him feel like a failure. He never understood how he, Frank Tisbury, had raised a homosexual son and a weak one at that. He blamed Sarah and now she wasn't giving him any attention he was annoyed at her all the time.

Without a doubt, the boy's suicide was Sarah's fault. She had been too soft with him, and it had turned him gay. Why hadn't he put his foot down more? Why hadn't he insisted that the boy join the armed forces or something? Well at least the boy kept it to himself and didn't embarrass Frank by telling people he was gay. What on earth would his work friends have said if they had known? What would the lads at the social club have said?

He was better off without him and perhaps now he should encourage Sarah to find a part-time job. Now she didn't have anyone else but Frank to look after, she might as well earn some money.

Frank could do with some extra holidays and reckoned he could also have a least two holidays a year without Sarah, if she got her act together and went back to work. The lads from the pub kept asking him to go to Talin, wherever that was, and fire some machine guns. Apparently, you could also eat sushi off a naked lady's chest in Talin. Frank noted that he didn't like sushi but reckoned that he could probably have chips or gravy or something more normal. Yes, thinking about himself licking Heinz beans off pert breasts cheered him up and took his mind off his stomachache.

FOURTEEN

Flipping the kettle switch on again, Bridget made herself the third cup of coffee in an hour. The early stages of the portrait were not going well. Despite having had two sittings with Verity, Bridget hadn't warmed to her at all. On the surface, she admired the strong woman in her swanky green suit but there was something about Verity that she couldn't put her finger on. She had met women like her before – sharp suited, emotionally absent, almost brutal but successful businesswomen who had found a way to break into a world dominated by men, albeit into a women's organisation in Verity's case.

Some of Bridget's friends had managed that back in the 1980s and it was even harder back then. Women had to behave and dress like men to get ahead in their careers. They did something called power dressing, which unlike Verity's powerful dress code, didn't include make up or nice colourful accessories, instead relying on boxy suits with large shoulder pads. Many of her friends with careers chose not to have children at all as there just weren't the systems in place to support working mums, let alone essentials like decent dishwashers and disposable nappies.

Bridget often wondered where on earth she was going with her career as an artist. According to her husband, she hadn't *really worked* for years, and this had been a sticking point between them for as long as she could remember. Bridget had painted and sold work whilst the kids were growing up and taught whenever she could. Over the years it transpired that in her husband's opinion, this wasn't real work. It didn't bring in a predictable monthly salary and he didn't see Bridget getting up early and leaving the house in smart work clothes. Clearly these were his criteria for a job as opposed to the work of a practicing artist. Bridget had increased her apparently *pretend work* once the kids were older, but he still moaned about it regularly.

It was an unresolvable issue and didn't warrant the effort required to try and change it. Bridget didn't really get why her husband felt the way he did about money and why he wore a subtle air of discontent all the time. They had a nice house, took a couple of holidays each year and could pay the bills. He had his hobbies, friends, lots of them in fact, and she painted, so over the years Bridget had learned to ignore the loaded looks that emanated from him whenever money was discussed.

Sipping the fresh coffee, Bridget scrolled through her phone and printed out some of the photos she had taken from the day in London. Although she never painted from photos directly, she would use them to experiment with Verity's posture and expression. They would also help build the background of the portrait and allow her to try different compositions. Some modern portraits favoured having the person quite small against a larger background which became as important as the person in front of it. Some portraits were painted so loosely it was difficult to know who the person was unless you read the title. Bridget wasn't sure yet how she would place Verity in the landscape of her office.

If she were a portrait painter through and through, she would probably make these decisions much quicker, but she wasn't. She was an artist who worked in a variety of ways and loved landscapes more than portraiture. All of her paintings were individual pieces, and she didn't have a tried and tested method or recipe like some artists seemed to follow. Overall, she felt this was a good thing but was never completely sure. Did it make her flaky, lack continuity or seem like she didn't have a strong painting persona? These questions ate away at her confidence way too often and were compounded by her scrolling on Instagram a little too often.

Battling her wobbly confidence, printing the photographs helped a little and Bridget pinned them on her studio wall. Finding the sketches she had made during both sittings, she Blu-tacked them next to the photos, so she could sit and have a long ponder. People underestimate the amount of time that artists sit and think. It might look like they are doing nothing, her husband certainly seemed to think so, but it was all going on inside. She considered the size, composition, palette of colours, how she might use the paint or what other media she might use. It was this stage of any painting that Bridget really enjoyed despite her wobbly confidence, and she knew that she had to resist making too many early decisions.

It was during one of these long ponders which were often lubricated by a glass of Malbec, that she noticed the text message from Verity's phone that she had jotted down on the edge of a sketch. The string of strange numbers and letters were scrawled in charcoal and were in danger of rubbing off completely. Bridget thought she had written down '6lbsQMreg@BS32urgent', but was it 6lbs or 616S? No, she remembered it definitely ended in 'BS' but was the second bit BS32 or was it BS82 or was it 8S32? It might even be 8532. She settled on it probably being BS32 because it sounded like part of a postcode, so she re-wrote the code in felt tip pen in her notebook. The distraction of the strange message, well and truly ended her relaxed pondering about the portrait. Instead, she allowed herself to wonder what the rest of the code might mean, why it was sent as a weird text message and why Verity needed a second mobile phone.

Dumping the coffee in favour of wine, Bridget resolved to get to know Verity much better as she uncorked the bottle of Malbec. To paint the best portrait of her she needed some different angles on Verity's personality and life in general.

'But the first thing you need Bridget is a nap,' she said aloud. 'Just forget about that second phone and the strange message – it's just a meaningless distraction.' But as she laid back on the sofa and pulled a blanket over her legs, strange letters, numbers and postcodes danced in front of her sleepy eyes as she drifted off.

FIFTEEN

Despite fantasizing about baked beans, AK47s and naked women, Frank was still feeling poorly. Sarah had insisted that he visit his GP who proceeded to prick his finger and tell him that his blood sugar was too high, and he was probably pre-diabetic. Frank huffed at this and pretended to listen as his doctor explained that all his symptoms, the stomach discomfort, the lethargy, the sweatiness, the strange taste in his mouth, could all be explained by the diabetes that was gathering pace and catching up with him. Frank agreed to take a daily tablet and cut down on sugar, but he had no intention of going on a diet or joining the gym and there was no chance he would be cutting down his drinking.

His GP knew Frank's type all too well and expected to see him again in a few months when his symptoms had worsened or something new had cropped up.

Once home, Sarah, the ever so attentive wife, asked how the appointment had gone, and Frank told her what the doctor had said. Sarah also knew that Frank would never make any major lifestyle changes as he never believed anything anyone else told him, especially a medical professional. Sarah also knew that the symptoms were unlikely to be diabetes alone but was pleased that this was now officially in his medical record.

‘Frank, I think we should make some changes to your diet. It’s easy for me to make some substitutions and you will hardly notice the difference love,’ Sarah offered in her kind and helpful voice.

Frank huffed and went back to his newspaper.

‘Okay, I’ll take that as a yes then. There are things I can do, Frank, that you won’t even notice, like sweetener in your tea instead of sugar and low-sugar marmalade, so you won’t feel like you’re missing out at all.’

This time Frank didn’t even huff.

Within two weeks of making some small dietary changes, Frank was dead. Sarah was right though, Frank didn’t notice the small changes she had made to his food, but he did continue feeling unwell and got steadily worse. One day, she came home from The Women’s League meeting and found Frank lying on the floor of the bathroom, barely conscious, breathing shallowly. He was blue and clammy, and his pulse was fading. She didn’t call an ambulance.

Leaning over him she whispered in his ear, ‘Give my beautiful son my never-ending love you horrid, horrid man.’

Closing the bathroom door Sarah paused for a moment, took a deep breath, and left the house. Having visited his doctor less than two weeks before, there would be no questions raised, no inquest carried out. She had followed the instructions she had been given to the letter, and it had worked like clockwork. Once in the car she called her new friend from The Women's League and arranged to meet her at the gin bar.

SIXTEEN

Eddie realised early on that the art group was, very much, what you made it. For Ralph it was about owls, well painting them at least, and Eddie wondered if he would move onto other birds or whether the owl was of special interest. He would ask him next time he got a chance.

For Sylvie it was mostly about chatting, gossip, getting messy and giggling. She often talked to Eddie about her friends and their lives, none of whom Eddie knew of course, but that didn't seem to bother her. The other group members seemed to all be working on a different painting every week, which mostly seemed to be pleasant landscapes of some kind, the sort of pictures you might see on a Victorian chocolate box lid. Eddie had never seen a Victorian chocolate box, but he had heard someone talk about them on a TV programme once and these paintings seemed very similar: a cottage or lake, lush green grass, pretty trees and often a dog, duck or other animal, all painted with soft hues and gentle tones.

It wasn't how *he* wanted to paint but he enjoyed the activities that Bridget set every week and enjoyed chatting to Sylvie. He also liked the different ages of people in the group and that they all came from very different walks of life. His work colleagues were mostly men, and his usual social circle were thirty something, professional men, so to chat to women at all, especially older women was quite enlightening. Older women, Eddie reflected, seemed to have much more interesting lives than his younger peers.

Since attending the painting group, Eddie had learnt that Sylvie had been married three times,

'Third time lucky,' she cheerfully chirped when talking about her latest husband Edgar. 'Edgar is good fun, lets me do whatever I want and… is good in bed,' she said slightly under her breath but with joy in her voice.

Eddie tried not to look shocked. Sylvie wasn't that old, probably around the same age as his mum and no one likes to think that their parents ever had sex, let alone were still at it. It transpired that Edgar was also fond of cocktails and quite wealthy, so Eddie could understand the attraction. Sylvie was making up for lost time and really enjoying her life. Eddie wondered what his life would be like in twenty years' time. Would Graham be up for cocktails and a giggle? Eddie doubted it, which made him feel a little sad, but no one really knew what the future held.

Eddie also really liked Bridget, but in a very different way to Sylvie. While Sylvie reminded him of the fun, chatty mum you wanted when you were growing up, Bridget

Sullivan was like an intelligent, cultured aunt that didn't over-share. Someone you could really trust and have conversations with into the early hours over a bottle of decent red wine. It took Eddie longer to get to know Bridget. As the teacher, she maintained a professional distance from the students, but over time Eddie noticed that Bridget liked talking to him and shared different things with him than she did with the others. Eddie also wondered if she was relieved to have someone younger in the group. Eddie was thirty-two and the next youngest was a woman called Sally who was mid-forties, took herself too seriously, seemed convinced she would be a successful artist and expected to be exhibiting at swanky Mayfair galleries.

There were a couple more women in their fifties, then Sylvie, and the rest were in their sixties or seventies, including Ralph. There was also Margaret who looked at least a hundred. She had glassy eyes, soft white hair and couldn't hear a thing. Remarkably she had her own teeth which she proudly showed everyone when she smiled, which was often, mostly as a response to questions and conversations she couldn't hear. Margaret didn't paint but preferred to draw churches with a soft pencil.

Looking round the room Eddie wondered whether he should be doing something more challenging or structured like an A level in Art or perhaps a foundation course, but he felt so at home in the group – it was like family, but without the arguments.

It was somewhat of a surprise, given Sylvie's usual cheerfulness, when she turned up to the group one day without the usual spring in her step.

'You okay, Sylvie?' Eddie asked as Sylvie placed some unopened letters on the table. The letters were clearly intended for the letterbox and the top one looked like a greeting card. It had a pale grey envelope with delicate Lily flowers embossed on it.

'Yes,' replied Sylvie, 'but I forgot to post these and there is a condolence card which needs sending today.' Sylvie indicated to the grey envelope, which was addressed to a Sarah Tisbury, 28 Nugent Close, Almondsbury, South Gloucestershire.

'Sorry to hear that,' said Eddie, clearly being polite as he desperately worked out what to say next. 'Was it someone you knew well?'

'Sort of. My friend Sarah, who I know through The Women's League. Her husband died suddenly last week, although he wasn't a very nice man. They lost their son a few months ago to suicide. Poor Sarah must be distraught.'

Although he was used to death of all kinds in his job, Eddie knew how painful suicide was for all involved and it must have hit the father badly, but he was wrong.

'Her husband was an arse and very anti-gay, or whatever the correct word for it is. He didn't know his son was gay and after Rory killed himself, he wasn't upset at all. It almost seemed like a relief to him.'

Eddie couldn't speak. He felt his stomach drop and heat rising in his chest. This wasn't the 1950s yet gay men were still being stigmatized. Eddie had been lucky that his parents were loving, accepting and supportive of his sexuality. Even though other family members weren't so understanding, he knew he had it a lot easier than some.

'I know he wasn't a nice man, but it's Sarah I feel for,' Sylvia continued. 'The card is for her really. I just hope she is getting lots of support from her friends at the League.'

Eddie didn't know what the League was, but he attempted to be helpful. 'Yes, the card is important, Sylvie. I can post it for you after the class, but it doesn't have postcode on it. I'll google it on my phone, and you can add it.' Eddie whipped out his phone and with the speed and ease of a millennial, he found the postcode. 'Do you have a pen?'.

'Only a Sharpie,' she replied, adding the postcode which now stood out a bit too clearly against the pale grey paper. They put the card back on the table as Bridget came over to tell them about today's painting activity.

'Today, my intrepid modern painters,' Bridget began, relieved that some people in the group wanted to paint something other than birds and cottages. 'We are going to create some painted backgrounds using random marks and paint. We are then going to see if we can find shapes in the randomness that could be people or structures or other things.' There was a glint in her eye. She loved this type of painting. She loved finding figures or animals or strange buildings in a painted surface, but she loved finding other things too, like the occasional vulva or penis. Could she share this naughty idea with them? Sylvie definitely, Eddie maybe, so she decided to see how it panned out.

Bridget sat and worked alongside the pair, getting up occasionally to help the other group members or make some hot drinks. They worked away spreading, pouring and scraping to create random surfaces under Bridget's instruction, which mostly comprised of 'just do what feels good' which made Sylvie titter.

As they filled the tabletop with painted rectangles of card, Bridget moved some things to create more space, and her eyes landed on the greeting card. How strange that Sylvie had written the postcode so clearly in felt tip pen. Bridget looked again. The address postcode was BS32 3EY. BS32. They were the same letters and number on the text message Verity had received. Yes, it was a postcode, the postcode area for Almondsbury, South Gloucestershire.

'Sylvie,' asked Bridget. 'I know this might sound strange, but that card you have there, what's it for? Someone's birthday? Do you have family in Almondsbury?'

Sylvie promptly told Bridget the same sad tale she had told Eddie earlier.

'I didn't know you were part of The Women's League,' Bridget added. 'I'm currently painting a portrait of Verity Scanlan, your CEO and soon to be president.' The words tumbled out of Bridget's mouth before she could stop them.

Sylvie let out a squeal and started talking twelve to the dozen about how amazing Verity was and all she had done for the League but then went on to admit that she had never actually met her. Bridget assumed that Sylvie was probably not the most discrete person and quickly told her that the portrait was not common knowledge. Sylvie pulled an imaginary zip across her lips, but it left Bridget unconvinced that she could keep this news to herself.

Once the class had been cleared away and Sylvie and Eddie had taken home several abstract paintings with hidden dogs, willies, skulls and the like, Bridget sat down and retrieved her notebook.

Next to the full text message from Verity's secret phone, she wrote:

Almondsbury, BS32 (3EY) and The Women's League.

Was it just coincidence that this postcode had appeared on the secret phone of the CEO of The Women's League, around the time that a man who lived in that same village had died? Perhaps The Women's League headquarters had some sort of alert system where Verity was notified every time a member dies, so they can send a card or something. No, it couldn't be that. They have thousands of members, and this was someone's husband not a member themselves. Anyway, Verity was the CEO and far too busy to be involved in things like that. Bridget's brain was running all over the place coming up with all sorts of ridiculous ideas.

Her brain often did this.

'For goodness,' sake Bridget, she chastised herself. 'Your mind is inventing things that aren't really there, just like when you over notice coincidences or imagine there are animals or people in your paintings. Get a grip woman!'

SEVENTEEN

Bridget resolved, albeit half-heartedly, to forget about the strange text message and focus on what she was meant to be doing – painting a portrait of Verity Scanlan and making sure it was bloody good. If well received, a good portrait of a high-profile figure like Verity could serve her well and lead to other work, so it was important not to get sidetracked. But being sidetracked was one of Bridget's favourite things and she justified it any way she possibly could. Yes, she smiled a little to herself. She could feel a good excuse bubbling inside, and it would allow her to do some digging.

'To make a good portrait, you need to get know this woman much better,' she told herself. And with that she decided to explore YouTube and watch some videos of Verity, perhaps some speeches she had given or something like that. Less than a minute later Bridget was staring at Verity's face and watching a recording made at something called a WED talk, filmed a couple of years ago. WED apparently stood for Women in Education. Bridget chuckled at this and wondered if the person who came up with acronym still had a job. WED just made her think of weddings which seemed like the opposite philosophy of this clearly feminist organisation.

Verity Scanlan's face was instantly recognisable. Her hair was slightly longer and a little less grey, but that was all. Her speech started as many often do – thanking people for inviting her and welcoming those in attendance. At first, this early version of Verity appeared softer than the Verity that Bridget had now met twice. She started by talking about the importance of girls and young women getting access to education and career opportunities. She noted how far this had come in the last hundred years or so since emancipation had begun. She was making soft but well intended eye contact with the young women in the room but then she changed gear. This younger Verity suddenly stood up straighter, put her hands on the lectern in front of her and leant forward towards her audience:

'But,' the word flew from Verity's mouth which was now not smiling, her right hand waggling a finger with its nail painted bright green. 'The world is still full of men that would rather see women stay at home, raise babies and pander to their every need. We have raised a generation of scared men who feel threatened by women and have now made it even harder for us.' Was that spittle escaping Verity's mouth? 'These men have found ways to keep women tied to the kitchen sink. For some, financial restrictions mean that the woman would be destitute if they left their husbands. Some women stay because they are scared for their children. Some women are psychologically manipulated to such an extent that they feel they wouldn't cope without a man…'

'Blimey,' Bridget said as she paused the video. It wasn't what she had been expecting, and she was more than a little shocked. Perhaps Verity was having a bad day when this speech was made, but except for the odd thumbs down and angry emoji, there were hundreds of comments agreeing with her.

The video had paused on Verity mid-rant and her eyes were cold, almost icy, as they bore into Bridget. They seemed bigger than Bridget remembered but her face looked different in other ways too. Her jaw and neck were tight, almost disjointed from the rest of her and it reminded Bridget of those disturbing Francis Bacon paintings with body parts in the wrong place, all twisted and red. The woman on this screen felt completely different to person at the start of the video and she wondered what a psychotherapist would make of her. It also reminded Bridget of those films of Hitler where he waved his finger in the air and it crossed her mind that Verity, like Hitler, looked like she wouldn't mind getting rid of a few people.

Bridget clicked on another video, one from ten years earlier when Verity had not long been head of The Women's League. In this video Verity's hair was longer with soft curls and she was wearing a dress paired with nice boots. This Verity was calmer, quieter but as she listened to her words, they were just as powerful, perhaps more so.

'We women are still stuck in the narrow, domestic walls of systematic marginalisation, being logical is more accepted than being emotional, and despite nearly sixty years of the contraceptive pill, it is still more acceptable and desirable for a young woman to be a virgin instead of possessing her sexual freedom.'

This earlier Verity really packed a punch with her words alone and didn't need to waggle her finger or jut her neck out. There was no venom, just powerful words that clearly moved people. What could have happened in the years between those two talks to change her so much?

Bridget glanced back to the video again and saw another shift in Verity's mood. Quieter and almost with a tinge of sadness.

'Let's not forget that the persistence of the patriarchy doesn't just hurt women, but also men who don't fit into traditional, masculine identities.' Oh, thought Bridget, there was none of that in the more recent talks. That sounded like she was fond of men or at least could see the damage that some men experienced through what Verity had just called toxic masculinity (that was a new term to Bridget, and she made a mental note to remember it).

Bridget wondered if Verity had any men in her life these days. She doubted this woman would ever want to be married. Perhaps she had brothers and of course a father would have possibly been around at some point. Did something happen to change Verity, something traumatic?

Bridget folded her laptop away and looked at the sketches and studies of Verity on the walls. This woman really was an enigma. She usually got the measure of people very quickly but there was truly something strange about Verity and she wasn't sure she liked it all.

EIGHTEEN

She wasn't sure that she would cope unless something changed. Some of her friends had spent years looking forward to the day their kids left home, but Clara McArthur had been dreading it, and the reality was worse than she could have imagined.

Her husband, Aaron, had retired early at a rather smug fifty-three years old, after a successful career in the city. Despite his age, he had kept himself very trim, had an attractive peppering of grey hair and wore very good clothes. She had tried to keep up with him, but the inevitable menopause had added extra pounds. Despite her natural beauty, she had never really been that interested in clothes, hair dos or make-up so she had felt like a frump for the last couple of years. Whenever she was allowed to attend his work do's, which wasn't very often, it was clear that his colleagues adored him, and she didn't fit in.

Smartly dressed men would make jokes that she didn't understand, often about work situations or people she didn't know. The women were always stunning. How did they manage to do that? These women worked full-time in the city and still managed to keep slim. Their hair was sleek and styled and they always had their nails done. The women too had their in jokes that they would share with Aaron, out of her earshot. Clara wasn't stupid – she knew what they thought of her.

Aaron had invested wisely alongside his lucrative day job and was so confident that he wouldn't need the state pension, he didn't bother keeping up his National Insurance contributions. Clara had wanted to top her contributions up, but he refused to help her saying that she wouldn't need the money, but this just made her feel even more trapped. After retiring, Aaron had kept his London flat and stayed there for a couple of evenings a week, preferring to stay in London after he socialised with his old work friends. It suited Clara as she felt suffocated by him being around too often in the daytime, which amplified how little they had in common. Worse still, she missed her children dreadfully and whilst she had secretly tried to find a job and recreate some sort of life for herself, it seemed impossible. Clara's age seemed against her, she had little work experience to speak of and every job application she made, was turned down. She had hoped that with a part-time job she could top up her pension contributions and feel a little less reliant on her husband, but that plan wasn't working out very well.

One Sunday afternoon in March, Clara and Aaron sat watching TV after finishing their Slimming Universe roast dinner. Aaron always insisted their cooked meal use only five of his fifteen daily 'Sins' so that the rest could go on his favourite evening drink – a dirty Martini (or two). The doorbell had rung, and Clara answered it expecting it be an Amazon parcel containing some new curtain ties. In an attempt to keep busy, she had started to re-decorate the house. She would have preferred to move nearer her grown-up children, but Aaron was adamant he was staying within commuting distance of London. The real reason for this, Clara would soon find out, was now standing on her front door.

It wasn't an Amazon delivery man but a tall, slender blonde in her early thirties with a young boy of about four years old hiding behind her slim legs. She also noticed a small tidy bump on this pretty woman's stomach and her own stomach lurched. No words were needed. She knew exactly what this was, and it all seemed such a sad cliché.

The young woman quietly asked to speak with Aaron and not knowing what else to do, Clara had left them for a few minutes. When the front door eventually closed, Aaron went back to the lounge and started to clean his golf clubs. He didn't say a thing to his wife but an hour later, he left the house saying he was going to London for the night. He gave no explanation to Clara.

Clara wasn't stupid and when Aaron arrived home the next evening, she confronted him. As he fixed his second dirty Martini, he attempted a feeble lie.

'I don't know who she was, Clara. I think she must have got the wrong address or something.'

Clara knew he was lying. She had listened to their conversation through the crack in the lounge door and anyway, the little boy had his eyes and his soft dark curls, there was no doubt about that. Aaron seemed think she was stupid. He seemed to think he could carry on as if nothing had happened. It seemed to Clara that Aaron had already decided that he didn't want a costly divorce. Nor did he want the restrictions of another marriage and young family to raise. He wanted the best of both worlds – freedom with this young woman and a warm bed and supper waiting with Clara. She laughed but at the same time felt something inside her die.

Thirty years of cooking dinner every night, cleaning the house, raising their children and looking after Aaron's every need, it all came into sharp focus. She had known, somewhere deep down inside, what his London sleepovers really were. Well, things would change and in a big way. She would talk to her friends at The Women's League and that supportive, strong group of women would help her find a way forward.

NINETEEN

Having watched the videos of Verity online and with a growing unease about the strange woman, it was no surprise that Bridget was very anxious about the next portrait session. In fact, there was more than a feeling of dread in her stomach as the day approached and even her well-tuned game plan didn't feel like it would work. What had she been thinking! She hadn't exactly warmed to the woman when they first met, but now she felt positively intimidated by the very thought of her. Thankfully Bridget's husband would always be at work when the portrait sittings took place as she didn't relish admitting to Verity that she even had a husband, let alone one she rather liked despite his moans about money.

Preparation was the key, and she readied herself by making a pot of fresh coffee and warming up the studio. It was February, quite chilly and sitting still for so long would make them both feel the cold, which wasn't conducive to feeling relaxed. Turning up the radiator, Bridget vowed to try and not let her recent online diggings affect how she felt about Verity. Her logical side knew that everyone in a public position developed a sort of persona, one that didn't necessarily reflect who they really were. She also told herself firmly that the whole secret text message thing, which Bridget's imagination had grown into an entire plot for a crime drama, was just her creative mind running away with itself, dragging her along for the ride.

When she arrived at the studio, Verity was already wearing the emerald green trouser suit this time paired with a rather striking maroon and black blouse. Her hair was not as closely styled as before, and Bridget was sure she could detect some weariness in Verity's eyes. No matter – it gave Bridget further ideas for the portrait, perhaps a way of introducing a little vulnerability to someone that rarely showed an iota of weakness. She had brought along a newspaper with her and despite Bridget's request that she just hold it as a prop rather than read it, Verity surreptitiously turned the pages when she thought Bridget wasn't looking.

People who don't paint or draw generally don't realise just how much artists really see – much more than you would imagine. They are masters of observation and Bridget often joked with her husband that not only did she have eyes in the back of her head, but they had much better sight than her real ones. So, when Verity's face which was usually devoid of emotion, started to brighten, Bridget noticed. In fact, the corners of her mouth lifted ever so slightly into a sickly strange smile which wasn't pleasant and immediately disrupted the fragile, creative flow Bridget had found.

'Shall I get us a fresh coffee?' Bridget quickly asked, her attention broken by the subtle change in Verity's manner.

Verity nodded and laid the paper on the floor, open at the same page that seemed to have provoked a change in her demeanour.

'I'll just pop to the lavatory,' Verity said. This time, slightly less formal than, 'I need a comfort break.'

Once she had left the room, Bridget looked at the newspaper page which was from the South Gloucestershire area. That was odd to start with. Why would a woman from London, visiting Wiltshire be reading a newspaper from South Gloucestershire? Bridget quickly scanned the pages without moving it. The stories were all the usual stuff you find in a local newspaper, local factory closure, the struggles of social care workers, local pub raises money for disabled child, tragedy strikes family for second time. Her eyes doubled back to that last story at the bottom of the page. It caught Bridget's attention, as she could see a mark made by sharp fingernail, next to the article. She quickly read the short piece:

The Tisburys, a local family from Almondsbury, have been dealt another second tragic blow, with the sudden death of Frank Tisbury. The family were still reeling from the death of their beloved son Rory, 22, who died recently. His widow, Sarah Tisbury, has asked that no flowers be sent to the funeral and donations made to either the Young Men's Suicide Trust or The Women's League who have been supporting her through this difficult time.

The door to the downstairs toilet banged shut and

Bridget quickly jumped back to the table to pour the coffee. Was Verity's strange smile because she was pleased that the local Women's League had been mentioned? No – it seemed different somehow. Bridget was certain it was more like an unpleasant smirk, and she was also certain she could detect a change in the woman's posture as she sat back down – she looked almost content. Why on earth would reading about a man's death make this strange woman happy?

Discombobulation was the only way Bridget could describe how she now felt, and it was seriously affecting her work. For the last hour she had been struggling to make pencil studies of Verity without seeing flashes of the angry face she had seen in those YouTube videos. She needed to urgently change tack, so she decided to get some paint out and think about Verity's clothes.

'That blouse is rather nice,' Bridget said, perhaps it would add some variation to the black, greys and greens, and it really did need it.

Taking advantage of Verity's better mood, Bridget asked if she could remove her jacket so she could paint the lovely blouse instead. Verity agreed and Bridget folded the jacket over the arm of the sofa behind the chair and returned to her easel. Sitting at the easel always made Bridget more relaxed as she could hide behind it and not have to worry too much about her own facial expressions. Both women relaxed, the energy lifted, and the second half of the session went much better. Bridget decided firmly that the blouse was the way to go and at the end of the sitting she showed Verity the study of the blouse, Verity agreed it looked great.

The women found a date for the next sitting and retrieving Verity's jacket, Bridget sent her off with a smile.

Once Verity had left, Bridget slumped down on the sofa feeling tired but a little happier with how the painting was going. Closing her tired eyes briefly, Bridget felt a gentle buzz against her thigh. The unexpected feeling jolted her, and she reached down to find an old mobile phone wedged down the side of the sofa. It was Verity's second phone. The screen was still lit from a new message, and Bridget read the text without hesitation. It read '4lbsOspecial@WD7urgent'. Bridget was just about to scribble the message down when her doorbell rang. It was Verity and her outline against the frosted glass door was clearly recognisable.

'Bugger,' she muttered under her breath. With no time to write the message down she started to say it over and over in her mind as she went to the front door, phone in hand. Bridget remembered to press the off button just in time so that Verity didn't see the lit screen.

As she opened the front door, gone was the more relaxed woman from earlier, replaced with stern features and slightly sweaty skin. Verity immediately spotted the phone in Bridget's hand, starring as she reached out for it.

'Thank goodness you found it, must dash, bye.' Verity's haste allowed Bridget to quickly scramble to her notebook and write down the text message before she forgot it.

TWENTY

Aaron had been pleasantly surprised how well Clara had accepted his denial of knowing Sasha. She hadn't questioned him at all. It had been nearly a month since Sasha had turned up on his doorstep with their four-year-old son, Henry. Although it was a bit of a surprise, he should have seen it coming. Sasha had become more and more clingy of late as her second pregnancy had progressed. In recent months she had started to ask him when he would be finally getting divorced so they could move to a bigger place and get married. Sasha had been under the impression that he had left his wife years ago and explained that his regular absences from their London flat were due to work meetings and conferences. He hadn't told her that he had already retired.

It had all been going swimmingly until she had got herself pregnant again and started to moan about wanting a bigger home and for him to be around more. Now on maternity leave from work, she had started to become suspicious of his absences and unbeknownst to Aaron had followed him one day. She had asked a friend to collect Henry from nursery, then using a spare mobile phone she had hidden in his car, she activated a tracking app which allowed her to follow him. As he headed away from Stansted airport instead of towards it, Sasha wondered whether perhaps her suspicions were founded.

He had told her about his evening flight from Stansted to Turin, where he would be for three days. This included a social day on the Saturday, meaning he would fly back on the Sunday morning. The weekend overlap meant Aaron could placate Clara by spending Saturday with her. He would then leave early Sunday, telling her he had to travel ready for a golf tournament on the Monday. He had this pattern of deception down to a tee.

What Sasha hadn't been ready for was the extent of his deception. As she watched him park his car outside the house that he told her had been sold when he separated from his wife, it became clear that he still owned the house and was very much still married. She had pondered what to do for a couple of days and then decided to pay his wife a visit and try and force Aaron to act.

Aaron had relaxed a little. Clara was still a bit pissed off with him but seemed to have accepted his lies about the whole situation. She seemed still happy to cook his dinner, have sex whenever he wanted and fix him his evening Martinis, so all was well in the world. He thought nothing of the slightly more bitter taste to the Dirty Martini, which he put down to the extra Olive he had added as a treat for himself. They were different Olives to the usual kind, larger and juicier and there were a couple of spare jars in the cupboard. He made a mental note to take one of the jars to the London flat, as he was running low. He idly popped an extra-large Olive in his mouth before settling down to watch some television.

Life was good. Two women, twice the sex, two separate lives, sorted.

Despite what felt like the ideal situation, Aaron wasn't feeling great. His energy levels had been poor of late, and he needed to stop having sex with Clara as he didn't have enough energy for both women. He was also struggling to run on the treadmill and had noticed that his skin had lost it usual glow. He was also having ongoing stomach aches and both Sasha and Clara had urged him to see a doctor.

Aaron visited his GP and told her how he had been a little stressed lately. His GP told him it was probably irritable bowel syndrome and that he needed to reduce his stress levels and perhaps a holiday was needed. Yes, a holiday would be a good idea. He would take Clara to keep her happy as he would soon need to spend more time with Sasha in the coming months, once the baby had arrived.

The following day as Sasha coaxed his penis to life, he found it difficult to maintain his erection. He made another Dirty Martini to help him relax, took two Viagra tablets, a long sniff on some poppers weirdly called 'Mr Fuk' and found it had the desired effect. Twenty minutes later and after a lot of exertion, albeit much more than usual, he released himself into Sasha and rolled over to sleep.

Aaron never woke up.

TWENTY-ONE

Like so many grown up sons, Eddie knew that he didn't visit his mum enough. Since starting his new job, he saw her even less and felt very guilty about it. He loved Anita dearly and they were closer than most of his friends and their mums. Eddie's dad had died about five years ago and it wasn't until he felt his mum was managing better and had made more friends, that he had felt comfortable about moving away from Hertfordshire.

Anita still lived in the family home where Eddie had grown up and despite Eddie's attempts to get her to downsize and move, she just wasn't ready. Anita was a quiet but confident woman who had a successful career in the NHS and left with a decent pension. She had retired to look after Eddie's dad when he had become poorly and just one year later, her husband passed away. She had returned to work part-time for a couple of years, but her heart wasn't in it and her beloved NHS had changed too much in her absence. These days she volunteered at the local hospice and after much encouragement from her friends had also recently joined her local Women's League.

It had been over a month since Eddie had last visited and to make up for it, he had brought her some flowers. No, not the sort you get from the petrol station, proper flowers. He would take his mum out for lunch and have a decent catch up. On his arrival he was slightly put out to find out that Anita needed to be back by 2pm as she was meeting some of her friends from The Women's League.

'Clara's husband, Aaron, died on Thursday,' Anita told Eddie with some urgency. 'And not in a good way either, so we are rallying round to help her.'

Eddie looked at her genuinely asking, 'Is there a good way to die, Mum?' but didn't expect the reply he received.

His mum took a deep breath and then whispered in a low voice, completely unnecessarily as they were alone in the house, 'He was shagging his mistress and just keeled over and died.'

Eddie was unable to keep his shock in check – not about the death but hearing his elderly mum using the word shagging.

'Clara found out a couple of weeks ago that he had a secret life in London, with a young son and everything. His girlfriend is even expecting another baby.' Anita drew breath and Eddie realised that this story would dominate his visit. 'And not only did the bastard not stop seeing her when Clara found out, he changed his will so that the other woman got as much as Clara if he died.'

At this even Eddie took a sharp intake of breath. 'Bloody hell, Mum, that's awful. So now she's not only a widow but she lost lots of money too,' said Eddie. 'Poor woman.'

'Nope, she is better off without the shit. He horded so much money, there's plenty left for Clara. It's just the shock of finding out about his double-life that was so hurtful and the bear-faced cheek of him wanting to keep both his wife and his mistress.'

Eddie had never seen his mum like this before. Usually, she was polite and wouldn't make judgements about other people, so her reaction was quite a shock.

'Would you like a glass of wine, Eddie or perhaps we should have a stronger drink. I do feel a little shaken up by all this.' It was only 10.30 in the morning and Eddie had never known his mum have a drink in the daytime, let alone before midday.

'I'm fine, Mum. I have to drive later.' Eddie was shocked as his mum downed a large Scotch in just two gulps. 'My friend, Sylvie, belongs to The Women's League and her friend also lost her husband rather suddenly, but thankfully this league thing does seem to support their members, just like you are doing with your friend.' Eddie paused before continuing, 'Shame I can't get Graham to join this league,' he joked.

His mum looked confused. 'But of course he couldn't, it's women only, Eddie'.

Eddie explained that he knew that and was only joking, but stopped himself saying that in many ways, equality would only be achieved if men could join women's groups and women could join men's groups. That idea would have been a bit of a stretch for his mum who, whilst accepting that Eddie had a husband and not a wife, was still rather traditional in many ways.

His mum continued, ‘And anyway, men wouldn’t like the same things as we do, would they, Eddie?’

Eddie didn’t reply but reflected that Graham would probably love to make chutney, listen to interesting talks or gossip with women – Eddie certainly did.

TWENTY-TWO

During an unseasonably warm Saturday in the spring, Eddie and Sylvie offered to help Bridget out at a local art fair. Whilst Bridget was grateful for the help, she was also slightly frustrated as she would much rather have been in a field somewhere, painting tree roots or rutted earth. The art fair was being held in one of those large, hangar size buildings on the estate of Cheltenham Racecourse. Perhaps it actually was a hangar, Bridget wasn't sure. No, it probably wasn't as she couldn't see why horses would need aeroplanes.

Sylvie was helping set up the small items for sale, including prints and greetings cards which seemed to be the done thing at these art fairs. When Bridget first had a stand at an art fair, everyone asked her if she had cards for sale and she hadn't and without exception, they all said she should. By the end of that day she went home in a bit of a mood and had chosen a couple of paintings and ordered a box of one hundred greetings card of each design. She still had ninety-six of one and ninety-three of the other left and could no longer stand the sight of either of them.

There were other unspoken rules about these art fairs that Bridget had learned the hard way. In the early days her stand had once been next to a chap whose work was all the same colour, all the same size and in identical frames. Her paintings were not, nowhere near in fact. Each painting was carefully framed by hand according to what suited the individual painting. Each painting was different to the next, the sizes were all very different too and it just reflected who Bridget really was. Despite selling lots of work at the fair, her neighbour had decided to give her his unsolicited advice. He was dressed in rather pointy silver shoes and sported a velvet waistcoat.

He genuinely twiddled his pointy moustache as he said, 'Your display is all over the place. Next time paint things the same size, like I do, and stick to one or two colour variations, oh, and the frames MUST be the same.'

At the time Bridget had been too shocked to reply at all and had just nodded, which probably came across as her agreeing with him, but the voice inside her was screaming bollocks! A true creative process doesn't work like that. I don't make the same painting over and over again just changing a small thing each time. His work looked like he had made it on a photocopier.

Next time, she made sure she wasn't his art fair neighbour; however, the silly man's words still rang in her ears as Eddie helped hang the paintings on the walls. Each time he unwrapped a painting, Bridget would hear him speak.

'Oh my, I just loooove this one. This is my absolute

favourite. Bridget you are so talented.' The lovely comments from kind and authentic Eddie finally drowned out the words of the man with the silver shoes.

Bridget didn't paint the accurately named chocolate box paintings that many people associated with landscape painting, instead finding inspiration in a range of sometimes odd and quite murky subjects. These included muddy places, abandoned places, trees stripped of their branches or leaves, and occasionally a polluted river. You could say she was interested in rather dystopian scenes or things that were basically dead or dying and this could sometimes be problematic when selling her work.

People would be interested in what the inspiration was behind a particular painting they wanted to buy so she often had to lie. She had learnt early in her professional career, that she needed to develop something called *artist bumble* which some might call artist bullshit. Here she would rattle on about the colours evoking something or other or the shapes alluding to a melancholic but gentle mood – those sorts of statements. She would manage to recall a random place and often pretend it was the starting point or inspiration for the painting. Overall, it worked a treat and people seemed satisfied. She was certain that if she told them the absolute truth, she would never sell any work.

Bridget knew that during these art fairs she would need to have all sorts of words and descriptions to hand when people made enquiries about paintings. She also knew that people would want to speak with her directly which also suited Sylvie and Eddie who could take money for cards, note down enquires or fetch the much-needed coffees.

‘You two should take a proper break,’ said Bridget. ‘The lunchtime rush is over now, and you better get to the café before they run out of decent sandwiches.’

‘It’s fine, Bridget. I’ve brought my own sandwich, but I’ll keep Eddie company in the café,’ said Sylvie and in a hushed tone she turned to Eddie saying, ‘I also have a little tipple for us, Eddie, just to make the afternoon flow.’

Five minutes later, Sylvie and Eddie were sitting in the aeroplane hangar café, nibbling on their sandwiches and discreetly sipping from Sylvie’s hip flask, hiding it when the waiting staff walked anywhere near their table. Finishing their lunch, they headed back to the stand and bought Bridget a sandwich.

‘It’s actually been quite quiet,’ said Bridget as she tucked into something which looked like a Chicken Tikka wrap that someone had forgotten to put the chicken in. ‘I seem to remember it being like this last time but it picked up mid-afternoon, so we might as well make the most of the down time.’ Taking turns with the only chair, the three friends chatted idly.

‘How’s your friend, Sylvie, the one who lost her husband?’ asked Eddie.

‘She is doing rather well,’ replied Sylvie. ‘I haven’t heard from her much since the funeral, but I’ve heard via other friends at The Women’s League that she’s perked up lately.’ Sylvie smiled and continued as she opened Facebook on her phone. ‘I’m so pleased. I think I mentioned that her husband wasn’t very nice, and it got worse after her son died but she seems to have a new lease of life, oh and a new hairdo,’ she added, clicking on a photo of Sarah.

Eddie looked at the photo of woman who clearly didn't look like she had recently lost her husband. Instead, she looked tanned and relaxed. 'Looks like she is on holiday, Sylvie.' He gestured to the location on the photo.

'Playa des Lagunas,' said Sylvie slowly as she tried to figure out where it was. 'Oh, it's in Ibiza apparently.'

'Blimey,' said Bridget. 'She *is* doing well, and is that someone's hand around her shoulder? Perhaps she really has moved on.'

'At least that gives me hope for my mum's friend who also just lost her husband,' Eddie said. 'She had just found out that he had a secret double life with a younger woman in London. He made it clear that he wanted to have his cake and eat it and wasn't going to leave either of them.'

'Oh, Eddie you are such a gossip. Do go on, dear'. Sylvie grinned.

'She was a friend of mum's from The Women's League, so at least they will look after her.'

At the mention of The Women's League, Bridget's ears pricked up. 'Where does your mum live, Eddie?'

'Hertfordshire, near Oxley, more like the outskirts of London, which apparently suited him as he could visit his mistress easily in their London flat.'

Initially Bridget didn't ask Eddie any more questions, but something was niggling her. Something didn't feel right, and she wasn't sure what it was. It just felt a little odd hearing about two members of The Women's League, who were clearly married to less-than-ideal men, who had died recently. Bridget supposed it could easily be explained by the age of those women at the League – fifty or sixty something with husbands who were the prime age for heart attacks and the like. But her imagination was starting to do its thing again.

'I'm just off the loo,' said Bridget, grabbing her notebook and phone. 'Won't be long.' She scurried off. Once in the toilet cubicle she looked up 'postcode finder' and 'Oxley, Hertfordshire. Her phone was slow and she had to hold it in the air to get a signal.

Realising she now had to stand on the toilet to read her phone, she wondered for a moment if she was finally losing the plot. Eventually her search returned the results. Postcodes starting with WD, in that area, notably WD7. She hurriedly opened her notebook to where she had written down the text message she had seen on Verity's phone during their sitting in London.

'4lbsOspecialWD7urgent'.

'WD7…WD7!' Bridget said out loud and then remembering she was still standing on a toilet, she sat down and quietly whispered to herself 'WD7…What the actual fuck.'

TWENTY-THREE

The Stapletons lived in a stunning country residence, in its own grounds, near Cirencester. Although it wasn't officially a manor house, Sebastian liked to call it Stapleton Manor. As a man in his early forties, Sebastian hated it when people shortened his name to Seb, thinking it made him sound like a singer from a boy band, although he didn't really know any boy bands. He was five foot five inches but insisted he was five foot six and a half inches rounding it up to five foot seven inches. He had very little hair but a significant paunch. Marrying into money, Sebastian didn't let people know that he was originally from a housing estate in Gloucester.

As a young boy, Sebastian had to walk to school through a park which separated the council estate from the wealthy parts of Gloucester with its Cathedral and private schools. He watched the posh boys play rugby and he would sometimes spy on them in the local cafes, listening in to their conversations. They were all called things like

Charles, Archie or Hugo. Sebastian, or Dean as he was known back then, would go home from school, stand in front of the mirror in his bedroom and practice speaking like the posh boys. He would also draw himself up to his fullest height and have imaginary conversations about horses, polo and *rugger*. He'd chosen Sebastian as his new name when he realised that being a Dean wasn't going to get him where he wanted to be in life. Stapleton as a surname was actually okay and keeping it was easier than changing it, so once he reached eighteen, he became Sebastian Stapleton and left Dean behind on the council estate.

At eighteen Sebastian moved to London, working hard to get a half decent job in a high street bank and eventually managed to secure a similar position with a better class of bank in the city. The character of Sebastian was really started to form as he hit his mid-twenties, and Dean was firmly in the past. Being surrounded by London bankers and stockbrokers, Sebastian fine-tuned his voice, speech patterns and topics of conversation. He joined a rowing club which was where he met the gorgeous but shy Olivia Montgomery. Researching her thoroughly, he discovered she was the only child of a minor peer in Oxfordshire who not only had family money but had founded one of the first computer companies in the UK. Her father was loaded, which meant she would be loaded too. Over the coming months he carried out a plan to woo poor Olivia, eventually marrying her within the year.

Over the following ten years, Sebastian endeared himself with her family and they purchased Stapleton *Manor* with the idea that Sebastian would run the small estate whilst Olivia looked after the children. But the children never came. Try as she might, Olivia did not fall pregnant and Sebastian was not happy about it, at all. After visiting a fertility clinic, he discovered that his sperm count was non-existent, but he never told Olivia. Instead, he claimed that the doctor had said he wasn't the problem. This was one of the many, many lies that Sebastian Stapleton told his lovely wife.

He always managed to turn things to his advantage, and he soon realised that rather than being a problem, being infertile meant he could sleep with as many women as he wanted without fear of getting them pregnant. He didn't even need to use condoms. Despite his slight paunch, he was good at talking to women, he was wealthy and had no problem finding women who also wanted a sweet night with no strings and no questions.

Olivia, understandably, was getting low and Sebastian also used that to his advantage. With her self-esteem already in its boots, he could easily manipulate her. On the rare occasions she tried to take some positive action, Sebastian found that a well-aimed slap followed by a string of apologies would easily stop her plans before they even started. He would explain how upsetting he found *her* infertility and how the thought of not having children caused his mood swings. Silver-tongued Sebastian was so good at psychological manipulation that gentle Olivia would end up thinking it was all her fault and even felt sorry for him.

However, Olivia did have a secret herself. Every Thursday evening, after Sebastian had left for his Gentleman's club, Olivia would drive to Cirencester for her local

Women's League meeting. She tentatively made friends and although she couldn't attend any other events, Thursday evening helped fill some of the gaping holes in her life. She could cope with Sebastian's temper, could easily cover up the bruises with make-up and she had accepted a life without children.

'I have a lovely life with Sebastian, a nice house and we are financially secure,' she would often say to her friends at the league. And Olivia believed this to a certain extent until one day she saw some unusual spotting on her pants accompanied by a strange rash around her vulva.

Taking a chum from The League with her, she made a doctor's appointment and was horrified to find she had a sexually transmitted disease. Despite telling the doctor and her friend that there was no way it was possible, realisation started to dawn, and Olivia could no longer put on a brave face. Tears fought their way out of her stoic face and as she dabbed her eyes, the make-up she had been using to hide the bruises washed away and the gentle face of Olivia started to tell a different story.

TWENTY-FOUR

Bridget struggled to keep her mouth shut as they drove home from the art fair. She had desperately wanted to tell Sylvie and Eddie what had been happening with the text messages, but she knew that they were only fledging suspicions, and it was way too early to share them. She knew she needed to figure out much more clearly what these messages meant and somehow find how they linked to the deaths of two men. Her attempts to convince herself she was being stupid, or that her imagination was running riot were in vain. The riot of thoughts was silenced by a stronger, louder feeling of unease.

'There is a difference between imagination and intuition,' she muttered to herself. Sometimes you must follow your intuition and trust it.

As soon as she was home, Bridget ran to the studio to get some headspace. She didn't stop to chat to her husband instead stuffing a slice of congealing pizza in her mouth and giving him a quick kiss. As she entered her studio, she was faced with the strangely smiling faces of Verity Scanlan covering her walls. The sketches and studies she had made of Verity now seemed a little scary and the woman's eyes were following Bridget round the room.

'For fuck's sake, Bridget, get a grip,' she said aloud as she laid a large sheet of paper on the studio floor, copying the two text messages she had seen on Verity's phone, onto the paper. She then drew a line from the first one and wrote BS32, Almondsbury, Tisbury on the end of it. She then drew another line from the second message and wrote, WD7, Oxley, Eddie's mum's friend's husband. What was his name? She wasn't sure he had mentioned it but never mind. So that was definitely a postcode, and the men did indeed die, but what did the rest of the text code mean? She didn't have a clue. Both men were not very nice, she knew that much and one of the women certainly didn't seem badly affected by her husband's death. Did she somehow kill her husband? She shuddered at the thought, but what did that have to do with Verity and the phone text messages? Bridget was just too confused by it all. She needed help, someone she could trust, someone who wouldn't completely laugh at her suspicions. Someone who knew much more about this sort of thing than she did.

TWENTY-FIVE

Sylvie was worried about her old friend Sarah Tisbury, especially after seeing her Ibiza Facebook post. She had wanted to visit Sarah and support her as much as she could following the death of her husband Frank so soon after losing her son, but she was having trouble getting hold of her.

Slightly concerned she had called the chair of her local Women's League and asked her if she had heard from Sarah. She informed Sylvie that Sarah had left the league and was on a world cruise with someone called Marco. Margaret, the chair of the local group, appeared completely at ease about it all, telling Sylvie that Sarah had seemed very happy when she had called to cancel her membership. She had told Margaret to give her love to all her friends and then quickly hung up.

'I could even hear the sounds of a Rumba in the background,' Margaret said, adding, 'Sarah seems to have found a completely new lease of life and said she was going to honour Rory's life by regaining hers to the fullest.'

Sylvie had mixed feelings about this and about Margaret, if she was honest, so she said as much. Wasn't Margaret at all concerned? Was it not slightly disrespectful that within a month of burying her husband, Sarah had run off with a Spanish lover. Shouldn't they do something to make sure this Marco wasn't taking advantage of her?

'No,' Margaret snapped rudely. 'Perhaps you should keep your nose out of it, let Sarah have some fun and stop fussing.'

Unsurprisingly and more than a little upset, Sylvie decided she would leave her old Women's League group and join a more local one. It was too far to drive since she had moved in with Edgar anyway, so it was probably a good idea. There was a branch of the League in Cirencester, which was closer, so Sylvie transferred her membership. After a couple of weeks, she realised that although they were rather posh, they were a nice group of women, and she quickly made friends.

TWENTY-SIX

Once Olivia Stapleton had recovered from the initial shock of realising that her husband was a liar, an abuser and had been cheating on her for years, she started to feel a little fire in her belly, that was quickly turning into a blaze.

Once she had ruled out this fire being the Sexually Transmitted Disease that her husband had given her, she looked at things a little differently. Despite being married to a man who had systematically belittled her and destroyed her confidence, she had more power than she had previously thought. However, Olivia needed to bide her time. She didn't confront Sebastian about the nasty itch he had generously donated to her. The antibiotics and cream the GP had prescribed were working well and she was feeling a lot better, so things carried on as normal, or so Sebastian thought.

He sat at the dining table, skimming his newspaper and checking his mobile phone every few minutes, while Olivia prepared his lunch. Several times a week Sebastian ate a ploughman's platter which included a chunk of cheese, a hunk of French baguette that she drove every morning to collect fresh from the village, and a ramekin dish filled with homemade chutney. Occasionally she would add some salad or a tomato, but this was always left untouched.

That afternoon, Olivia was getting the train to Rutshire to visit her elderly father. Her mother had died a couple of years ago and he and Olivia were closer than ever now, given that she was his only child. On the train, Olivia tried to compose her thoughts, so she could tell her father what had been going on, without getting too upset. He picked her up from the station and she soon found herself crying. The kind but strong old man pulled the car over and held his daughter in his arms as she told him what she suspected. As he wiped her tears away, he could see the bruises Sebastian had left on her cheekbone the previous week which were now yellowing as they aged. Her father stifled a tear and managed to keep calm as her story unfolded.

'Olivia, before we do anything, we need to make a case against this man. We need evidence, hard evidence of what he has been up to, and I know what we should do,' he continued, telling Olivia about a private detective that he had once hired to unearth some corporate sabotage in his company.

'The detective agency also deal with domestic problems. I can call the, when we get home.'

TWENTY-SEVEN

Bridget didn't know what to do with herself. She was halfway through painting a portrait of a woman who she suspected may somehow be connected to the death of someone, but she didn't have a clue what to do with her suspicions. Was she going mad or was there something really going on? She desperately needed to speak to someone, but it would have to wait.

'Oh well, at least the portrait's going well, Bridget,' she muttered in an attempt to calm down ahead of what might be a difficult day.

It was usually at this point in the process that the sitter would visit her at the studio and see what progress she had made. It also meant that Bridget would receive the second instalment payment. Having already received and immediately spent the initial deposit, she was more than keen to be paid as the recent art fair sales hadn't been good and the second payment would also serve as a sweetener for her husband. As well as meeting to discuss the progress of the portrait and the next payment, Bridget also had a little plan up her sleeve.

Verity had texted ahead announcing that Anthea would also be coming along, as technically she was the one who commissioned the portrait. Anthea would meet Verity at the local railway station, and they would get a taxi to the studio together.

As she greeted the women at the studio door, Bridget sensed that neither was at all happy. Anthea had lost the chirpy, chatty nature she had seen during their brief meeting in London and was now quiet and pensive. Verity also seemed to be struggling but managed to greet Bridget and chat casually as they walked into the studio. Bridget, however, had started to really get to know this woman, her facial expressions, the subtle changes in her demeanour that showed how she really felt, and she could tell that Verity was having to work hard to keep her cool. Bridget made some coffee and the three women stood in front of the partially completed portrait of Verity. To Bridget's relief, Verity's mood relaxed and lifted as she took in the work so far.

'My goodness,' she said, 'this is stunning. I look so strong and…umm… vibrant, and I love how the blouse is looking.'

It's doubtful that anyone other than a portrait artist understands the relief that arrives at this particular moment. The utter feeling of bliss that emerges, knowing that what you have made, is being received well. Bridget beamed inside and out.

'Obviously it's a long way from being finished, but I'm

pleased with it so far,' she said, consciously sucking up all the lovely happy chemicals that were swimming around her body. 'And I think I'll include the book that you brought with you that first meeting,' Bridget added casually, setting her little plan in motion.

'I can't remember what book it was. What did I bring with me?'

'The life and times of Lucrezia Borgia,' Bridget said lightly, and at that very moment, it felt like a bomb had dropped in the room.

Anthea's face rose in colour, and she had to turn away. Bridget could have sworn she said something under her breath but didn't catch it. Conversely, the colour drained from Verity's face, but she didn't miss a beat.

'Oh, I wouldn't bother. I actually never got round to reading that book. Why not include a different book? I'm currently reading *A Handmaid's Tale*, that's a feminist text with lots of complexity – why not put that in instead?'

Now it was Bridget's turn to stumble over her words. 'That's quite a book,' she said. 'I just wonder if it's a little too umm… I don't know…a bit controversial perhaps.' Bridget immediately realised that the conversation was spiralling out of control. Verity turned on Bridget with a venomous look in her eyes.

'Controversial…controversial?' she repeated the word. 'Good God, woman you haven't got a clue, have you? No idea what men around the world put thousands of women through every day. Next you will be telling me you are happily married and wouldn't change a thing.' Verity clenched her teeth.

Bridget's happy chemicals had now well and truly left her system.

'Okay, let's not worry about it for now,' said Bridget quietly, shocked at how well her plan had worked but also more than a little scared. 'We can figure it out later.' She could see Anthea nodding furiously as she gathered up her belongings, clearly eager to make a quick exit.

After a few more minutes of uncomfortable chit chat, mostly around how nice the coffee was, Bridget brought their attention back to the agreeable aspects of the portrait, making sure that her next payment wasn't in jeopardy. The strange pair of women quickly drained their mugs and left. Closing the studio door, Bridget flopped onto the sofa and breathed the biggest sigh of relief possible.

TWENTY-EIGHT

As soon as the taxi rounded the corner away from Bridget's studio, Anthea let rip as much as she could with her voice hushed so the taxi driver couldn't hear.

'How could you be so stupid, Verity? A fucking book about one of the most famous female poisoners in history. What the fuck were you thinking?' Without giving Verity the opportunity to reply she continued, 'And then, you made it worse by saying another book about man haters. For fuck's sake, Verity you can be really stupid sometimes.'

'The Borgia book wasn't the problem, Anthea, but your reaction was really fucking weird. God knows what that bloody artist thinks about us both after that debacle,' Verity shouted in a whispery voice. 'And why are you so tetchy, Anthea? What the bloody hell is wrong with you?'

Anthea produced her phone and showed Verity a small London news item, titled 'Suspected poisoning of four-year-old boy'.

Verity was confused 'What's that about?'

'It seems Clara McArthur's husband took a jar of olives from his house to his London flat where he stayed with his lover and young son. And the stupid woman gave her boy some of our *special* olives.'

'Oh shit.' Verity's face paled again.

'Luckily, we have a League member in the local police who wangled a visit to the woman, and she managed to remove the olives before they started testing things in the flat, so it will be impossible to trace. But it was a close thing, Verity, and it has really shaken me. I mean, the boy is okay. She took him to the children's hospital, and he recovered quickly but it really shook me. Nothing like this has happened before but I'm bloody relieved that we got to the olives in time.'

Verity was quiet for a moment before saying, 'If the worst had happened, well that doesn't bear thinking about, but you did well to rescue the situation, Anthea. We just need to make sure that all our safeguards are still in place. I'm sorry about what happened in the studio. Bridget is clueless and is not a threat. If I thought she would be, I wouldn't have agreed to the portrait.'

Bridget, however, was far from clueless. The behaviour of the two women had provided her with many things to ponder. She just needed someone to be Watson to her burgeoning internal Sherlock Holmes and she finally knew who to ask.

TWENTY-NINE

Olivia girded herself as she opened the buff manila folder the man had given to her, earlier that day. They had arranged to meet in a Starbucks, which he said was always noisy and would make it difficult for people to listen in. The man looked totally ordinary to Olivia, nothing like she thought a private investigator would look like. He had sadness in his eyes as he passed her the file and he told her to read it later, perhaps with a whisky. He also told her to line up a good friend to talk to after she had finished reading about Dean.

'Dean? Who's Dean?'

The investigator didn't reply, but later that day, Olivia found out exactly who Dean was.

Once she had arrived at her friend's house, the one from The Women's League who she had initially confided in, Olivia had politely asked for a large scotch and opened the manila folder. She read the documents cover to cover, pausing every now and then to let out a cry of utter disbelief. The whisky sat untouched. Once she had finished reading, she passed the folder to her friend who also read it all and made use of the whisky instead. They sat for a while, Olivia struggling to speak.

‘I think it’s time to take action, real action this time, lasting action, Olivia,’ her friend said.

‘Yes, but what?’

THIRTY

The Jam Maker

Nobody pays much attention to garden sheds. Such a normal part of both urban and rural life, they are almost invisible as they nestle amongst overgrown bushes and trees in the gardens they call home. Just as the humble garden shed sits unnoticed, so do the things that take place in these funny, little, wooden structures.

One particularly ordinary shed sat invisible at the end of a particularly ordinary country garden. In the summertime, butterflies buzzed around the sprawling buddleia bush as the scent of soft, pink roses filled the air. Right now, in early spring, the shrubs were still bare, the earth dank, and the only scent was a strange, sickly-sweet smell emanating from the shed, whose windows were fogged with condensation.

Pushing the door open to make sure the shed was well

ventilated, a figure wearing an apron and a hair net removed their FFP2 mask, taking a moment to breathe in the fresh, damp air before going back inside. Taking a small vial from the shelf, they measured the exact quantity required and added it to the hot, sticky mixture, gently bubbling on the stove. Taking great care to stir the mixture without any splashes or spills, they turned off the gas to let the mixture cool.

THIRTY-ONE

Olivia scanned the QR code and the automated delivery box door swung open. She removed the parcel contained inside and drove home straight away, not listening to the radio, not playing any music, just staring straight ahead at the road in front. She knew what the parcel contained.

Once back in her kitchen, she lifted the Kilner jars out and placed five of them in the cupboard, leaving one on the kitchen worktop. The label read 'Green Onion Chutney' and she opened the jar giving it a cautious sniff.

It just smelt like chutney.

An hour later Sebastian arrived in the kitchen for his Ploughman's supper. He had already told Olivia he was going out with friends in Cheltenham for the evening and would be home very late, if at all. She acknowledged this and smiled sweetly, noticing him scratch his crotch a little longer than usual as he sat down at the table.

Twenty minutes later he had finished his supper of Stilton, chutney and crusty bread. Olivia had chosen the strongly flavoured mature Stilton just in case, and Sebastian was now washing it all down with a glass of port. Olivia told him that she didn't feel very well and was off for a lie down. Once he had left the house, she came back downstairs, washed up and poured herself a glass of wine. She had been told what to expect and how to behave over the coming weeks, but it was going to be difficult to contain her rage.

Then she remembered that Sebastian, Dean, or whatever his name was, had lied and manipulated her for fifteen years and her rage hardened into cold determination. Olivia was young enough to rebuild her life after he had gone, she might even be able to have some kids of her own. She was only thirty-nine and many women had children into their forties.

She didn't even need to get married again – she had enough money to do it on her own. After a second glass of wine, she turned on the TV and found an episode of Midsomer Murders.

THIRTY-TWO

The visit from Anthea and Verity had really upset Bridget and although she had kept her calm at the time, she had spent the next hour crying and trying to rationalise what had just happened. Her mobile phone pinged, and she was relieved to see that the second instalment for the portrait had thankfully been paid by The Women's League.

'Why do I have to paint these bloody portraits?' It took so much out of her every time, for all sorts of different reasons, but this current situation really was beyond the pale. If she didn't need to worry about money, life as a painter would be so different.

She believed deep down that she could up her game if she didn't need to constantly satisfy her husband's insecurities by taking portrait commissions which she hated and although she didn't mind running the painting group, it did take up energy and time that she could ill afford. She was in her late fifties now and her energy levels were not as they had been in her forties and much less than in her thirties. Bridget also felt that time was running out professionally and although she often tried to reassure herself by reading articles about female artists that flourished in their seventies or eighties, she knew that women like that were very much in the minority. Sometimes she felt completely stuck.

Letting her eyes wander around the studio, Bridget's gaze settled on the half-finished portrait of Verity. As she locked eyes with her, she felt like Verity was laughing at her.

'Think you are something special do you, Bridget?' Verity's imaginary voice said. 'You're an old, washed-up artist who will never do anything remarkable with your work,' the mocking voice continued. 'You are a disgrace to the women who fought against the patriarchy to give you your freedom and this is how you use it.'

Bridget wasn't sure she actually believed that, but it still hit her hard in that vulnerable moment. Verity's voice in her head did not let up, 'You can't make decent money painting and only survive because of your husband's job.' Those last words hurt her, even though they were spoken by her own mind. Unfortunately, she knew there was some truth in that comment and her mind had fed on her deepest fears about herself.

'Fuck you,' she said quietly. 'Fuck you, Verity,' she shouted out loud this time. 'Fuck you and your posh job, your posh clothes and your evil fucking soul.' Oh this felt better. 'I don't know what your fucking organisation is up to, but I will figure it out!' Bridget was now standing up and found herself picking up the pot of green paint she had been using to paint the emerald trousers in the portrait. She threw it at the wall of photos and sketches. Yes, this is what she needed to do. 'Fuck you, fuck your dark, ugly office, your cold heart and your fucking bitching face.'

At that last fuck, Bridget realised she had a Stanley knife in her hand and was carving through Verity's face. The canvas split beautifully and within two more slices, Verity's face fell away from the painting. Realising she had wrecked the painting she decided that she might as well make it worthwhile, so she cut up the loose piece of canvas into tiny pieces and burnt them in the fire along with several sketches from the sittings.

Later that afternoon, as the burning smell started to fade, Bridget couldn't avoid the obvious realisation – she had to start a new portrait from scratch. She had already been paid the second instalment and there was no other option.

THIRTY-THREE

The slightly mature blonde that Sebastian had pulled in the sticky-floored bar, turned out to be nearly as old as his mother.

'Never mind,' he told himself. 'Needs must.'

Olivia hadn't been putting out lately, citing women's problems which had started to really piss him off. He hadn't had much to drink that night as his stomach was playing up. In fact, he hadn't felt well lately at all, and Olivia had booked a doctor's appointment for him the following week. Dropping his trousers, he used his hand to steady himself on the chair next to the bed, but his legs felt odd. They felt weak and slightly numb, mostly around his feet. He stumbled a little.

His lady friend murmured in a rather raspy voice, 'Careful love, you don't want to hurt yourself before we've had our fun.' She pulled him alongside her and he chuckled, not willing to admit he wasn't feeling quite right. 'Let's get going then, lad,' she continued, reaching down his Y-fronts and struggling to find his non-existent penis. After a few minutes trying to coax it to life, she huffed. ‘Come on boy, let’s see what you can do.’

Sebastian couldn’t do anything, well his penis couldn’t. His stomach was still aching, his legs felt funny and now his groin was feeling strange, not exactly weak but numb.

A better man might have apologised or explained what was happening or at least offered to give his lady friend some pleasure, but Sebastian was not a better man. He mumbled something rude about his lady friend not being pretty enough and started to get dressed. Going to the bathroom he relieved himself before quickly exiting the cheap hotel room. Forgetting himself for a moment, he left fifty quid on the side telling her to get a taxi home.

‘I’m not a fucking prostitute,’ the woman yelled as he closed the door.

Sebastian couldn’t go home, he didn’t feel well enough to drive home and Olivia wasn’t expecting him anyway, so at the hotel reception he paid for another room and went straight back into the lift. Once in the new room he rushed to the toilet and only just made it in time, letting go of what felt like three days’ worth of food.

‘Jesus, it must have been that Chicken Madras.’

With his legs feeling slightly better now, he stood up and splashed some water in his face and looked at himself in the mirror. Perhaps he had had a lucky escape with that woman earlier, she was way too old for him. He assured himself that he was still a good-looking bloke, and this was just a rough day. But Sebastian had noticed that his hair had thinned in recent weeks, although his roots were getting darker somehow. At least that distracted from the hair loss.

Had Sebastian been a chemist or expert in neurology or toxicology, he might have suspected that something else was going on. Had Sebastian taken himself to the hospital and had a blood test, it's unlikely that the blood test would have shown a toxic level of Thallium in his blood as most regular laboratories didn't screen for it. Had Sebastian realised he was slowly being poisoned, he might have stopped eating the same things day in, day out. But Sebastian didn't know any of this. He attended his GP appointment and was told to cut down on alcohol and fatty foods, but he rapidly deteriorated in the coming weeks and one day, he fell asleep in another strange hotel bedroom, after another failed sexual encounter, with his pants around his ankles.

He never woke up.

THIRTY-FOUR

The new Women's League group in Cirencester was a lot nicer and much more relaxed than Sylvie had expected and by late Spring she was feeling upbeat. Her new League friends in Cirencester had encouraged her to start cold water swimming and whilst she still currently hated it, Sylvie was confident she would start loving it soon.

'If Davina McCall likes it, it must be good,' she kept saying to Edgar, trying to convince herself, more than him.

They had also introduced her to some new authors, some of which were on the more rigorous side of feminist literature. It had certainly been enlightening, but Sylvie took it in her stride and laughed about it with Edgar when she got home from the meetings. Edgar kept her grounded, but in a fun way and always handed her a nice gin and tonic when she came through the door. He didn't belittle the feminist theories that Sylvie tried to explain to him, he listened, adding his own point of view which was always quite balanced.

One of the unexpected surprises of joining the Cirencester League was that Sylvie had met Eddie's aunt, Linda. Although at first neither of the women knew that Eddie was a friend in common, but when the meeting minutes listed Linda Best as the secretary, Sylvie decided to ask.

'I have a young friend who's a Best,' Sylvie offered.

'Rather common name really,' replied Linda. 'Although most people our age think of George Best, the footballer from the seventies or perhaps it was the sixties, I can't really remember.'

They both laughed.

'My friend's a policeman who attends my local art group,' Sylvie added, at which point they realised the joint connection. From then on, they often chatted about *young* Eddie and the happenings at the art group and during one gin lubricated chat, Sylvie let it slip that Bridget was painting a portrait of Verity Scanlan.

'Sod it,' said Sylvie. 'That was meant to be a secret. I get a bit over excited sometimes and forget who is meant to know what.' She quickly swore Linda to secrecy.

'No need to worry but if it helps, I'll tell you something about Verity,' Linda whispered. 'I really don't like Verity Scanlan. I worked for The League years ago, often reporting to Verity. She was nice for the first couple of years and then something happened, and she changed, almost overnight.'

Sylvie moved closer to Linda. 'Do you know what happened?'

Linda shook her head. 'We all had different theories, but she used to wear a wedding ring and one day we noticed it was missing. Whether she had a bad divorce or something, I don't know. It felt more than that.'

Linda paused, took a deep breath in, making Sylvie realise that she had a lot more to say. 'Someone said that they thought they saw some bruises on her arm one day, but that could have been anything, and we never saw any again. Someone else thought she had lost a lot of weight, worrying so. Someone else said she kept vanishing to the toilet and would come back much calmer and settled and people wondered if she was taking drugs. There was so much gossip flying about, but nothing was ever proved and after a few years we just accepted the new version of Verity. Since then she has been bitter, hard-nosed and not someone you want to get on the wrong side of. Anyway, this was over fifteen years ago, and she has done great things for The Women's League since so she must have got over whatever happened.'

Sylvie was shocked. Not least because Linda appeared to be a gossip but also because of the theories about Verity.

Linda continued, 'Anyway, you can make your own mind up, Sylvie. She's apparently gracing us with her presence at our gala ball and is giving the after-dinner speech. You could bring a guest too. Men are allowed, so we could invite Eddie as your plus one. I haven't seen him for ages.' She beamed at this idea. Sylvie was still grappling with the gossip about Verity and without much thought, nodded in agreement.

'That's sorted then, I'll put you down for a ticket and get one for Eddie too. It's black tie so we need to make sure he has something suitable to wear,' Linda said in a matter-of-fact voice.

Sylvie hadn't listened properly as she was thinking about the portrait of Verity and wondered what Bridget would make of all this gossip. In recent months Sylvie and Bridget had become closer and she wondered if she should tell her all this speculation about Verity. Perhaps Bridget already knew about it all or had known Verity for years and that's why she was chosen to do the portrait in the first place.

Pondering more, Sylvie wondered whether that was the reason that Bridget kept the portrait a secret as she felt some loyalty to Verity. She quietened her thoughts.

No, Bridget was a good person and definitely wouldn't be impressed if Sylvie gossiped to her about Verity.

THIRTY-FIVE

'I am such a bad person,' Bridget said as she stared at the portrait. A gaping hole was now where Verity's face should have been.

There was no way she was going to tell her husband that she had destroyed the portrait. Not only would it wreck the carefully crafted story she had told him about the timescales, but he would also probably find out what her real fee for a portrait was, which was way more than he thought. He would also find out that she had spent, well, squirrelled away most of the money to fund her trips and residencies. Over the years she had maintained the illusion that she worked slowly and didn't earn much from each commission, to prevent her husband turning her into a production line. Bridget was, as she reflected, quite cunning and not terribly honest with him about many things, but especially money.

Bridget had flung an old sheet over the damaged portrait, to hide the mess. She hadn't looked at it for a couple of days, worried that Verity might somehow start shouting at her from her disfigured painted face. Although Verity's whole face, including her mouth were missing, Bridget knew that her imagination would easily accommodate for this and still allow the portrait to speak to her like the others always did. But what happened was more surprising. After staring at the sheet for what felt like hours, Bridget slid the paint splattered fabric off and sat back down to look at her handy work.

The Verity-face shaped hole was now filled with a view of the studio behind the painting. Through the hole Bridget could see the wall of charcoal sketches she had made of Verity. It made a weird patchwork of mini-Verity faces. As she thought about it more, it occurred to Bridget that it was almost like Verity's outward facing persona had been stripped away, enabling multiple versions of her to be exposed. It made for a fascinating type of portrait and grabbing her phone, she took multiple photos of the damaged portrait with the background wall showing through, just as she could see it at that very moment. Knowing she had to start a new painting, Bridget mused whether these strange images would inform the new portrait somehow. She printed several of the photos out, added them to the wall of charcoal sketches and started to stretch a new canvas.

'No point in delaying the inevitable,' she muttered, confident that by the end of the day she would have the beginnings of a new portrait, perhaps an even better one.

THIRTY-SIX

He hated to admit it, but Eddie was worried that he had made a big mistake in taking this new job and moving away. He had uprooted Graham who was doing okay but Eddie hadn't made any work friends yet despite being in his new job for several months.

'Friendships take time,' Graham had reassured him.

Eddie was bored at work. All the Murder Investigation Team in South Gloucestershire seemed to do was survive on *possible* murders that *might* have taken place.

One such suspicious death was reported by a coroner who had examined the body of a man found naked at a place called Severn Beach. Eddie had been excited when he was asked to visit Severn Beach and make some preliminary investigations. For reasons which on reflection could only be put down to desperation, he took some swimming trunks and a towel with him. It was only once he had left home that he remembered it was March and probably too cold to swim.

'Never mind,' he told himself. 'I'll have a nice stroll on the beach and an ice cream at least.'

Perhaps he would take Graham there at the weekend – they could have fish and chips and a cosy pint afterwards.

As Eddie left the motorway and drove through the flat, desolate village, he couldn't see any signs of holiday life. No holiday chalets or camping sites. No shops selling buckets and spades and no amusement arcades either. He thought it strange until he parked up and walked towards the seawall. Anticipating a sandy or at least shingly beach, Eddie was dismayed to only find large concrete lumps, soon followed by mud and pebbles. The mud stretched out into the distance, blending into shallow trickles of murky water and eventually into a slither of brown, flat water. This… this was the beach? It was Severn Beach. To the left the slither of brown water extended into the flat horizon with no discernible features. To the right, almost shadowing the *beach* was the towering, grey motorway bridge, stretching to Wales.

Whatever had he been thinking? What a disappointment. For a moment it had cheered him up to think that a nice beach was fairly close to work. It would have been a silver lining to the grey cloud that his new place of work was turning out to be. But Severn Beach was not a beach of any sort and certainly not silver, sunny or shiny.

At least he had left his swimming shorts and towel in the car – that would have been embarrassing. He was due to meet up with his colleague Amita and make some local enquiries about the body but as he turned to phone her, he found her already walking towards him. They quickly found the location where the body had been discovered and made enquires at the houses close to the site. After a long morning of door knocking and conversations which were unproductive, they both agreed it was vital to visit the nearest pub and question the locals over some much-needed refreshments.

If Severn Beach needed to change its name to avoid being reported under the Trade Descriptions Act, the Sailors' Rest needed to do the same. There were no boats here, no evidence of boats, no old structures which alluded to boats or ships, no rowing boats, no sailing dinghies not even a paddle board. Nothing that said sailor of any kind and the pub itself showed little evidence of being restful either. This was evident from the moment they crunched on the broken glass on the pavement by the entrance door.

'Sorry about that, the cleaner's not turned up,' said a spotty-faced barman. 'It was a bit spicy in here last night,' he continued as he rubbed a bruise on his check.

'No rest for the sailors last night then,' chuckled Eddie, quickly realising that this joke was lost on this boy who was now wiping down a sticky bar stool, with an even stickier cloth.

'Did you want to order some drinks, some beer or maybe wine for the lady?' asked the barman.

Eddie wondered if this acne laden boy was even old enough to serve alcohol but put that thought aside as he produced his warrant card and introduced himself and Amita.

'No, we are investigating the body that was found on the beach a couple of days ago.'

'All sorts get washed up here – it's the strong tide you see. Second biggest tidal drop in the world. Over fifteen metres sometimes. We find dead farm animals, children's play equipment and even found a life size plastic elephant once.'

Eddie stifled a shocked laugh. Severn Beach was not only an un-beach, but also a weird place.

'Perhaps you might be able to identify the body that was found,' Eddie said, as the bar boy nodded. 'He was naked so obviously had no ID on him. The photo isn't nice so only look if you feel comfortable.'

The boy reached his hand out and Amita showed him a photo of the man's head and shoulders.

'Oh man. Aw nah.' He wasn't shocked but instantly upset. 'That's Bungo. Aww that's such a bloody shame, dude,' he said somehow acquiring a vague Australian accent as he spoke. 'He was such a decent bloke was Bungo. Obsessed with the Bore and trying to surf it. For years he banged on about surfing it naked. Looks like he tried but got into trouble.' Shaking his head, the barman looked a little sad but summoned a shout to the whole pub which was empty apart from two other people also nursing bruises. 'Lads! Bungo's gone and drowned – the stupid fucker!' Facing Eddie and Amita now he felt it was important to explain that Bungo was one of his best customers and without him his takings would plummet.

And that was the end of Eddie's suspicious death. He had secretly hoped it was a murder, but it turned out the be the strange tale of an Australian man (why would you leave the sandy beaches of Australia and the lovely weather?) to live in a place that pretended to have a beach. A man who was obsessed with surfing something called the Severn Bore naked and unfortunately drowned.

Death through misadventure was the final verdict. Well at least this flurry of activity had provided a break from the routine and Eddie had learned a few things. Severn Beach wasn't a beach, the Severn Bore was basically a small wave produced inland a couple of days a year when the tide was just right, and it shouldn't be surfed naked.

On the way back to the station, Eddie resolved to have a chat with his boss. Perhaps there was something he could do to keep a little more motivated or maybe he could move sideways to a different job.

Whatever it was Eddie knew that something needed to happen soon, or he would die of boredom.

THIRTY-SEVEN

Sylvie was chomping at the bit. She had so much she wanted to talk to Eddie and Bridget about and it felt much more than a week has passed since their last art group. A private chat with Bridget about Verity would have to wait until after the other group members had left but she could talk to Eddie as they painted, sketched or whatever Bridget had planned for the day.

As usual Ralph and his owl arrived first after Sylvie, followed by all the regulars milling around and collecting water, desk easels and the other materials they needed. Eddie overheard a conversation between Margo, who was convinced she was a superb artist and elderly Margaret who had discreetly turned off her hearing aid as soon as Margo approached. Margo was ranting about how she had taken her work into several galleries locally, and they had all declined to sell her work, suggesting a local craft shop might be more appropriate. Margo had been so annoyed and had instead submitted one of her paintings to the Royal Academy Summer Exhibition.

'It's exceptionally hard to get your work in,' she told Margaret, who couldn't hear a thing Margo was saying but amazingly seemed to be nodding and shaking her head in the correct places.

'How clever' thought Sylvie, giving an internal chuckle.

Margo continued her rant saying, 'And do you know what the Royal Academy said?'

Sylvie at this point noticed that it wouldn't have mattered whether Margaret gave a nod or shook her head at that point as either would have suited the question. 'They said yes, but I must frame the painting and ship it to London to arrive on an exact date and it mustn't be wrapped. I mean, how on earth am I meant to do that?'

Bridget had intervened at this point. 'What a great achievement, I can help you find a suitable framer and courier.' She helpfully told Margo the rough cost of framing and shipping which turned her a little white.

Returning to her chair, Margo quietened significantly, and the group settled into their usual activities.

Coming over to Eddie and Sylvie, Bridget said brightly, 'I have a treat for you two today. I thought you could take it in turns to do a portrait of each other.' Both Eddie and Sylvie were unable to hide the look of terror on their faces. 'Don't worry, don't worry,' Bridget said quickly after seeing their faces. 'It'll be fun, and I know you will get so much from it and there is one other thing…' Bridget tapped the table in a fake drumroll, '…you are going to do it upside down.'

'Oh Bridget, I really don't think I can do that, it sounds terribly hard. Can't we just do it standing the right way up, I get so dizzy these days and think I'll probably be sick,' Sylvie said.

Bridget and Eddie both let out a howl of laughter and didn't stop quickly enough for Sylvie's liking.

'No silly, you draw Eddie the wrong way up, but you will be the right way up.' Bridget tried to suppress her amusement.

As Sylvie breathed a sigh of relief, Eddie continued chuckling while Bridget gathered some materials before Sylvie changed her mind. Eddie didn't seem phased at all and in fact, seemed excited by the idea.

Once they were up and running, with Eddie drawing Sylvie first, using charcoal and a nice, sharpened rubber, Bridget left them to it.

Returning later she gave Eddie a couple of pointers, saying he wasn't allowed to turn it the right way up until he was finished. She then left them to it and went to see how the rest of the group was getting on.

'I hear I am taking you on a date in a couple of weeks' time,' said Eddie.

'I beg your pardon young man,' Sylvie said, feigning shock as she smiled. 'I'm way too old for you and we are both happily married. So where are we going?' she asked.

'My auntie called me and invited me to a Women's League do and apparently I'm your plus one.'

Sylvie laughed. 'Oh goodness me, I completely forgot about that. You don't have to go Eddie. I can ask Edgar if you'd rather not, but Linda seemed to think it would be good for you to meet some new people.'

'Yes,' said Eddie, 'unlike my mum, she likes to get involved in people's lives and thinks she has a solution for everything.'

'Back in the day, we would call someone like that a busybody,' Sylvie said, instantly recalling all the gossip Linda had told her about Verity. 'But she means well, Eddie. Anyway, the League's big evening dos are always good fun, and all sorts of people go. We could take a hip flask again and have sneaky prinks in the taxi.' Sylvie tittered a little at this thought.

'I'd love to come with you, Sylvie, if that's okay with Edgar. I've been feeling bored and a bit lonely lately. My job isn't quite working out as well as I'd hoped,' Eddie continued and filled Sylvie in about the rather quiet murder squad and the recent suspicious death at Severn Beach. This had them both laughing as they wondered why you would want to surf naked in England.

The funny pair of friends now switched round with Sylvie taking her turn at drawing Eddie upside down. As they settled in, all was quiet in the studio. Sylvie was concentrating furiously on trying to draw Eddie's left eye and was sneakily trying to turn her head sideways in an attempt to cheat.

Suddenly, the peace and quiet was shattered by Ralph saying rather loudly, 'I have finished. I am done with this blasted owl. I am not painting his bloody claws or feathers anymore!'

The whole room erupted into applause, which wasn't

entirely appropriate, but everyone knew Ralph had been working on the owl for months and this was a momentous moment. Bridget propped his owl against a plain wall for all to admire and opened a celebratory pack of chocolate Hobnobs. The room settled back to happy chit-chat with a gentle undercurrent of celebration.

Ralph went home with a big smile and instructions to think about what he might want to work on next. Sylvie made plans with Eddie about the ball the following week and also asked Bridget if she could have a chat after people had left but Bridget told her she had already had a meeting planned with Eddie. To Sylvie, a meeting sounded important, so she resigned herself to talking to Bridget another time.

THIRTY-EIGHT

'You are doing really well, Eddie,' Bridget said. 'The portrait exercise today was super, and I really think that having you here has helped Sylvie no end. She's so young at heart and before you arrived, I think she was getting a little stuck. How are *you* finding the class though?'

'I'm enjoying it. I mean, I know I am a bit strange being the youngest but…'

'Thank God though, Eddie,' Bridget interrupted. 'You bring some energy and laughs with you.'

'I've been struggling with my work lately, Bridget. Coming here is a welcome change.' He explained about his boredom at work and the worry that he had upended his life and now thinking it hadn't been the right thing to do. He omitted the story about the dead, naked surfer on Severn Beach as he didn't know Bridget quite the way he knew Sylvie and just now Bridget looked a little serious.

'Well, if you are bored, perhaps what I'm going to tell

you might help. At the very least it might help settle my mind about something.' Bridget shuffled in her seat a little and Eddie sensed that she was feeling uneasy, so he decided to try and help her relax first.

'What's the painting you have been working on?' he said, gesturing to the large easel, covered by the sheet. 'We have all been wondering and didn't want to ask, although Sylvie seemed to know something about it; she told me it was confidential.'

Bridget adjusted herself in her seat and started to speak. 'The portrait is the starting point of everything I am about to tell you, Eddie. You'll have to bear with me though, it's all rather confusing and at the end of it you might think I'm bonkers.' She slipped off the sheet to reveal the damaged portrait.

Eddie just starred at the painting and the gaping hole that had previously been someone's face.

'Oh my God, Bridget. Did someone attack your work? This is definitely a police matter. I can call someone for you. Did they break into the studio? Do you know who it was? This is bloody awful.'

Bridget struggled to interrupt his outburst, 'No, Eddie, it wasn't a break in. It was me. I um…cut the face out of the painting.'

Eddie looked confused before Bridget quickly continued, 'It's not really why I wanted to talk to you but it's all tangled up together. Let me explain.'

Eddie sat quietly as Bridget explained about the portrait commission was of Verity Scanlan, head of The Women's

League. Eddie nodded saying he knew what The Women's League was.

'The first time I met her, she came here, that's what usually happens. I didn't exactly dislike her, but I didn't warm to her either.' Bridget shuffled her feet a little. 'To be honest, I don't often like the people whose portraits I am commissioned to paint, but financially, it's unavoidable.'

Eddie hadn't really given much thought as to how things worked financially for an artist. He assumed that Bridget must run a couple of classes a week, sell two or three paintings a month and then do the occasional art fair. He had seen her sell a couple of painting at the art fair but hadn't really thought much beyond that.

Bridget continued her story about Verity. 'The second sitting always takes place at the person's home or place of work, so I met her in her London office a few weeks later. She needed the toilet and left her phones out on the coffee table, but having two phones is a bit odd, isn't it?'

Eddie thought for a moment, turning his head from side to side in a pondering action. 'Not that unusual these days. If you are in a high up job where it's essential to have a mobile, you might have a work mobile and a personal phone too.'

Bridget looked a little surprised. 'I struggle to remember to charge one,' she said. 'But it was the thing that happened next that intrigued me. One of phones vibrated when she was out of the room. I just so happened to be rearranging the items on the table to draw them. That's all part of the process, having some personal items with you that might be included in the portrait. Anyway, I glanced at the phone to see a rather odd message on it.' Bridget showed Eddie the sketch on the wall which still had the text written on it. 'It's strange, isn't it?'

Eddie had to agree it was a little strange and Bridget continued explaining how she had been trying to figure out the different numbers and letters in the message eventually deciding it was the first part of a postcode covering Almondsbury in South Gloucestershire.

'That's near where I work, Bridget. It's a nice little village. The text looks like a delivery notification. I sometimes get sent those when a parcel is being delivered. You click on it and it tells you when the parcel is going to arrive – well supposedly,' he added.

'No, it wasn't one of those,' interjected Bridget. 'I mean Verity lives in London so why would she be tracking a parcel in South Gloucestershire and something else happened a couple of weeks later that made me start thinking more about it. You remember that Sylvie had a condolence card to send to her friend, that was the same postcode area, Eddie.'

At this Eddie shook his head. 'I really don't know what that has to with anything.'

'Okay,' said Bridget. 'I forgot to say that when I was in Verity's office, she came back in and noticed she had left the old phone out and quickly, too quickly in my opinion, snatched it up and put it away, as if she was worried about leaving it on display. At the time I thought it a little odd, but for the rest of the sitting, she had a very different face on her.'

Eddie laughed. 'What do you mean by a different face?'

'I'm a portrait painter, well I paint a lot of portraits and when you've been studying people's faces for forty years you tend to notice things that other people don't. I could see how different she was after leaving this secret phone on display. She was tetchy, talked even less and her eyes seemed to be searching me to see if I had seen something I shouldn't have.'

Sighing a little dismissively, Eddie said, 'So it's a secret phone now is it? Look I really don't see anything suspicious about this. Are you somehow saying that Verity knew about the death of Sylvie's friend's husband?'

Bridget looked frustrated. 'I haven't finished telling you it all yet, Eddie. Please try to be open minded, I know I am older than you but I'm not completely doolally. I know this all sounds completely random but there is something else.'

Eddie nodded, trying not to sigh too loudly.

'When Verity came here last week, the same phone fell down the side of my sofa. I only found it when it vibrated after she'd left.'

Eddie quickly interjected, 'And you just happened to look at her private text messages again, did you?'

Bridget looked a bit embarrassed, but it didn't stop her. 'Yes, and it was a similar text, this time with a different postcode. This time it was…' she fumbled with her note-book and eventually said, 'WD7 which apparently is Oxley, in Hertfordshire and I just wondered whether we, I mean you, could look into any strange events linked to Verity or perhaps The Women's League. I mean I know it's a bit of a long shot, but I just can't get this all out of my head and …'

But Eddie had stopped listening when she had

mentioned Oxley. 'My mum lives near Oxley,' he said flatly.

'Oh, that could be helpful,' Bridget said. 'You must know some local policemen.'

'No,' said Eddie, 'No, that's not the point Bridget. I mean I do know some local officers, but I don't need to ask them anything. I already know of at least one sudden death of a middle-aged man recently. It's the husband of one of someone Mum knows through The Women's League.'

At that moment, they both went very quiet before Bridget eventually asked, 'What happened to him? I mean how do you know about this?'

Eddie wasn't sure whether to tell her what he knew, but as he hadn't been told in an official capacity, he decided he would.

'Mum has a friend at The Women's League, a nice lady called Clara. I met her once,' he said.

At the mention of The Women's League, Bridget took a sharp intake of breath.

'When I visited Mum a couple of weeks ago, she said that Clara's husband, I can't remember his name, had died rather suddenly and in a compromising situation.'

'I recall you mentioning something about it to Sylvie at the art fair, but what do you mean by a compromising situation. Do you mean…?'

To avoid hearing another mature lady use the world shagging, Eddie quickly told Bridget how the man had been leading a second life for years and his pregnant girlfriend had turned up on his doorstep with her young son in tow and that three weeks later he was dead.

‘Yes,’ said Eddie feeling his face blush. ‘He died during or after a sex session with his girlfriend, I didn’t ask Mum for the details.’

‘He actually died while he was fucking?’ said Bridget, at which Eddie winced while nodding and wondering why he found it so difficult to hear older women say words like shagging and fucking. Was he a prude?

Bridget refocussed saying, ‘The Women’s League, that’s the issue.’ Eddie felt confused, but Bridget persevered, ‘The wives of these dead men were both members of The Women’s League. And according to your mum and Sylvie, both men were utter shits.’

Eddie tried to listen to Bridget and understand what she was thinking but he also knew how easy it was to imagine a connection between the two deaths, one that just wasn’t there. Both men were in the same demographic and that particular demographic was one where their wives would likely attend The Women’s League. It was just a question of numbers. But it was obvious to Eddie that Bridget was way too invested in the story she had woven in her head.

‘The Women’s League, Eddie. Verity Scanlan, the woman with the secret phone. She’s Chief Executive Officer of The Women’s League, and she is receiving text messages that are something to do with these two sudden deaths.’ Bridget almost spat out the last sentence. ‘I know it seems ridiculous, but I can’t get my head around the coincidences and she really is a strange woman.’

‘Bridget, lots of people are strange, that doesn’t make them killers which is what you are saying, isn’t it?’ Although he was trying to calm Bridget’s suspicions, underneath something was niggling at Eddie. Her dogged suspicions had planted a little seed of doubt. What if there was something in this? No, of course, there wasn't. There must be a simple and reasonable explanation for all of this.

'I know this all sounds like a mad conspiracy theory, but these texts seem directive somehow. Oh and I forgot to mention the newspaper.' Bridget briefly told Eddie about Verity's reaction to the article about Frank Tisbury's death and Eddie had to admit he could see how she ended up with twenty-nine by adding only two plus four. 'Could you just do a little digging around and see if other sudden deaths are related to The Women's League somehow, please?'

'Give me time to think about this all, Bridget. Drop me an email with the details of the texts, the men's names, the newspaper article and I'll give it some thought.'

After this uncomfortable concession, Eddie finished his tea rather quickly and left the studio mumbling that he had was late for dinner.

THIRTY-NINE

Later that evening while mindlessly scrubbing away at the wok, Eddie's mind started to ponder what Bridget had told him. Yes, he could understand slightly where Bridget had got these strange ideas from but how to explore them further was going to be tricky.

'Hey,' Graham suddenly said, coming up behind him and planting a kiss on his head. 'I appreciate your eagerness to wash up, but woks aren't really meant to be scrubbed. It took me months to get that lovely non-stick surface.'

Eddie stopped scrubbing at the delicate surface of the pan and turned to face Graham. 'Sorry, I'm just struggling with a lot of things at the moment.' He'd wanted to talk to Graham for weeks and took the opportunity to explain how his job wasn't turning out as he had hoped and how he felt guilty for uprooting Graham from his life in London. He also told Graham about the dead, naked surfer which thankfully made them both laugh.

Eager to reassure him, Graham said, 'The way I see it is that you are married to a really good looking bloke who loves you, you have a decent job and you have made some friends at the art group, even if they are all pretty old. You had a good laugh at Severn Non-Beach – you really must take me there, even if it's just for a pint in the Sailors' Unrest.'

Eddie smiled. Graham was always so calm and positive.

His lovely husband took a breath and continued, 'And you nearly had a murder to solve, even if it was just a daft, naked Australian who drowned on the world's smallest wave. I imagine there'll be another murder to solve soon, this time a real one.' As those last words left Graham lips, it occurred to Eddie that he might already have a murder to solve, possibly two.

'It's funny you should say that. Something odd happened today after the art group and it's been playing on my mind all evening.' Eddie poured them both a glass of wine and settled down to tell Graham about his strange conversation with Bridget and her rather mad ramblings, but how he was now thinking there might just be something in it.

'Eddie,' Graham said without hesitation. 'It actually sounds to me like she's onto something and I think you should find a way to explore her suspicions, even if you have to do it in your own time.' He then went on to tell Eddie about a true crime podcast he had listened to where the murderer had killed people using poison letters. 'You could be uncovering the crime of the century, Eddie love, just think about that. The worse that could happen is that it is all complete nonsense.'

'Actually, the worse that could happen is I get sacked,' Eddie said. 'I'll do something about it, but I need to tread carefully at work. I need to think of a way of investigating without getting into trouble and I'm not sure how to do that.' He took a purposeful breath and at that moment he felt a bit excited for the first time in a long time. Pondering this surprising feeling he added, 'It certainly will test my detective skills, if nothing else.'

FORTY

It had been over fifteen years since they had set up the Jam Maker programme and they had lost count of how many women they had helped by relieving them of their husbands and partners. The world was better off without the abusers, rapists, misogynists and tyrants of all kinds they had helped to remove.

The first time had not been easy.

She had been very different back then. Back before it all began, Verity had been a strong woman, principled but also loving and passionate.

No one knew that many years ago Verity had had a baby. Her bump had shown so very little it was easy to keep her pregnancy and family life a complete secret, which is what she wanted as she feared it would change things at work. Although she never doubted that she would love her child unconditionally, she also knew that she would end up talking about nipple shields, mastitis, and weaning. The anticipated talk about nappies, the different types and their relative benefits and drawbacks, was something she couldn't bear the thought of. She was intelligent, well read and could think of a thousand things better to talk about. So, she devised a plan to have her baby in secret and keep it separate from her world at work.

Around six months into her pregnancy Verity realised that she wouldn't be able to hide her bump much longer. She wove a story about having a relative in the United States who was dying and with her being the only surviving relative, she had to cross the Atlantic to sort out her affairs. She arranged a three month sabbatical which she planned later to extend by saying she herself had become seriously ill whilst in the states. This would give her enough time to have the baby and get through the first few months without detection. The mysterious illness would also help explain why she looked tired upon her return to work.

Richard, Verity's husband was not keen on the idea. In fact, he had never been keen on having a family at all, liking the money and freedom he and Verity had as DINKs (Dual Income No Kids). He was angry when Verity had fallen pregnant, angry that she wanted to keep it and even angrier that she then decided to conceal the pregnancy and birth which he thought was pointless. In truth their relationship was rocky at best before her pregnancy, started to fail during the pregnancy and was barely limping along in the months following the birth.

He didn't like the attention the baby demanded, even with help from a live-in nanny from Norlands, who had signed an NDA and was sworn to secrecy about the baby's birth. He resented that at the end of a day's work he couldn't just have a beer, watch some TV and have sex with his wife. Verity, having gone back to work when the baby was three months old, just wanted to sleep. Richard made it no secret that he hadn't wanted the baby and just wanted his old life back. In his opinion the only upside to this whole shit show was the young nanny who had joined their household.

Sophie was twenty-two, gentle and always attentive to Richard, nothing like Verity who he now viewed as hard-nosed and completely disinterested in him. The situation was a cliché at best. He and Sophie were discreet, with him popping home for a quickie at lunchtimes. Verity would never find out as she was always at work. Despite the unexpected benefits of having a nanny, Richard still didn't like the baby. In fact, he never used *its* name which was Harry, who was a gentle, funny baby boy.

He hadn't planned to kill the boy, it just seemed to happen. Richard had come home late after a night of drinking with his single friends, risked a quick blow job from Sophie without waking Verity and then casually looked in on the baby. All it took was a soft cushion over the baby's sleeping face and within minutes he was gone. He knew that babies sometimes died in their sleep for no known reason, so he knew there would be no real investigation.

In the months after Harry died, Richard dutifully supported Verity, saying the right things at the right time but he already knew that once she was over it he would leave the marriage and start over. Sophie had quickly found a new flat and new job and settled into what she thought was going to be a new life with Richard. However, Richard thought differently. To him she was just an occasional shag with no strings, but Sophie wanted to marry him after he divorced Verity.

Eventually she broached the topic and without even drawing breath, he said, 'No fucking way. I'm not falling into that trap again.'

Shocked and hurt, poor Sophie had threatened to tell Verity everything, so Richard was forced to leave his marriage sooner than he planned.

But Richard didn't know that Sophie had seen him enter Harry's room the night he died. The following morning she noticed a cushion was out of place because she always tidied them into the same pattern each evening. She had noticed the lack of shock on his face when Harry was discovered. She wasn't stupid, she had seen how little interest he had in the baby, and she knew exactly what had taken place that horrible night.

Starting to see things clearer and knowing that he was never going to move in with her, let alone marry her, Sophie decided to exact her revenge on Richard. One Sunday morning she arrived at Verity's house to find the poor woman utterly broken and looking like she had nothing to live for. Recruiting strength and resolve beyond her age, Sophie made Verity a cup of tea, sat her down and told her everything. Verity hadn't flinched, even when she heard about their affair, not even when Sophie told her what she'd see that night and that she believed Richard had killed Harry.

Sophie left the house and Verity never heard from her

again. A cold, steel blanket descended upon her as she sat in that kitchen, shocked by what Sophie had told her but deep down not surprised. After several days without crying or any outward signs of upset, Verity returned to work. No one at work knew about the baby and now they never would. But the Verity who returned to her job at The Women's League that day, was a very different woman. Within a year she had recruited Anthea as her PA and they had become firm friends.

Within six months Richard had died from natural causes.

FORTY-ONE

Long before she became Verity Scanlan's PA, Anthea Broadbent had what seemed like an ordinary life. She lived in a small village, on the outskirts of Oxford and worked part-time for the local GP practice as a receptionist. Her husband had a good job, a reasonable car and dutifully mowed the garden lawn each Sunday. It was that sort of place. Anthea knew everyone in the village, and they all knew her. She was the sort of lady you could turn to for anything and when The Women's League started a new branch in her village, Anthea joined without hesitation. In fact, Anthea spent little time at home, because despite what the villagers in Much Worthy thought, Anthea's life was less than happy.

Learning at thirty that she was infertile, Anthea and her husband were both devastated. In fact, he couldn't cope and during the years that followed, he took it out on poor Anthea. He undermined her, controlled her excessively and he blamed her for everything, destroying her confidence in a few short years. At the time poor Anthea didn't understand what was happening to her. Eventually, perhaps mercifully, he left their marriage. As Anthea tried to carry on life without him, she found to her surprise that she didn't miss him as much as she had expected.

After a straightforward divorce, Anthea started dating Robert Clearwater, a local policeman who lived in the same village. Originally working in forensic science, Rob had decided he needed a more active job and joined the police force, eventually working with domestic abuse cases. He had watched Anthea's life over the years and knew that her husband was not what he seemed. After Anthea's husband left, she and Rob became friends, with the friendship eventually turning to love. Rob nursed her psychological wounds, helped her rebuild her life and encouraged her to apply for a job in London with The Women's League, as Verity Scanlan's personal assistant.

Verity and Anthea were both surprised at how much they liked each other. Their working friendship became strong and trustworthy, so much so that Verity eventually told Anthea about baby Harry, his death and the horrendous pain she had suffered due to Richard.

One quiet Sunday, Anthea invited Verity over for Sunday lunch with her and Rob. Anthea had discreetly told him about Verity's ordeal, knowing Rob could be completely trusted. Over jam roly-poly and custard, jam courtesy of The Women's League of course, Rob told Verity about his work in domestic abuse and some of the awful circumstances he had investigated. He told her how very few convictions were obtained and how many men escaped scot-free and possibly went on to commit further acts of abuse and violence.

As the three friends opened a bottle of port, Rob collected some cheese and chutney from the kitchen, noting how lucky they were to have an endless supply of jam, chutney and other preserves via the Women's League. Verity was quick to tell Rob that the League did much more than just jam making, and these days supported women all over the world in all sorts of ways.

But as she spoke Rob had become very quiet. He spooned the onion marmalade onto his cracker, and gently said, 'But what if these marvellous jam making talents could be put to better use – used in such a way that would benefit society and do what the justice system seems unable to do?'

FORTY-TWO

Bridget felt disappointed and a little stupid, as she reflected on Eddie's lack of interest about the text messages and the deaths she thought were connected. Without seeing what she had seen, Bridget understood that she sounded like a rambling, old woman with a few screws loose. However, she had hoped that Eddie would at least look on his police computer and see if there was anything similar happening elsewhere, but perhaps that wasn't as easy as it was on Midsomer Murders or CSI. These days it seemed like to do anything you had to fill in three forms, give consent to something to do something else and then you still needed your identity checking. This, the stranglehold that admin seemed to have over everything, was another reason Bridget avoided getting a *normal* job.

More than disappointed, Bridget was worried how their conversation might change Eddie's opinion of her. It was so good having someone younger in her art group, someone who was willing to give new things a go and who was happy to chat with Sylvie. Bridget really hoped he didn't stop coming to the group. Eddie had some real talent for drawing and painting, which she wanted to nurture. As she thought about Eddie and the group, she remembered how lovely it had been at the last session when everyone was engaged, happy, chatting and even laughing at times. The joy, and relief, that filled the room when Ralph announced that he had finished his owl was something she should value more, instead of being distracted by horrid portraits and stupid imaginary murders.

In that moment she decided she would let go of the stupid text message, death thing, whatever it was and more likely, wasn't. She needed a new project, something she could immerse herself in and although she still needed to work on the new portrait of Verity, she knew she had enough space in her week. What would energise her right now? What would she like to do that would fill her head and heart and not leave any space for ridiculous fantasies? The weather had improved so without hesitation, Bridget packed a bag with a sketch book, pencil case and drawing board. She made a flask of tea and a sandwich, grabbed her coat and drove off the driveway, only to stop down the road to pick a random place to spend a few hours sketching.

'Okay,' she said to herself. 'I'll close my eyes and pick a random place on the road map and just go wherever my finger lands.' She made a mental note to only include places an hour or so from home. Her finger landed in the middle of the River Severn. 'Bugger,' she said aloud. 'I'll just go as near as I can, see what's there and draw for a couple of hours regardless.' As Bridget followed the automated route finder towards the pin, she noticed it was directing her to Severn Beach. This delighted her; she loved a beach.

Arriving at Severn Beach, she experienced disappointment. However artists tend to have a different way of looking at the world. Initial thoughts such as What a dump, Where is the sand? and Why would anyone call this a beach? were quickly silenced as Bridget looked out across the river towards Wales. The tide was far out, and the glistening mud seemed to stretch on for miles. She sat down on one of the concrete boulders and poured some tea from her flask. Looking into the distance, she could see the water of the estuary.

Opening her pencil case, she took out her material of choice – charcoal. She loved the soft lines and blocks of black and grey that willow charcoal made. If you wanted a dark tone, it would oblige and if you fixed the surface with hair spray, the dark tone would stay. You could also use the charcoal to cover a whole piece of paper and then use a rubber or finger to draw into the surface. She always got covered in black and didn't care, in fact having black marks on her face and arms made her feel very happy. Drawing the mud in front of her and the shapes that the water made as it fell away with the receding tide, was addictive. From that first position, she made four large drawings. Eating her sandwich with her blackened hands, she noticed the remains of a fire that someone had made which left a mixture of charred wood and rubbish. Not many people would think fondly when seeing litter left in this way, but Bridget immediately got up and selected two or three bits of charred wood – basically more charcoal with which she could use to draw.

Free drawing materials, she thought to herself as she turned her body to face the other direction, giving herself a completely different view of the mud and its fascinating, wet gorges and clefts. She focussed on one big drawing this time and joyfully scooped up some mud and used that to draw with too. By the end of the morning, she had five drawings and was covered in mud and charcoal. She felt so much better, and all thoughts of murders and strange codes faded, as if they were sinking into the River Severn mud.

FORTY-THREE

When Glenda Grant had called her good friend at The Women's League in Bolton, she knew exactly what she was doing. They had arranged to meet after the regular League meeting, and the women sat chatting in Glenda's car. To an outsider, the pair looked like they were just catching up, probably supporting each other through tricky times. But Glenda wasn't just having a tricky time at home. She was planning to rid herself of her husband William and needed some help.

In recent weeks Glenda had reached the limit of her patience and was no longer willing to keep the status quo at home. As so often happens, something had tipped her over the edge – a straw that broke the camel's back.

William, her husband of thirty years had forced himself on their niece whilst drunk at a family wedding. William had instantly forgotten about it, but their niece didn't. When she failed to reach her target grades at A level, she'd broken down in tears and told her mum, Glenda's sister-in-law, everything. More like a giant tree trunk than a straw, this is what had broken the proverbial camel's back. The camel's back that had already been burdened by years of financial abuse and a growing unease about her husband's recent behaviour around younger women. Glenda had already started to change their finances in an attempt to protect herself, but things quickly unravelled. Her new financial advisor was horrified at what William had been doing with their money, but for Glenda it was William's behaviour towards young girls that was impossible to stomach.

Their niece had been seventeen when he sexually assaulted her, Glenda had already noticed that William seemed unable to judge the age of younger girls and women. He had made inappropriate remarks about girls as young as twelve, justifying it by saying he thought they looked older. He hadn't been like this when they first married, but as he got older, his interest in young girls seemed to have bubbled up from somewhere. Before confronting him about the assault on their niece, she had decided to explore his laptop and see if there was any other worrying activity. Sadly, Glenda had found plenty. His online skills were not very good, and he had left a trail of incriminating activity so large it could probably be seen from the moon, as someone in cyber detection later remarked.

Glenda decided to tell him about her financial re-jig before tackling the assault of their niece and it hadn't gone well. He told her that he had financial commitments he couldn't meet if she put her salary in a different account. When she asked what these financial commitments were, he wouldn't say and became annoyed at her questions. On closer inspection of his internet activity she was horrified to discover that William had been paying for child pornography materials pretty much since the internet had started. It felt to Glenda that William was now upping his game and taking it into the real world.

Thinking about it made Glenda feel sick. She couldn't believe he had been doing this for years and using her money to finance his sick desires. She had worked full-time all of her adult life, including when the children were growing up and she had so little to show for it. He had told her he was managing her pension but she discovered that there was no pension in her name. At fifty-two she could try to make up some pension payments, but before all this she had been hoping to reduce her hours. On her modest salary working in social care, she would be working full-time for many years to come.

Did she want to live those years with a man unhealthily obsessed with young women and girls? A man who also had spent her pension on child pornography. Nope. So here she was, sitting in her car, ordering the means with which to end her husband's life.

FORTY-FOUR

Finally summoning up the bravery to speak to his boss about his job and how it wasn't challenging enough, Eddie managed to avoid adding that in his opinion there needed to be a few more murders in South Gloucestershire. In response, his boss sat him down and carried out a much-needed Personal Development Review Plan, with work goals, learning activities and something called outcomes. Despite not really knowing what an outcome was, it made Eddie feel a lot better about having uprooted his and Graham's life. To add to his brighter mood, he received an email inviting him to a two-day policing conference in Manchester called *Detecting the future: research, methods and innovation*. Eddie felt more excited than he had done for months.

'You are going to have such a great time,' said Graham, sounding just as excited as Eddie. 'Many years ago I went on a work conference and made friendships that lasted for years. You know Sleepy? I met him on the first day at a conference in Liverpool and several hangovers later we were inseparable. All I can remember of that conference is sitting through hours of talks and presentations, trying not to snore. I think I had about four Red Bulls each day to keep me awake as I was presenting a paper and chairing several sessions!' Graham was chuckling as he recalled this memory.

'So that's how Sleepy got his name then – I did wonder,' Eddie said. He had met Sleepy several times and adored him.

'Nope, that's not it. He fell asleep on a chair lift once when we went skiing. He went all the way back down the mountain, before falling off. Thankfully the lift was not that high when he fell off and he landed on the nursery slopes with several groups of six-year-olds zooming past him on skis. Within a day, the whole ski resort seemed to know about the stupid Englishman who feel asleep on the lift and then fell off.'

Graham laughed even more this time and Eddie wondered whether he would have funny stories to tell when he was older. Although only ten years older than him, Graham seemed to have had such an eventful, interesting life, which made Eddie even more determined to do new things at home and hopefully at work too.

Later that evening Graham booked Eddie into the conference hotel. He had insisted that it would be more fun staying in the thick of it all, even if it was a little more expensive than a Premier Inn. They also printed out the conference programme and looked at all the sessions available, snoring at the ones that looked boring and laughing at the ones with the snazzy names which were clearly intended to attract attention, without any indication of what the talk was about.

'This is my favourite one, look at this.' Graham smiled as he pointed to a session entitled, *The Policeman's Balls: how to keep all your balls in the air and what to do if you drop one*.

Eddie laughed too saying, 'Police officers do have a sense of humour you know.'

'You have, Eddie, but I'm not sure about some of your colleagues I've met.'

Graham's comment was immediately backed up as he pointed to another session called, *A highly effective, 29 stage process for efficiently labelling evidence*.

'I rest my case.'

FORTY-FIVE

Having received a text saying '3lbsSJstrong@BL2' the Jam Maker knew they needed to make a batch of strawberry jam, with a special added ingredient. This added ingredient varied, sometimes it was run of the mill arsenic, occasionally ricin or The Jam Maker's favourite, thallium. The jam would then be sent to an electronic drop box, in this case, near Bolton. The Jam Maker had been making this particular jam from the very start, perfecting the recipe and developing different strengths of poison depending on the requirements.

Strawberry jam was easy: the taste was strong, it had different textures and natural little seeds that helped mask particles of undissolved arsenic. Another good thing about Strawberry jam was that it had multiple uses. You could have it on toast, crumpets or scones - jam first, then cream, obviously. You could use it to make jam roly-poly, jam tarts or other puddings and there were many tasty strawberry drinks that could be flavoured using the jam.

When Anthea Broadbent entered the steamy garden shed which had been converted into a small laboratory many years ago, she looked fondly at the man standing at the worktop with his back to her. It was unseasonably warm, and Rob was naked except for a pinny, heat gloves and a gas mask. Mahler was playing loudly on the old record player, which was his favourite music for cooking whether in this little shed or their normal kitchen. Slowly Anthea crept up behind him and without him noticing, she slid her hands around his groin and cupped his balls. She hadn't realised that at that very moment, he was carefully pouring hot, molten, poisoned jam into an equally hot glass jar. The shock of having his balls grabbed, albeit gently, caused him to knock the jam pot which spilled over the counter and onto Anthea's hand as she removed it from under his pinny.

'Fuck,' yelled Rob, 'What are you doing? Never surprise a naked man when he is cooking, especially something hot!' As he looked down, he gasped when he saw Anthea's hand dripping in hot jam and the terrified look on her face. 'Oh my God, are you okay, my love,' he said, rushing her to the sink, running cold water over her hands and washing off the sticky jam.

Anthea was in so much pain she thought she might faint, but as the cool water eased the pain slightly, her thoughts turned to the poisonous contents. 'Oh god, will it kill me? Oh my God, oh my God, what should we do?'

Rob quickly dragged a chair to the sink and sat her down, making sure to keep her hand under the cold water. 'It's okay, old thing. It wasn't touching your skin for very long and it would need to be ingested to cause a real problem. Just stay there and I'll get you a brandy.'

Later, once they were back in the kitchen of their cosy cottage and they had both had another brandy, Anthea's colour was returning, and Rob was feeling calmer. They both reflected on how lucky they had been that this was the first real accident in over fifteen years of jam-making and how it could have been much, much worse. Rob always made more jam than necessary so despite losing around half a pound they could still send out five jars of jam to Bolton which would be plenty.

As they lifted the gauze that was covering Anthea's hand, they were horrified to see how badly burnt it was. She would have to go to hospital, there was no choice but a middle-aged woman who had burnt her hand whilst making jam wouldn't be at all suspicious.

They waited an hour for the brandy to leave their systems a little, and Rob quickly drove Anthea to the local minor injury unit where after four hours of waiting, her hand was dressed and bandaged. She was also given some antibiotics because of the size of the burn. Once home and feeling a little better she told Rob she wouldn't be taking the antibiotics as she had the Cirencester Gala Ball on Saturday and she didn't want to miss out on the prosecco.

Rob, always stunned at both her stoicism and determination to have fun, planted a soft kiss on her head.

'I'm so sorry about your hand, old bean, but take solace in the fact that the jam will help make another woman's life much better.'

'Yes,' replied Anthea, 'I know it will.'

FORTY-SIX

Flicking on the kettle in her studio, Bridget was feeling much brighter following her trip to Severn Non-Beach. It had been a long, wet winter and she resolved that next year, she must get outside more. Perhaps she could arrange some sort of residency on a remote island where you could warm up in a little cabin after a day's drawing in some stark, mysterious, foreign landscape. Norway, or Iceland maybe or perhaps the Outer Hebrides – yes, that felt like a good plan. It was such a relief from constantly thinking about Verity Scanlan, the bloody portrait and the whole imaginary murder story she had constructed in her ridiculous, beautiful mind.

No one would ever understand how her imagination, the essential ingredient in her work, could be so draining at times. The mere spark of an idea or sideways glance at something out of the corner of her eye, could start a full-blown imaginary world or epic story worthy of a Hollywood film. At the same time, her imagination could twist her perception, feed her anxiety and drain her of energy. Then there were the dreams. At least with age she had learned to temper the horrid daytime visions, but at night in the depth of sleep, she was powerless. Mercifully the violent dreams were usually short and lacked detail, but upon waking, her imagination would fill the gaps. Thankfully, not all her vivid dreams were completely unpleasant. Her favourite ones were the James Bond style, action dreams, where she was the hero who climbed, ran, skied and sometimes shot or fought people in hand-to-hand combat. They were real, visceral, full-sensory experiences and she often would wake from them exhausted. She had tried writing down her dreams, which several therapists suggested might help but they were such sensory rich dreams, there was little narrative she could easily put words to. She had also tried to draw her dreams, but again, they were so fast moving, so complex that a single image would not suffice.

Bridget had lived with this rampant, vivid imagination all her adult life and still recalled when it first started to take on a life of its own. She had been around eighteen, fallen in love with her husband and just started to branch out into the wider world beyond her sheltered upbringing. Looking back, it felt like falling in love had lit a fuse inside her which had been connected to a huge bomb – a bomb made of a strange mix of emotions, hormones and imagination. Early on this resulted in quite unpleasant visions of her husband dying in all sorts of ways. She would see his death, the emotional fallout, the funeral and even the aftermath, all in detailed visions. Later in life she had learned to understand her creative mind much better, but during times of stress, poor sleep or when she didn't have enough to occupy herself, her creative imagination would torment her. Such it had been in recent months with the portrait of Verity Scanlan, so when she received an email, from Anthea Clearwater, all her previous imaginings came flooding back.

The subject line had simply read: Finalising a date to unveil the portrait.

Bridget had decided not to open the email until the new portrait was nearly complete. For the last couple of weeks, she had chastised herself for destroying the portrait and how she had let her anger and imagination win. Mercifully the remnants of Verity's portrait had been quiet of late, perhaps shocked at what Bridget had done to it.

Despite her general dislike of the woman, Bridget had been pleased with some parts of the previous portrait, she decided to keep the same composition but build in hidden elements to allude to other sides of Verity's personality. Outside of her own observations and suspicions, Sylvie had eventually shared with her what Linda had told her about Verity's stark personality change years ago. Recruiting Verity's outward, more positivity personality into the portrait, whilst somehow alluding to these changes felt more compassionate, so Bridget started painting with a kinder heart. She squeezed a different palette of oil colours onto her mixing board and whilst she would still use the emerald green, it would now be alongside pinks and peaches.

The smell of the paint pleased her and for an intense couple of hours, Bridget painted without stopping. As she painted, she kept the colours clear and bright, carefully avoiding too much mixing and muddying. As she traced the contours of Verity's face, she noticed how much like a landscape a face really was and this helped. If she treated her face like a landscape Bridget found she could disconnect from her feelings about Verity and all the unpleasant ideas her mind had created. She would still include the personal items she had planned, but she could now treat these as elements in a landscape. The book, with its straight lines became a leaning building in Bridget's mind, the phones square and iconic, were like paving slabs. As she was about to add the second *secret* phone, Bridget was startled by a strong, clear voice coming from inside her.

'You're right about that secret phone, Bridget, but perhaps wait until Verity has seen the portrait before you add it.'

'Hmm, okay then,' Bridget replied to the voice as she put down her paintbrush.

FORTY-SEVEN

Glenda had always been a patient person, but as the truth about her husband ate away at her, she struggled to keep calm as she waited for the poisoned jam to take effect. She had unwrapped the jam as soon as she got home from the collection box and started figuring out how to administer it straight away. Willliam loved strawberry jam and strawberry flavour things, so it was going to be easy. One week after she had started to use the special jam, she had encouraged William to attend a GP appointment, saying he looked tired and pale and did he realise that he hadn't been eating much in recent weeks.

'The quack didn't find anything wrong with me, so that's good, eh!' William chuckled as he tucked into his lunch. 'He told me to try and eat a little more and to eat things I enjoy and if I don't feel better in a couple of weeks, he would do some other tests.'

Glenda smiled back. This gave her the perfect excuse to

feed him some extra portions, which funnily enough, would contain as many strawberry flavours as she could think of.

‘Aww that’s good,’ she replied softly with her back to him, so he didn’t see her face. Glenda moved to open the oven door and removed a tray of freshly baked scones, the gorgeous smell filling the kitchen. ‘I’ve made a fresh batch of scones for later.’

Over the next couple of weeks, William tucked into jam roly-poly pudding with strawberry custard, strawberry gâteaux and anything else Glenda could think of that she could put jam in. He had a couple of jam tarts in his packed lunch every day, alternating with a Victoria sponge filled with, of course, a thick layer of strawberry jam. William lapped it up and although he *was* starting to feel unwell, Glenda reassured him that the GP would look into it, and he should relax. The following few days she ramped up her efforts, serving him a couple of cocktails in the evening, including a version of a French Martini with strawberry instead of raspberry.

Unsurprisingly, it wasn’t long before William was showing clear signs of being poisoned. Consulting with her contact at The Women’s League, Glenda was advised to encourage him to take a couple of days off work, at the same time ramping up his intake of jam. William agreed but said he needed to go into work to collect a laptop so he could work from home. Unknown to Glenda he also took a spare jar of strawberry jam he had found in the kitchen cupboard. William had been meaning to make a donation to the communal food in the work fridge and decided that a jar of jam was a good idea. He was also a little bored of strawberry jam, but not wanting to upset Glenda, he decided not to tell her.

William deposited the attractive pot of homemade strawberry jam in the work fridge and was pleased that he had finally got round to giving something to the FFFF as it was known – the free food fridge fund. As he bent over to put the jam in the fridge, he started to feel very unwell. It was here in the works kitchen, late that Friday afternoon, that William collapsed in front of Tina the cleaner. Within the hour he was in the Accident and Emergency department at Bolton hospital, undergoing urgent assessment.

Glenda, the dutiful wife brought him in a small snack, but soon realised it wasn't necessary.

FORTY-EIGHT

Bridget was feeling much happier. Outside of some last-minute additions, the portrait of Verity was nearly finished, and she was relieved that Verity and the whole bloody saga was nearly over. It had taken up way too much time and energy and she had spent most of the income already, knowing that the final payment would only serve to pay off some of the credit card bill she had built up in recent months.

'Oh well,' she muttered, 'You never know what might come of these things.'

What Bridget meant was that paid commissions usually came via word of mouth, so perhaps someone would see or hear about Verity's portrait, and it would generate more work, but hopefully not one as torturous as this portrait had been. With a high-profile portrait such as Verity's, there would likely be some articles in magazines or online blogs that would help generate interest and although she longed not to have to paint portraits, she did get a thrill from seeing her work in print.

At the art group later that week, Eddie didn't turn up. Sylvie mentioned that Eddie had a busy week coming up including going to The Women's League Gala Ball with her and was off to a work conference the following week.

'I told Eddie he should spend some time with Graham and he shouldn't worry about missing one week of art class.' Sylvie glowed as she added this detail, as if she was looking after the son she had always wanted.

Despite Sylvie explaining Eddie's absence, Bridget wasn't entirely convinced. Was Eddie avoiding her because of their discussion about Verity and the text messages? Oh well, if Eddie stayed away again, she would call him, apologise and find some way to get him back to the class.

As the group settled down, there was an undercurrent of excitement. Bridget pulled up a chair and Ralph proudly announced that he was starting a new painting this week and it was going to be a robin. The group responded to this announcement with such encouragement that Bridget had to bite her tongue and swallow down what she really wanted to say.

'Not another bloody bird! Why Ralph, why? It's just more claws and feathers to torture yourself with and it's not even Christmas.'

No, Bridget had long ago learnt what do so and say in these situations, so she smiled, nodded and encouragingly asked Ralph what materials he needed to get started.

FORTY-NINE

William Grant had been a very unwell man and despite the hospital's efforts, they couldn't find out what was wrong with him. They were waiting for blood test results to come back from the laboratory, but before the results came back, William was dead. Even if they had received the blood test results in time, it would have been unlikely they would have detected the presence of the poison, as they didn't routinely check for it.

Had it not been a busy Friday evening in A&E, William might have been seen by a more experienced doctor, one that wasn't covering A&E alongside twelve hospital wards, on his own. A more experienced physician may have suspected poisoning of some kind, perhaps ordered some different blood tests and maybe tried administering carbon as a precaution. But the exhausted junior doctor who saw to William, had already been on shift for fourteen hours and just went through the motions. He did ask Glenda if there was anyway William could have been poisoned or whether he had been eating anything different of late.

As her husband slipped away, the poison of recent weeks was aided by an undiagnosed heart condition, not uncommon for a man of William's age. When the heart monitor started bleeping furiously, Glenda did not alert the staff. Instead, she cleverly unplugged the monitor by tangling the cable around her chair leg, which pulled the plug out as she carefully moved her chair backwards. The subsequent alarm mingled with all the other alarms merrily going off in the unit and no one came running.

Once sure that William was dead, she went to the toilet, shed a solitary tear mostly for the years of lies she had uncovered and at how desperately stupid she felt. Once back in the cubicle, Glenda plugged the monitor back in and quickly called out for help, feigning shock and upset.

'I just popped to the toilet and when I came back, the monitor was going mad and…'

The NHS did their thing, quickly, professionally and with love. Despite the staff all being overstretched, exhausted and run off their feet, they did everything they could for William, but nothing could be done. The amazing staff then took care of Glenda who was trying to react as anyone would expect in these circumstances.

'No. No thank you. I just want to get a taxi home,' Glenda said through glistening eyes when asked if they could call someone. She needed to get home, get rid of the jam and clean the kitchen as quickly as possible. Things hadn't gone to plan at all. William was never meant to die in hospital, and she was starting to worry. She feigned some sobs in the back of the car and managed to thank the taxi driver with sufficiently red, puffy eyes.

Once indoors, Glenda called her contact at The Women's League who gave her immediate instructions about what to do. This included getting rid of any unused jam and how to dispose of it safely. She told her contact there was only a scrapping of jam in one jar plus one unopened jar in the cupboard.

When Glenda got to the cupboard she froze. The last jar was missing. She was certain there had been another unopened pot and she counted the used jars just in case. Shit. There were only four so there was definitely one missing. Shit, shit. This couldn't be happening. The sinking feeling in her stomach was starting to make her feel nauseous but she carried out the rest of the instructions which included opening a new jar of shop bought strawberry jam, emptying some of it into the sink and crushing a few crumbs of bread into the top to make it look used. Glenda put every item of crockery, cutlery, glassware, bakeware and utensils that she owned, into the dishwasher and put them on a hot wash, putting them away before allowing anyone else into the house. She had known that this would need to happen so she had been careful to only use a set amount of crockery and cutlery over the last few weeks, but as she bleached the worktops, changed his toothbrush and anything that might contain trace elements of the poison, she could not stop worrying about the missing jar of jam.

Glenda was desperate to speak with someone. She needed to tell the League about the lost jam but at the same time, she was scared what they might say. Early on they had made it clear that if something went wrong, they would cease contact, and she would be on her own. Swallowing down her panic, Glenda decided not to tell them.

His work colleagues started telephoning Glenda the following week to express their condolences. There is only so much that can be said during these sort of phone calls, and despite the usual, well-intentioned and caring questions the conversation eventually shifted to the caller's life.

'How are you, Glenda?'

'Must have been such a shock for you?'

'When might the funeral be?'

'My cousin dropped dead suddenly, and they never found out why.'

'It must have been the stress of the job.'

'Did you know Geoff, because he is the one we all reckon will die next!'

Glenda knew that even the kindest people struggle to know what to say under these circumstances, but when well-intentioned callers started to mention that a few people at William's work had been ill lately, she knew instantly what had happened to the missing jam.

Glenda needed a plan. She wasn't going to let this mishap wreck her life, especially after William had left her with little money and even less dignity. No, she knew what she needed to do and set about her plan to retrieve the jam. Early the next day, she drove to William's work-place – a factory on the outskirts of Bolton. The receptionist was surprised to see her, and Glenda made all the right noises expected from a recently bereaved wife, noting with curiosity that she didn't feel sad at all. Glenda explained that she had come to collect William's belongings.

'Can I wait in the staff kitchen while you find them, please?'

'Of course,' said the kind receptionist who took her to the staff kitchen, made her a coffee and then went off to pack up William's things. Once alone in the kitchen, Glenda furiously searched the cupboard for the jam, eventually finding it in the fridge. Dismayed to see it was nearly empty, she quickly put it in her handbag, just as the kitchen door opened.

'Glenda, my love,' said Donald the managing director, who she had met many times over the past twenty years.

Hearing his voice, Glenda quickly grabbed the milk to provide an explanation for her rummaging in the fridge.

'We are all so sorry for your loss. It was such a shock. How are you doing?'

'Oh, as well as can be expected, Don. I just thought I would pop in and collect some of his things.'

Donald nodded solemnly.

'He'd been feeling under the weather for a couple of weeks and was just waiting for some blood tests to come back. He only came into work on Friday to collect his laptop and arrange some time off.' As Glenda spoke, she had to fight the urge to rush out of the room, knowing that a longer, more tear laden conversation would be useful right now. She reached inside her bag to find a tissue and blew her nose which helpfully made her eyes puff up.

'We are all here for you, Glenda. Mind you, we've had a run of sickness here this last week. You don't think William had something which was contagious do you?' As this thought crossed Donald's mind, he took an obvious step away from Glenda.

Glenda felt prickling heat rising up her neck, around the sides of her face and struggled to reply. 'No, I'm sure that's not the case, Don. They think it was his heart, but they don't really know.'

Misinterpreting her reddened face as upset, Donald quickly said, 'Oh I didn't mean to upset you. Glenda. It just crossed my mind to tell you in case the doctors were wondering what made him so ill so quickly. I mean one minute he was laughing and joking with the office girls, the next, well… umm sorry… I'm not very good at these things.'

Inside, Glenda painfully repeated to herself *laughing and joking with the office girls*, yes of course he was, the bloody pervert. She really wished Donald would leave now as she was struggling to keep it together. Thankfully she spied the lovely young receptionist approaching with a cardboard box; she would soon be out of here. Donald, however, was still talking.

'Yes, I had to call Occupational Health about the staff being sick, especially with William's sudden death, so they've arranged some checks to be carried out. I will make sure they leave you alone though, Glenda. Please do take care and let us know the funeral arrangements when you have them.'

Ice cold fear instantly swept over Glenda. She hadn't thought about Occupational Health becoming involved. Fuck. As Donald left the kitchen, the receptionist entered with the cardboard box. Glenda failed to notice the uncomfortable look on the girl's face, as she was busy trying not to vomit. What the fuck was she going to do? If they tested all the kitchen food and utensils in the works kitchen, they would discover traces of poison and despite her removing the jam, the employees would remember it. Shit, shit, shit.

The young receptionist didn't meet Glenda's eyes as she passed her the cardboard box, which was lucky for Glenda as she wasn't sure what her face might be giving away. Hopefully the girl would just put Glenda's weirdness down to grief and shock. Grabbing the box, Glenda thanked her quickly and left straight away to avoid further chit chat. On the way back home, she did indeed pull over and vomit until she had nothing left to bring up.

Closing her front door, Glenda shakily tried to call the contact number she had been told only to call in an emergency. She tried it a few times but there was no reply. In an attempt to keep busy, she started to unpack the box of William's possessions from his office. Here she found a coffee mug which said, World's best uncle. Glenda screamed manically. There were also some old birthday cards and car magazines – the usual crap that ends up in your office drawer when you have worked somewhere for a long time.

At the bottom she found a large brown envelope and what she saw inside, caused her to stomach to churn once more. A small pile of photos of all the girls in their family, nieces, younger in-laws, all as young teenagers, some even younger. In another envelope were photos of even younger girls that Glenda didn't recognise. Her mouth, having been filled with an acidic taste for the last couple of hours, was now dry. She couldn't speak, she couldn't cry, she couldn't shout. Placing the envelope in the kitchen sink, she set fire to the whole thing, watching every image burn to ashes.

Glenda didn't know that the lovely receptionist packing William's things, had seen the photos and discretely put them in the brown envelope. Nor did Glenda know that within a day of her retrieving the jam, a solitary member of the local environmental health department visited the kitchen at William's work place. She had taken swabs of all the items in the cupboard and confiscated all the food in the fridge, reprimanding the company for not keeping food labelled or dated. Nor did Glenda know that the same Environmental Health Officer had spoken to all the company employees who had been off sick in the last couple of weeks The only thing the employees could remember eating that was different from usual, was the strawberry jam that William had brought into work, the week before he died.

That same jam that had now disappeared from the fridge.

FIFTY

Eddie had arranged for Graham to pick up Sylvie and drive them both to The Women's League Annual Gala Ball in Cirencester. Unlike Eddie, who was sporting a rather nice dinner jacket and bow tie he had borrowed, Graham was wearing jogging bottoms, an old fisherman's sweater and two days of stubble to accompany his sticky-up hair.

'You look gorgeous,' Graham had made a point of saying to Eddie as they left the house. Looking down at his own clothes he continued, 'Cinderella here will finish the hoovering and collect you from your do at midnight.'

Eddie laughed.

'Take a left here, first house on the right, that's Sylvie's house there,' Eddie said, exiting the car as Graham pulled over. 'Won't be a mo.' As Eddie rang the bell, Sylvie must have been waiting right by the front door, as she opened it immediately.

'Goodness, you scrub up well.'

'So do you. No paint splatters on us today, eh!'

Sylvie was wearing a midnight blue, floor length dress with a sequined top. Despite her advancing years, she looked amazing with her hair half up, half down.

Eddie smiled broadly as he took her arm.

'Don't wait up!' chirped Sylvie towards the back of the house as Eddie closed the front door. 'I've pulled a younger man and who knows what we'll get up to!' She laughed and this made her look even more fabulous.

A short drive later, they pulled up outside the Regency Rooms in Cirencester and joined the line of smartly dressed couples entering the ball. Eddie was surprised to see people of all ages. He thought The Women's League was just middle aged and older women but there were also couples in their thirties and forties and even some same sex couples. Eddie found the seating plan and was pleased to see that they were sitting on the same table as his Auntie Linda, Jim, his uncle and some other people that Sylvie knew. Eddie sat between Linda and Sylvie, which meant he could chat to them both. The Maître D' opened the dinner service, and they tucked into their starters.

As their first course was cleared away, Sylvie explained to Eddie that Verity Scanlan was the head of The Women's League, something like president or chief executive, she wasn't sure. She gestured to a striking, auburn-haired woman sitting at the top table who was wearing a deep turquoise trouser suit with a peacock print blouse. Eddie could see by the way this woman dressed and held herself, that she was powerful. Her hair was curly with flecks of grey, cut into a fashionable style with one side longer than the other.

'Not many people could carry off a hair style like that,' he noted.

Leaning into Eddie further, Sylvie whispered, 'I'll tell you a secret, Eddie. Bridget has been commissioned to paint her – to paint Verity!' Sylvie was clearly excited about knowing this secret and was beaming as she continued, 'I imagine she has nearly finished it by now, but you mustn't tell anyone.'

Eddie, who already knew this, didn't want to disappoint Sylvie and feigned both surprise and delight. Little did Sylvie know that Bridget had recently destroyed the portrait of Verity; he would be keeping that to himself. Eddie prayed that Bridget had started a new portrait. He had been worried that her concerns and suspicions were causing her to struggle with the new portrait. He was also feeling guilty about dismissing Bridget's suspicions, but until he had some concrete evidence, he couldn't collude with her. It occurred to him that tonight might be an ideal opportunity to poke around a little and perhaps he should do more than just hide away and chat to his auntie and Sylvie all night.

'And that lady sitting next to Verity is Anthea Clearwater, her PA. They have been together for years. Well not *together* together, but they've worked closely for years now.'

As Sylvie looked at Anthea, she saw that one of her hands was bandaged. 'Goodness, I wonder what happened.

She seems to have injured her hand,' and without seeming to need to breathe, Sylvie continued, 'I doubt that she can type or drive or anything with that. Poor thing – I'll find out what happened later.'

After listening to Sylvie explain who was who, Eddie needed a drink and ordered a bottle of Prosecco, knowing that both he and Sylvie would both enjoy it way too much. It became the first of three bottles the pair consumed that evening and evaporated very quickly as they sat through numerous welcome speeches and the longer address from Verity who was clearly the headline act.

So, this is the famous Verity, thought Eddie, paying as much attention to her speech as he could whilst keeping an eye on Sylvie's over generous top-ups.

As Verity stood to welcoming applause, she pulled herself up straighter, summoning the full power of her body. She started informally, thanking those who had invited her, congratulating the local branch for their seventy-five years of service and how she felt privileged to lead The Women's League into the future. It was at this point that Verity shifted gear and changed tone. Initially it took Eddie by surprise but as he listened, he started to see something very different emerging from her. With increasing pace and power, Verity demanded a new, stronger wave of power for women, that went way beyond feminism and way beyond traditional notions of equality. She seemed to be calling for complete role reversals in business, education and politics. For men to stand aside and let women sort out the mess that men had created, which Eddie found himself agreeing with to a certain extent. However, there was an unspoken subtext to her speech – we need to teach men how it feels to be subjugated, chained to the home and something Eddie didn't understand about sorting out the wheat from the chaff. He made a mental note to ask Graham what that meant.

Eddie turned and whispered to Sylvie, 'Did she just say what I think she did?'

But Sylvie didn't reply. She seemed completely unaware of Eddie. She was transfixed by Verity's words and presence, in fact all the women in the room seemed mesmerised by her. The men, Eddie included, didn't know what to do with themselves and shifted uncomfortably in their seats, as if they were trying to sink into the carpet or walls. Eddie tried to focus on Verity's words again, noticing how clever she was. She wasn't overtly calling for anything bad to happen, it was just subtly alluded to. Eddie was both amazed and scared and couldn't understand the complicated feelings he was having towards this woman. He was starting to see what had unsettled Bridget and why this woman's energy had fed her conspiratory ideas.

Eddie was relieved when Verity finished her speech and found himself clapping along but he felt very conflicted about her ideas and beliefs, let alone the actions they might provoke. He topped up his and Sylvie's glass and took a big glug of Prosecco.

'Isn't she marvellous, Eddie,' cooed both his auntie and Sylvie in unison, still in state of reverie.

'I am a bit overwhelmed,' Eddie said, trying to find something neutral to say and still wondering if, as a man, whether he might be lynched later that evening. 'She certainly knows how to rouse people, even if it's a bit

Hitlerish,' he said this second bit under his breath. 'Sylvs, shall we get some air?'

'Did you just call me Sylvs?' laughed Sylvie. 'Since when have you called me Sylvs?'

She tittered as they walked outside into the sculpture garden. As Sylvie's titters calmed, they both realised that the fresh air had been a very good idea, and they sucked in big gulps. Not long after, Anthea walked into the garden, also seeming to need some air. Seeing her chance, Sylvie bounced over to her, excitement immediately returning.

'Anthea. Hi, it's Sylvie, we met a few years ago, I used to belong to Almondsbury but recently moved to Cirencester. This is my gay friend Eddie – he's my plus one for the evening.'

'My friend Eddie would have been sufficient, Sylvie,' said Eddie. 'Nice to meet you, Anthea,' and wasting no time asked, 'What happened to your hand? Looks very painful.'

Anthea seemed discombobulated by this question and stumbled over her answer, 'Oh just a bad scald from my kettle.' She drew breath to explain further but Sylvie jumped in.

'Must have been a lot of water, Anthea, it goes all the way up to your elbow, how on earth did that happen?'

Noticing that Sylvie's voice was getting louder and that she wasn't being terribly sensitive, Eddie realised that she had probably had a lot more Prosecco than he thought. He wished Anthea a speedy recovery and whisked Sylvie back inside saying, 'I think they are serving pudding and rumour has it there might be port later.'

'Oh goody, although I am a little light heady, already, Eddie. Ooo, already Eddie, that rhymes!'

Back inside, Sylvie seemed intent on gossiping and told Linda about Anthea's burn.

'Oh, that's strange; she told Mandy it was an oven burn.'

Pudding was served and took very little time to eat.

'Why do they always make the portions so small?' Linda moaned. 'What I would really like is a big slice of spotted dick.'

As Linda said dick Sylvie tittered, making Eddie splutter the raspberry jus from his cheesecake everywhere, which made Sylvie laugh even more. As they were halfway through the third bottle of prosecco, Linda poured Sylvie a coffee in a vain attempt to stem her friend's inebriated state.

'Sylvie, forget Anthea's hand, I have some much more interesting gossip.' Linda leaned over Eddie to replace Sylvie's Prosecco with the coffee. 'I've just found out from Marge that a member up north is being questioned over the death of her husband. Apparently, he died in hospital last week and no one thought anything of it, until people he worked with started to become ill as well. And because he died in hospital, there will be a post mortem.'

Linda continued talking but Eddie couldn't hear anything. His heart had dropped into his stomach and his hearing had gone all fuzzy as if he was going to faint. It could have been the Prosecco, but did Linda say that the women's husband had died, and his wife was suspected of killing him? The words swam round Eddie's head in a hazy vacuum. Coming back to the room Eddie asked his auntie to repeat what she just said.

'I said she's been ARRESTED,' Linda stopped abruptly, realising she was almost shouting, and because the music had paused between songs, the whole table had heard what she had said. Continuing she whispered, 'Arrested under suspicion of poisoning her husband.'

Hearing this, Eddie suddenly felt unwell. He felt the blood leave his hands, then arms, then feet. He gave his apologies and rushed out, managing to get to the gents' just in time. Propping himself up at the sink, he looked in the mirror and saw how pale he looked. 'What the fuck?' he muttered to himself as he splashed his face with water. Immediately, the recent conversation with Bridget rushed back into his head. Although he had already decided to tentatively explore her suspicions, he hadn't expected to find any evidence of it being true, but now…

'What the actual fuck,' he said again, this time out loud. Thankfully the gents' was empty, not surprising given he was vastly outnumbered by women tonight. He quickly typed a text to both Graham and Bridget, saying, 'I think I've found another death related to The Women's League.' He knew Bridget wouldn't read it for several days but there were already two ticks by Graham's message, meaning he had read it straightaway, and he was now replying.

'Christ on a bike! I'll pick you up at midnight and don't get yourself murdered (winking smiley emoji). I'm cleaning the oven. Love you, from Cinderella G.'

Eddie struggled to get through the rest of the evening. He knew he mustn't discuss it with Sylvie – she was way too drunk to be discreet. Eddie had sobered up rapidly and only drunk Red Bull for the rest of the evening, but on reflection, it was a mistake. Not only did Eddie struggle to sleep once home, when he finally dropped off, he had the most awful dreams which involved being chased by hundreds of smiling, silver-haired ladies in evening gowns who were trying to kill him.

FIFTY-ONE

It was 11.05am and the man in his early forties jumped as his mum opened his bedroom door.

'Wakey, wakey, Trevor. I'm off to Bingo, love. I've left your lunch in the microwave and your breakfast is here.' She placed the boiled egg with its top carefully removed and the lines of lovingly cut toast on his desk, adding, 'I've left the washing out so keep an eye out for rain, will you, love?' But she knew that her son was a terribly busy man and probably wouldn't notice.

Trevor, aka SherlokH, was the creator and administrator of a website called 221b. This unimaginatively titled site was an online detective forum comprised mostly of middle-aged people who had spare time on their hands. Some were disillusioned conspiracy theorists, who found their voices ignored in the over-crowded conspiracy world, so they had turned to armchair detection instead. Others were wannabee detectives, some turned down by the police force due to minor criminal convictions in their youth and others because they just didn't fit the mould. Another smaller group included those turned down by GCHQ, as are most apparently. The rest were just regular people who were a little bored watching too many re-runs of CSI, Taggart or Poirot and decided *real* action was needed instead.

The various activities of this online community included members scouring their local newspapers, inquest findings and court proceedings, in the hope of finding interesting information that might help unsolved crimes and cold cases. Trevor, aka SherlokH, would then select interesting cases, do a bit more research and if it looked like it had potential, he would add it to the Investigation Hub. This hub contained many digital investigations, each with its own online mind-map, where members could add any titbits of information they had found, make links and comment. These links were often tenuous and pointed to a trait that members had in common – overactive imaginations, a heightened ability to notice patterns and magical thinking – a theory that psychologists and psychiatrists use to denounce everything they can't easily explain.

Trevor checked and moderated all links but didn't often exclude things. It was only the links which mentioned aliens, time travel and blackholes that he didn't allow; this was a serious detective community and Trevor's day job. He believed that what others, including the police, might see as a rather tenuous link and not worthy of consideration, had often been proved the key to solving a case.

He was proud of the online community which had helped find several missing persons (many of whom didn't want to be found) and various lost pets. They had also found lost family heirlooms which also helped the police solve several burglaries and a couple of art fraud cases. Trevor also knew that the police used the 221b website anonymously and whilst he would have liked their acknowledgement, he was just happy to help. The income from the site helped pay his broadband bill, the household food bill and paid for Trevor and his mum to take a holiday in Blackpool every summer.

As Trevor dipped the last soldier, sadly realising there was only the white bit of the egg left, he noticed that someone had added a new investigation thread to the website. It concerned the mysterious death of a man in Bolton, alongside the illness of many of his co-workers. He knew that it was likely a case of food poisoning at a workplace and nothing else, but it provided a new case for his followers and contributors to explore. Trevor approved the thread without hesitation and added the Bolton case to the Investigation Hub. He needed a snappy title and decided on *The Bolt-On Poisoner* which played to the location of the occurrence, a juicy but unlikely explanation of what had happened and the fact that William Grant's place of work was a factory that made nuts and bolts.

'You genius, SherlokH,' he chuckled to himself as he added the files and information including various hash tags. He was just about to close his laptop down when he noticed a file that had already been added, which gave further information about Glenda Grant, the wife of the dead man. It made a passing mention that she was a member of The Women's League and whilst Trevor had no clue what that was, he added it as a hash tag just in case.

FIFTY-TWO

Eddie was ridiculously excited about attending the policing conference in Manchester. Although he had worked for the police for over eight years, he had never really wanted to or even considered attending the event, which boasted attendance of over a thousand police staff. Eddie had idly pondered whether the criminal population of the UK might use this as an opportunity to indulge in a bit of illegal activity but doubted it since most attendees were unlikely to be grass roots police officers taken off the beat.

As much as he was looking forward to the conference, staying in a swanky hotel was even more exciting. He and Graham rarely stayed in hotels, preferring to camp or stay in an Airbnb, so it was a rare treat. Pushing open the door to the hotel room, he had an immediate urge to jump up and down on the immaculate bed but remembered he was a policeman in his thirties, not a nine-year-old boy and anyway, he didn't want to crumple the pristine sheets. He then realised he had two beds, two double beds – what was that about? Were two couples meant to sleep in the same room? That sounded a bit weird or perhaps each person had a whole double bed to themselves? Either way he decided to jump on one bed and leave the other bed smooth and crisp. No one would ever know.

The two-day conference was due to start the following morning, and Eddie was looking forward to a decent sleep. He hadn't slept well since the revelations from the Gala Ball. He had tried to talk to Graham about it, but it all just went around and around his head. Without any possible way of getting more information about all the incidents, including the recent arrest of a woman in Bolton, there was little more he could do. He unpacked his things and decided to eat in the hotel bar before getting an early night.

The bar was large with about twenty small tables, each with two or three chairs. Nearly all the tables were occupied by a solitary man or woman, all eating or fiddling on their phones. Eddie guessed that they were probably all attending the policing conference – the clue was the bright blue paperwork they had all been sent in advance, which sat on most of the tables. Eddie hoped that by tomorrow evening he might have made one or two friends, and the restaurant would look less like a singles speed-dating event. Tonight though, they all looked a bit nervous, uncertain how to break the ice and wondering what tomorrow might hold. He resolved that if they were all sat like this again tomorrow evening, he would invite everyone out for a drink in the city centre. He hadn't had a big night out for some time, well, if you excluded the Gala Ball which had sadly left a sour taste in his mouth. No, Eddie fancied a proper night out – he just needed to make a friend or two tomorrow.

Unaccustomed as he was to these kinds of events, by mid-morning coffee the following day, Eddie was starting to think that the chances of finding a friend to go clubbing with, were increasingly unlikely. The first morning was dominated by long, boring talks from important people Eddie should have known, but didn't. They droned on about policy, the future of policing, political issues and even how climate change and AI would change the force. At one point Eddie fell asleep. It was one of those micro-naps where your own snoring wakes you up and you hope no one heard you. The chap sitting next to him stifled a laugh and that was all that was needed – the gentle, knowing smile of a stranger, soon to be friend. Smiling back, Eddie saw the chap was a similar age, but with long tied back hair which made him look too trendy to be a policeman. They got chatting during the tea break and Eddie soon found out that his name was Simon and he lived near Birmingham. He worked on domestic abuse cases and was considering a complete change of career.

'I only came to the conference to help me decide whether to leave the force and do something different or whether to stay. The type of cases I work are so stressful, plus the strain it puts on my own marriage and trying to raise two young daughters. Sometimes it's just too much.'

Simon seemed nice and he and Eddie arranged to meet up for lunch, after their chosen seminar sessions. Eddie didn't really know what the difference was between a paper session, a seminar and a workshop, except for the duration of each and that workshop inferred he would have to participate somehow, so he avoided those.

His first session was *A Policeman's Balls: how to keep all your balls in the air and what to do if you drop some* which he had only chosen because he and Graham had found the title funny. Not the best reason to choose an hour-long session that he now had to sit through.

However, the session was rather enlightening, and he learned that some police officers had so much work to juggle that they were stressed and needed strategies to cope. Given how little work Eddie had to do each day, this renewed his doubts about his current job. However, he also learned that not having enough to do was also stressful which was a complete revelation to him and went some way to explaining why he felt the way he did. Eddie's challenge, it transpired, was to pick up some new balls but also examine his own balls more closely. This meant considering whether he could take on a new work challenge or responsibility to make his existing work more fulfilling. He couldn't wait to tell Graham this, and was sure he would offer to help examine Eddie's balls somehow.

The description of the next session was a little more obvious, *The rise of the armchair detective and the role of internet sleuthing communities*. It appeared that the more accurate the session title was, the less likely people were to attend. The balls session was completely rammed but this one was almost empty except for an officer who looked close to retirement who clearly hated wannabee detectives; a young female officer who felt completely the opposite, and two other people who turned up late looking as though they were lost.

Eddie opted to sit next to the female officer as she seemed more open to chatting and actually understood the potential of the internet.

The session was fascinating, and the presenter gave a balanced view of both the dangers of these online communities but also the potential help they could be to law enforcement especially in the case of complex, unsolved crimes. He showed screen shots of some of the online sites and how they worked. Some you had to pay to join, others relied heavily on advertising and were more trouble than they were worth. Some sites were even run by ex-police detectives or private investigators who wanted to use their skills differently. One popular site was run by an officer who had been injured in the line of duty and was now confined to a wheelchair. His website, he said, helped him to continue to do work that he loved.

As the presenter acknowledged the downsides to these online communities, it gave the older attendee a massive opportunity to rant about how dangerous the websites were, how they were used by vigilantes, how they caused harm to families affected by major crime and how they distorted the facts which made detection more difficult.

Eddie knew that this man was correct in many ways, but once the presenter got a word in edgeways and invited others to talk, Samara, the younger woman gave a very different point of view. She spoke about how these communities were able to put together a much wider picture than the police were able to. They could ask questions informally, drawing on the *hive mind* which was much bigger than official channels. Eddie nodded vigorously to all of her comments.

Samara gave an example of a case in the US where a serial killer who had been operating for over twenty years, was unable to be caught as he made a point of changing his *MO* every time and only carried out one murder in each US state. The killer was only caught by the police working with one of these online communities. It had been something to do with a unique brand of bubble-gum that the murderer liked and was only sold in certain places, or something very strange like that. Eddie couldn't later remember exactly what it was, but the point was that without the online community bringing lots of random ideas and information to their online mapping system, it would never have been figured out. As Eddie listened to the presenter and Samara nodded in agreement, something started to form inside Eddie's mind. It flickered away like a light bulb trying to come to life, but he couldn't see what it was yet.

Back in his hotel room, Eddie decided it was time to give Bridget a call to clear the air and talk about The Women's League and the woman recently arrested in Bolton. He hadn't yet had a reply to his hastily sent text from the ball. He had also messaged her, apologising that he couldn't come to the last art group, but she hadn't replied to that either. Checking his phone, Eddie realised he had actually sent her two WhatsApp messages and neither displayed a tick by them.

'Bridget!' Eddie couldn't hide his relief at finally speaking to her, 'Did you get any of my messages?'

‘How are you, Eddie?’ said Bridget.

‘I’m fine but a lot has happened and I’ve just realised that you haven’t received any of my messages,’ Eddie said.

‘Eddie, I can’t hear you very well… the signal isn’t good... that will be my end as I’m in the garden trying to get a frog that looks lost, back to my neighbour’s pond… that’s it, off you go little one. Righto, I’ll get back to the house then I’ll be able to hear better.’ Eddie could hear some light puffing and a door close. ‘Yes, it’s good to hear from you, I was getting a little worried that I had upset you.’

‘Not at all. You know I went to The Women’s League ball with Sylvie last week, well apparently there has been a suspicious death somewhere near Bolton and the wife who is a League member has been arrested…Bridget are you still there?’

Bridget, now back in her kitchen, was idly stirring a cup of tea. She immediately stopped. ‘What did you say, Eddie?’ She thought she knew what he had said but needed confirmation.

‘A Women’s’ League member has been arrested in Bolton. I don’t have details, but her husband died suddenly, and she is being questioned about it. She’s suspected of poisoning him.’ Eddie wished he had more to tell Bridget, but he had left for the conference straight after the ball and been too busy to do anything. ‘Bridget, did you hear what I said?’

‘Yes, I’m just a bit shocked. I have spent the last couple of days trying to forget about it all and convince myself that I had made it all up in my head but now you’re saying there may be some truth in my suspicions?' She stumbled over her words and realised she needed to sit down.

'Listen, I'm still not convinced about it all, but I wasn't completely dismissing what you said, I just needed to find out more and think about it. Now this Bolton thing has come up, it gives me something more concrete to look into.' Eddie was trying to strike a balance between apologising to Bridget whilst not being completely sucked in. He wasn't sure he was succeeding but Bridget was still listening. 'Look, I'm at a conference right now, so I can't do much.' He omitted to mention he was just about to go on a big, boozy night out. 'But I've had an idea and I think you could help.'

Eddie told Bridget about the online detective forums he had just learnt about. 'I think we should join a few and see what we can find out about. Perhaps any other unexplained deaths or information that might be related to The Women's League. Graham can't help at the moment, and we can't ask Sylvie because she's too close to the League, and I would hate to upset her again.' Eddie took a big breath in, surprised that Bridget didn't jump in straight away. 'I know I can trust you, Bridget and I think you have an insight into the minds of these people, certainly more so than me. What do you think?'

Still a little shocked and now grappling with the fact that perhaps her imagination hadn't made it all up after all, Bridget quietly said, 'I'm not great on the computer, Eddie, but I'll try and help if I can.' She sighed a little before speaking rather quietly. 'It's just that after we talked about all this before, Eddie, I felt so silly and I've persuaded myself that it was just my ridiculous, creative mind and…'

Eddie cut her off quickly realising that his lovely friend had been beating herself up since they last spoke.

'I know, Bridget and I'm sorry, but now we know about this case in Bolton, we can both go into this with a more level head. Yes, we will probably find that we were wrong or just maybe, something bigger is happening. We don't know right now, but this way we can explore a little more before I jeopardize my career by talking to someone at work.' Eddie hadn't realised how much he needed help from Bridget and that yes, he was worried about his career. He couldn't just go bowling into work with the evidence he had, which of course wasn't evidence, it was just a handful of vague suspicions and coincidences.

'I've sent you an email, Bridget, that way you can click the link on your computer. It'll be easier than on your phone. Sign up to a couple of the websites, but don't add anything, just read stuff and explore the site structure. I know there'll be a way of searching using key words, but we can do that together when I'm back – just have a mooch around for now. Oh, and whatever you do, don't use your real name, make up a user identity or avatar name of whatever they want. Call yourself Cyril or something innocuous. I've got to go – speak soon.'

Eddie hung up the call and tried to relax as he pulled on his favourite T-shirt. He had dumped a lot of information on Bridget, but he knew that she was tough and much more internet savvy than she liked to think. He quickly checked his hair, sprayed on an extra squirt of aftershave and left to meet Simon in the lobby.

‘Manchester here I come!’ he said grinning to himself.

FIFTY-THREE

Manchester exceeded Eddie's expectations of a great night out. He and Simon had immediately clicked and whilst Eddie had to constantly remind himself that both were happily married, he noted that he rarely felt such an immediate connection with someone. They started off in the usual way, in a pub with a couple of beers, but by 10.30pm it had progressed to cocktails in fancy bars and the inevitable decision to find a night club. Simon, it seemed, was not only fed up with his job which had really taken its toll on him, he also needed time away from his family. He and his wife had three children under three years old: twin boys and baby girl. He proudly told Eddie their names which Eddie promptly forgot. Trying later to recall their names to Graham, he thought they were John, Paul and Georgina but realised he made that up in his head as there had been a Beatles' song playing at the time and he was four Mojitos in.

Eventually the new friends found themselves in a

night club near the conference hotel. The owner of the club was pleased his club was nearly full on a Wednesday, numbers swollen by off-duty policeman attending the conference. The night club wasn't the sort of place Eddie would usually go, but wasn't that the point of being away from home? He yelled into Simon's ear during the Drum and Bass set. Eddie was never sure how to dance to Drum and Bass and found himself doing a kind of knee bend whilst punching the air, interspersing this with the occasional double-arm, fast wave. Later, when the music changed to Techno, he discovered he was doing identical moves.

'Come and meet Tommo,' Simon yelled in Eddie's ear and gestured to a group of men standing at the bar, who were just about to down shots of varying colours.

'Three, two, one, yessssss,' the men chorused.

Eddie noted that they were a little older than he and Simon and would most definitely regret their choices tomorrow.

'I just met Tommo today. He's from Bolton, but you'll love him'.

At the mention of Bolton, Eddie's ears pricked up a little.

'Tommoooo!' shouted Simon as if the two had been friends for years, even though they'd only met earlier during a workshop called *Diversity: Balls come in all shapes, sizes and colours*. What was it about the police service and balls, Eddie wondered.

'Tommo, meet Eddie, you'll love him'.

Tommo pumped Eddie's hand enthusiastically, before

introducing himself as Thomas, father of five who worked in the murder investigation team.

'Father of five!' Eddie couldn't help himself and his face clearly gave away what he was thinking.

Thomas chuckled saying 'Well, seven really as we are a blended family, with my other two staying every other weekend and they are all girls, all of them and please, no jokes about starting my own football team.'

Eddie immediately liked Tommo, he was warm, friendly and very chatty. Eddie wondered whether his chattiness was due to life at home being so busy that he relished a couple of days where he could talk as much as he liked. Eddie bought the three of them a jug of a cocktail called an Americanito which was basically a ginger Mojito with a little Stars and Stripes flag stuck in it. It went down very easily. They chatted about life and work and Eddie shared how he was a bit bored at work due to the lack of murders in South Glos. Neither of his new friends had heard of South Glos.

'Consider yourself lucky, mate,' Thomas said in a tone which seemed way too sober to Eddie. 'My team's run off its feet all the time and we just got a really complex case in this week, which has stretched us to the limit.' Eddie and Simon both leant in to hear more. The Americanito had relaxed Tommo's tongue and he added, 'We just arrested a woman on suspicion of killing her husband and she seemed to have poisoned his work colleagues as well, but none of them died, thankfully.'

Eddie gulped and said nothing, gesturing for Tommo to say more.

'We think she removed the poisoned food from his

work's fridge before anyone found it, but traces were left in the kitchen. Nothing found in her kitchen at home, soooo she was really careful.' His elongated so gave away just how loose his tongue was.

Simon had only listened to the first few words and was now making a bee line for the dance floor, in a very wobbly fashion.

Eddie, desperate to ask something, cupped his hand over Tommo's ear and tried not to yell too much or sound too interested, 'And how do you think she poisoned him, Tommo?'

Tommo hesitated before leaning over to Eddie and with a cupped hand which failed to do its job, he yelled, 'Something sweet, mate, probably a sandwich filling or toast topper. Chocolate spread, marmalade or maybe jam, that kinda thing.' Tommo immediately jumped up shouting, 'Woooo hoooo, gotta dance to this mate, it's Blur.' He vanished onto the dance floor.

Eddie put down his ginger Mojito with its little flag now soggy and sagging and left the club in shock.

FIFTY-FOUR

As soon as he got back to his hotel room he downed a strong coffee and turned on his laptop. Signing up to several online investigation forums, he spent the remainder of the night figuring out how they worked, and which ones seemed to be the best. Knowing he wouldn't have time tomorrow, Eddie also emailed Bridget about the revelations from Tommo, telling her to include the search term 'jam' on the detective sites. Once he was finished, he managed to grab an unrefreshing two-hour sleep before going down to breakfast.

Eddie saw neither Simon nor Tommo at breakfast. Most of the dining tables which were quiet the previous morning, were now filled with small clusters of people chatting lightly and all bearing the signs of a late night and budding new friendships. The waitress gave Eddie a knowing look as he ordered a Red Bull, a pot of coffee and a full English Breakfast. He checked his emails and was pleased to see one from Bridget.

'Got your email. Will do.'

Eddie sighed, well at least she had agreed to help and hopefully next time she would reply with more than one sentence, especially once she read about his discoveries last night.

Finishing his cooked breakfast Eddie buttered his toast and reached for a little pot of marmalade on the table. Perhaps not, he thought as his stomach turned over. He looked at the other little jam pots on the breakfast table and put a strawberry one in his pocket to remind him what Tommo has said about poisoned marmalade or jam.

'As if I'm likely to forget that!'

The morning seminar sessions were achingly slow, and Eddie wondered if every single person at the conference had been partying the previous night. Everyone seemed subdued and definitely more dishevelled than the previous morning when they had been fresh-faced and ironed. After the morning coffee break and despite topping up his caffeine levels, Eddie's hangover and lack of sleep started to kick in. He desperately wanted to nip back to his room for a nap but didn't want to miss the next seminar session. It was titled *From Greeks to Geeks – poisoning through the ages. What modern policing could learn*. Eddie wondered if the subtitle was purely added to make the subject seem relevant for the conference.

The hour-long seminar was torture and Eddie struggled not to fall asleep. He wished he had given it a miss. The presenter was so boring and had a monotone voice which he clearly knew was a problem and had decided to liven up his talk by adding jokes, tenuously related to the seminar.

Seeming proud of this, the presenter chuckled to himself before he had even told the jokes.

‘I poisoned my wife’s pita dip,’ he said, his chest bouncing as he laughed to himself. ‘The police charged me with hummus-cide.’ The presenter laughed much too loudly, which was useful as it masked the fact that the audience were just shaking their heads.

Eddie wondered how long this torture would go on. His stomach was suffering with all the booze, caffeine in the middle of the night, little sleep, more caffeine, fried food, more caffeine and then a chocolate muffin. He already felt like he had poisoned himself and talk of poison was not helping. Rushing out of the seminar early, he grabbed the handout as he left, just hearing the presenter’s next joke which confirmed to Eddie that leaving was the right decision.

‘Did you hear about the Germans who got food poisoning? It was the wurst.’

Back in his room, Eddie flopped onto the bed and grabbed a couple of hours sleep before the afternoon session. He didn’t check his phone or emails as he knew he would get sucked back into the unfolding situation by Bridget. His mind however, had other ideas, and as he nodded off it treated him to a dream where he was swimming naked in a pool filled with strawberry jam, watched by a group of middle-aged police officers. He couldn’t get out of the pool as the sides were too slippery and he eventually slipped under the surface to meet a very sticky end. As he jerked awake, he chastised himself saying that Red Bull was no longer his friend.

Hauling himself out of bed after the unrefreshing nap he returned to the conference for the final session, eventually found Simon and Tommo, who had only just made it out of bed. They all chuckled about the previous night's activities which had abruptly ended when the night club owner realised his club was full of coppers and decided the risks of his various illegal activities were too great, so he had chucked them out early.

Early was apparently 4am instead of 6am so Simon and Tommo had found another establishment which saw them dancing on the tables and consuming more dodgy cocktails until 7am. The men all remarked that it was a top night, exchanged contact details and vowed to keep in touch. With his eyes truly open to a new side of police life, Eddie got the train home exhausted, happy, and with a lot of work to do.

FIFTY-FIVE

Knowing that he would be less than impressed, Bridget had kept her thoughts and suspicions about The Women's League to herself and not shared anything with her husband. He was already of the opinion that she was too easily distracted and wasted time on strange activities – time that would have been better spent earning money. If things got more complicated, she would tell him, but not yet. She was used to keeping things from him – it was just easier that way. Putting this aside and buoyed by Eddie's discovery of a new murder in Bolton, Bridget started exploring the world of online investigation.

Her online skills were basic at best, at worse they could be described as primitive, but Bridget could get by if her laptop behaved itself. Following the recent discussion with Eddie, some of which she hadn't heard properly, she opened his email

'Include jam as a search term,' she muttered to herself as she read Eddie's email.

Bridget opened the first link Eddie had sent and noted that the website forum was called Christie's Army. The about section explained, unnecessarily in Bridget's opinion, it was named after Agatha Christie, and they saw themselves as an army of amateur detectives solving crimes that the police didn't see as important or had tried and failed.

This rationale was echoed by most of the other websites who names included, Sherlock's Underground Network, and CSI Alive, which Bridget thought she recognised from a TV show, but this one apparently stood for Canterbury Sleuths Investigate. Although her favourite forum was called Poirot's Pedants, she decided to focus on Christie's Army as it looked like a more professional site, and it was on the second page of a Google search. Her nephew had told her once she shouldn't click on the first links that appeared on Google as that usually meant the site had paid money to be there. She wanted to ask why that was a problem, but she trusted him.

He regularly fixed and cleaned up her laptop saying with an air of frustration as he typed and tutted, 'It's not broken, Gitty, you just keep clicking on things you shouldn't and downloading unhelpful shit.'

To be part of Christie's Army Bridget had to provide her email address which she did and was informed that it would be used to alert her of new developments on cases (as well as offers, news and messages from partner organisations unless she ticked the privacy box, which, of course, she didn't). This was followed by a quick video which showed Bridget how to use the website, which she diligently watched and then instantly forgot, so now it was up to her.

Bridget stared at the screen and had never seen such a complicated website page. Eventually she found a search box shaped like a magnifying glass. Clicking on the icon which also contained a little fingerprint, she could see options for a simple search and advanced search. The more advanced search asked for key words and had options for filtering the search results, which immediately made her head hurt so she opted for a simple search. As Eddie had told her about jam, she typed JAM in the empty search box. Clicking the fingerprint, the funny magnifying glass moved about as if it were looking at different things all over the screen. So clever, she thought. Within a few seconds her search results had appeared on screen:

47 ongoing cases included the word JAM; 543 individual comments mentioning JAM; 1895 links to external cases mentioning JAM.

'What the…how on earth am I meant to look through all those? This is ridiculous.' She wasn't sure what to do, so she saved the search and decided to just open one of the forty-seven cases that included the word JAM. This opened a new tab with the case title clearly named at the top, *Missing Jamaican Women: Doncaster, 1997*.

'Oh bugger,' Bridget said out loud, quickly closing the tab and opening the next one which showed a case entitled, *British man missing in Jamaica: Kingston, 2001*.

Closing this and opening the third case, she guessed what was coming, *Murdered Jamaican man: Liverpool, 2004*.

'Okay, so searching for jam is not a good idea,' she muttered under her breath. Somehow, I need to search for jam but not words with jam in them. 'How do I do that?' She scanned the screen for the talking paper clip that used to her help her years ago. Not finding it, Bridget decided to call her nephew who wearily suggested she look at the Help pages on the website.

'And, Gitty, if you get stuck, I could come over on Wednesday to help.'

Clicking on the help page, Bridget found another video called How to improve your search results and settled down to watch this. The helpful video showed her how to exclude certain items and narrow searches down and avoid the search term being included in other longer words, which had been one of her problems.

Following the instructions her JAM search now brought back better results.

4 ongoing cases that include the word JAM; 76 individual comments mentioning JAM; 673 links to external cases mentioning JAM.

That was better, Bridget thought brightly but glancing at the clock she realised she had already spent two hours fumbling about on this website and had achieved nothing. She replied to Eddie's email and then decided to call it a day. Opening up her email, she was dismayed to discover she had eighty-five new emails.

'What the fuck,' she screeched. The first new one was a welcome email from Christie's Army. Fair enough. The second one congratulated her on her first search. The third email offered her a special discount on membership, giving all the benefits of said membership which was reduced to only £49 for the year if she signed up today and featured a little clock, counting down the hours and minutes to when the discount would run out. The other eighty-two emails all had similar titles:

Search alert JAM: someone in Middlesborough has used the word JAM in their comments, or Search alert JAM: new link to external case in Moldova.

What on earth had she done! This was only about an hour's worth of searching. By the time her nephew came over in a couple of days' time, there would be thousands of them. She grabbed her phone and frantically called him again. He seemed so calm and talked her through how to unsubscribe, as if it was a regular occurrence for him.

'What is this website anyway, Gitty? You haven't been scammed, have you? We did talk about only giving your email out to people and sites you know, didn't we?'

She loved her nephew, but right now he was sounding very patronizing. On reflection, maybe he had a point she thought as she deleted the emails which had already increased in number. Without telling her nephew about the site and its purpose she thanked him and wrote Eddie an email.

'Not sure I'm techy enough to help with all this. Just got 83 emails from just one of those websites. Whatever you do, don't just put JAM in the search box.

Hope you are not too hung over, best wishes, Bridget Sullivan.'

As she closed her laptop she wondered, not the first time, what on earth she was doing.

FIFTY-SIX

When things had started to go wrong, Glenda Grant knew that she would be completely on her own. After her visit to William's office, she had called the emergency contact number at The Women's League but there had been no answer and eventually the number had been disconnected. Glenda had been warned that this would happen if things went wrong or the authorities got involved, but even the friendly member from her local group seemed to have vanished into thin air.

'She works away for months at a time. I doubt she will be back before the end of the year,' her local leader told her.

In the days before her arrest, Glenda tried to bring the funeral forward, telling the funeral directors that a family member had to go back to the States urgently and could they have the cremation in the next couple of days if a cancellation came up.

The funeral director had asked her politely, but with a distinct smirk,

'Under what circumstances do you imagine someone cancels a funeral? People don't tend to resurrect. Anyway, the police haven't released the body.'

Despite having taken precautions and done exactly what she had been told to, Glenda knew it had not been enough, so when officers from Bolton police department arrived at her front door, she wasn't surprised. She sat with an unsmiling female police officer as forensic officers swabbed her kitchen surfaces and gathered items for testing. Glenda knew there was little point in arguing but when she saw an officer come downstairs with William's laptop in hand, she had to say something.

'Do you really need to take that laptop? It has all our family photos on it, and I need it to arrange the funeral.' This wasn't the truth, but it was all she could think to say at the time. Glenda knew that if they searched the laptop, they would find evidence of William's activities including pornographic images of young girls. Apart from the disgust she felt, she knew it would raise further questions about his death.

'I'm sorry, Mrs Grant, we need it.' With that, the police officers and the raft of people in white overalls had left her house. Less than forty-eight hours later, Glenda Grant was in custody and charged with the murder of her husband.

FIFTY-SEVEN

Bridget had managed to get to grips with one of the investigation websites a little, but it had taken two days of struggle with nothing useful found. Thankfully she managed to unsubscribe to most of the notification emails as she had been receiving around two hundred a day. On the third day, she turned on her laptop to get to grips with another investigation site but quickly remembered that both Verity and Anthea were due to visit later that day to see the almost finished portrait and to plan the forthcoming unveiling.

Her stomach dropped at the thought of the two women visiting her again, especially since she and Eddie had started to explore the strange deaths in earnest. The thought sent a chill through her. Were these women, these middle class, ordinary women really killers? Bridget knew that her mind could conjure up all sorts of strange things as it had done so on many occasions, but she couldn't easily imagine Verity or Anthea performing the deed themselves.

That slightly more rational thought didn't calm her growing feeling of unease as the afternoon visit approached.

The women travelled separately to see Bridget with Anthea's husband driving her from Oxfordshire as her hand was still heavily bandaged and Verity driving from Wales where she had been on a tour of Women's League groups. Anthea arrived earlier than expected much to Bridget's annoyance as she wanted to prepare her studio and make it look like she had been furiously working on the portrait, which was far from the truth.

As she opened the studio door, the woman standing there was nothing like the bright, friendly, chatty Anthea that Bridget had met in London a few months earlier. Apart from the obviously bandaged hand, Anthea looked tired, worn and had lost weight.

'I'm sorry for being early, Bridget, but my husband is meeting up with a group of old colleagues from the police force and had to drop me off first.'

Hearing this Bridget made a mental note to tell Eddie about Anthea's husband being in the police, as it might turn out to be important. She politely offered her a cup of tea and Anthea accepted. Whilst making the tea, Bridget casually asked what had happened to her hand.

'Oh, it's healing well now, just some small burns I got from an old kettle which I should have thrown out years ago,' she said, gently patting the bandage. 'The handle broke and the whole thing dropped boiling water on me. I'm hoping to have a smaller dressing put on later this week so I can start driving again. It's been such a pain having to be chauffeured round by my husband,' she added, looking even more depleted.

Verity arrived just as Bridget was pouring the tea. She also looked very different to the first time they had met. Her hair was wind swept and her grey roots were more prominent than Bridget had painted. At first she wondered if it was just the effect of having been in windy, wet Wales for a few days, but as the meeting progressed it became clear that all was not well with the two women.

'I'm just pouring some tea for us, Verity. Would you like some?' asked Bridget.

'God no,' Verity said rather rudely, quickly remembering herself and saying, 'Sorry, I meant that I only drink coffee, would you mind?'

Realising she had run out of *proper* coffee Bridget explained she would pop over to her house and get some, leaving the women alone together. As she walked back up the path to the studio a few minutes later, she could hear raised voices and decided to listen in at the door, for a moment.

'What the fuck are we going to do about that stupid woman up north, Anthea? This could cause us no end of problems,' Verity hissed.

'We've cut all communication with her and our member has gone away for a couple of months, so there is no trail. At the start she was told that if anything happened, she should destroy her SIM, clean up thoroughly and practice her back stories. We can only trust that she has done that,' said Anthea.

'But no one's ever been arrested before. Do we know

what happened? The papers are also reporting illness at the man's place of work. Is it related? We might have to send someone to see her or something. I am getting really worried about it all, Anthea.'

'No, we can't risk anyone seeing her. Anything that happens is up to her now and if she gets charged, I doubt very much that she will implicate anyone else.'

At this point, Bridget realised she had been gone long enough. She backed up a few steps and made loud noises, pretending to spill the coffee so the women didn't think she'd heard their conversation.

'Shit, shit, oh no, it's okay,' she said loudly. 'Only spilt some of the coffee,' Bridget bumbled loudly as she entered the studio. 'Here we go Verity, I'll just pour you a fresh cup.'

The women had already stopped talking and were busy pretending to look around the studio and at the studies of Verity that Bridget had blu-tacked to the wall.

Bridget beckoned the women to sit and took some calming breaths, reminding herself that she had hidden the damaged painting, and that the replacement painting was surprisingly better than the first one. She was confident that Verity would like it because Bridget herself liked it, which was unusual. She also reminded herself that she had high standards for her work which always stood her in good stead.

'Here we go,' said Bridget as she lifted off the sheet covering the nearly complete portrait. As the sheet slid to the ground, the three women found themselves looking at a magnificent painting of Verity, painted in bright hues of turquoise and soft pinks, set against the dark interior of her office. To the viewer, there was absolutely no doubt that the person in the portrait was a charismatic leader in her field. Her hair, although showing her unique one-sided bob, was painted in soft, auburn curls with just a suggestion of grey. The gold of her hair glowed against the optically opposite colour of her green suit. The blouse had been a good choice giving a burst of pattern and texture against the flatter, strong colour of the suit. Verity looked strong and beautiful but there was an unmistakable air of intrigue. On the coffee table in front of her, Bridget had included a mobile phone and the outline of a second which also looked like a bookmark poking out from under the book. The book itself did not have a title – this would be added later. Bridget also planned to add in another couple of items, depending on how the following weeks panned out.

Verity took a sharp breath in and looked like she might cry before her face lifted into a huge smile. Anthea went to clap but remembered her bandaged hand and clapped on her leg instead.

'It's just amazing, Bridget. Nothing like I was expecting but I really love it.' Verity sounded so earnest and authentic that just for a moment Bridget forgot she might be some sort of serial killer.

'Oh Bridget,' cooed Anthea. 'I knew you were the right choice for this commission, it's just superb, isn't it, Verity? I can't wait to see it framed and to show it to the world.'

Anthea had regained some of the energy that Bridget had seen in her the first time they'd met and was very pleased they had both reacted well.

All Bridget had to do now was make some minor changes before the final presentation and unveiling. However, despite her initial feelings of relief, she knew that this time was different. Usually, the joy of knowing that a portrait had been well received would feed Bridget and help fuel her through the final stages of completion. Today was different; her feelings of unease quickly replaced the momentary relief. If she and Eddie were correct about their suspicions, what would that make these two ordinary middle-aged, middle-class women standing in her studio right now? What would become of this portrait and more than that, what might these two unassuming women do if they found out what she suspected?

Bridget quickly reminded herself that she didn't really *know* anything. Her imagination had a strangle hold around her rational mind and she needed it to soften its grip.

Talk about something practical before you start losing it, she told herself. Running into the storeroom, she retrieved some sample mouldings and started a discussion about framing the painting, which kept all three women busy for ages. Eventually they also put a date in the diary for the unveiling which would take place at the London headquarters at a special drinks reception in four weeks' time. Four weeks and this would be all over, well at least her direct contact with Verity and Anthea would be.

Four weeks.

She could do this, she just needed to keep her cool and at some point, probably talk to her husband about what had been happening, but not yet.

Once Verity and Anthea left the studio, Bridget breathed

a sigh of relief and felt the sickly feeling in her stomach subside a little. At least for now she could relax. She would forget about it all for a day or two and then tell Eddie that she needed to ease up on the investigation – it was taking too much out of her, and she was more tired than she realised. Yes, that's what she would do.

FIFTY-EIGHT

Back in her car, Verity waved goodbye to Anthea and the fake smile dropped from her face instantly. Unbeknownst to both Bridget and Anthea, Verity had also been struggling to keep her calm whilst they had sat and happily discussed framing and wine choices for the unveiling. Earlier, while they had been casually looking around the studio, intrigued by the sketches and studies of Verity, one jumped out at her and stopped her in her tracks. As she looked at the simple charcoal sketch that she had made of her in London, Verity noticed that Bridget had written something down the side of the paper and attempted to rub it out. However, the charcoal had left clear outlines, and Verity immediately recognised the small collection of letters and numbers. It had been the text message that she had received during the London sitting. At first she thought she had imagined it and was reluctant to stare at the sketch any longer but as she flicked her eyes back to take a second look, she could see the message as clear as day.

Verity's head flopped into her hands. Her fingers started to massage her head but quickly it turned into painful pulling of her hair and her fingernails started to dig into her scalp. Why on earth had Bridget written that message down? How did she see the text message? What did this stupid woman think she was doing? Verity's stomach started to flip over and over but her well-honed nerves of steel kicked in and she calmed herself, relaxing her fingers before she left marks on her skin. She also decided not to tell Anthea. She would wait and see what, if anything, happened. She doubted that Bridget, the old, slightly dim artist wouldn't have a clue what the text code meant. They had designed the message system carefully so that no one could decode it, unless you knew exactly what it all meant.

Despite this, Verity struggled to shake off the worry. What with the stupid woman in Bolton getting herself arrested, she was already on edge, and this just added to her growing feelings of dread.

FIFTY-NINE

As the art group gathered at Bridget's, the atmosphere felt markedly different. Ralph was quiet and when he did speak, he was grumpy. Now working on his new bird project, a robin, he kept muttering under his breath saying, 'Bloody birds… why did I choose another bloody bird… bloody claws…' As well as Ralph's bad mood, Margaret was missing. Bridget had taken a call from her granddaughter earlier that day, who told her that Margaret was in hospital after having a bad stroke and doubted she would be coming back to the group. When Bridget told the group this news, everyone was clearly upset, and the room became even quieter.

To soothe the unpleasantly quiet room, which was usually filled with chatter, Bridget put the radio on, deciding that Classic FM was a good choice. Once you ignored the ageist advertisements for Life Insurance for the over fifties, will writing services, stairlifts and cruises for older people, the classical music worked its magic and the energy in the studio lifted.

Bridget found some artist books with examples of interesting ways to paint birds and sat down with Ralph to talk through them. She also showed him some different ways to use the paint and brushes in the hope that it might free him up and stop him doing the same thing whilst expecting different results. He seemed to take on board what she said, but ten minutes later, was happily making the same marks in the same way, with the same results he had been getting for months. Bridget knew that this was one of the things she had to accept. As a teacher you could only show people different ways of doing things, support them to have a go, but you always had to let go of your own ideas and let the student do what they wanted regardless of the outcome. If you couldn't, teaching people to paint was torture.

Not that Bridget found teaching adults easy – it was much harder than people thought. Young children were free spirited and much more fun to teach, but of course you couldn't really run daytime groups as the children were at school, and you couldn't really charge the same sort of prices as adults. Adults on the other hand, were less free spirited and had grown up with a lifetime of unhelpful beliefs about art. Most held set views of what constituted a good painting and always wanted to leave the class with a finished, framed painting. This really pissed Bridget off, but she could never admit it.

This was one of the reasons why Bridget loved having Sylvie and Eddie, in the group. Sylvie willingly went along with anything Bridget suggested and enjoyed the process regardless and Eddie seemed keen to really learn. He listened to Bridget's suggestions but was also happy to challenge her. She wondered why he ended up being a policeman instead of having a creative career, but she knew many examples of people who had different sides to their life: Leonardo da Vinci was both a great artist and engineer; as well as being a famous bass guitar player, Brian May was also a doctor of astrophysics.

Happy that she had both of them in her art group, Bridget settled Sylvie and Eddie down to copy a section of a Monet's waterlilies. The aim was to explore his palette of colours, which involved enlarging Monet's paintings on her laptop, so they could see how the colours were laid next to each other. She left them happily chatting and squeezing tubes of acrylic colour.

'How are you finding your new WL group, Sylvie?' Eddie asked. He had a raft of questions he was desperate to ask but needed her to relax and he knew this would make her smile.

'WL group!' Sylvie replied with a smile 'Get you! It's good, quite different from my old League group but still lovely,' Sylvie mused as she mixed white with a little Indian yellow and rose pink, to make a soft peachy colour.

'In what way?' Eddie asked.

'Well, they're a bit posher I suppose, and sometimes I feel rather normal or even poor, to be honest. They all seem to have ponies, or double-barrelled names, you know the sort of thing.'

'Well, my Auntie Linda isn't like that. She's always

worked you know, and she even had a job at the League years ago,' Eddie added.

'Yes, she told me about that. Did you know she worked for Verity?'

Eddie did not know this and had to stop himself from sounding too interested. He must tread lightly, he told himself. 'How long ago was that? I expect I was still a child.'

Sylvie pondered for a moment. 'I think she said Verity was in her early or mid-thirties, so maybe fifteen years ago or more.'

Eddie reckoned that he would have been a grumpy teenager around then.

'Linda told me that around that time something must've happened because Verity changed almost overnight, and no one ever figured out why.' Eddie was listening intently now and Sylvie, bless her, continued without prompting 'When Linda first started working for her, she was happier and calmer and then over the space of a few weeks she lost weight and became much more, umm what did Linda say, more aggressive. No, that's horrible, stronger perhaps.' Sylvie slowed at this point, wondering if she had spoken out of turn, but then whispered, 'Apparently, she stopped wearing her wedding ring, so everyone assumed that it was something to do with her marriage.'

Eddie casually asked, 'Does she have any children?' thinking it was a perfectly reasonable question.

'Pfff, of course not. She isn't really the type. She is just too…um…I'm not sure how to put it.' Sylvie was clearly embarrassed as she failed to conceal her all too obvious thoughts about Verity.

'But she was married,' Eddie said.

'Apparently so, but it can't have lasted, and most people think it ended very suddenly.'

Eddie now wondered what happened to end Verity's marriage and, more importantly, what had become of Mr Verity Scanlan. Where was he now? Would he talk to Eddie? That would be helpful, and he doubted there was a better way to find out more about the mysterious Verity.

The odd couple, Eddie in his thirties with his short blonde, spikey hair and Sylvie, in her late sixties with greying hair tastefully styled into soft curls, settled down and resumed their painterly exploration of Claude Monet's famous waterlilies. According to Bridget they produced some gorgeous studies. Ralph although dismissing Bridget's suggestions, seemed happier with his efforts at painting the robin.

After a brief discussion the group agreed they would send a get well soon card to Margaret and to this end, Bridget found what she called an old canvas and cut a square out of it which featured a vase of painted flowers. Ignoring the horror of the art group as she sliced through what seemed to them like a perfectly good painting of the interior of the studio, Bridget then stuck the square onto a folded piece of white card.

'Instant greeting card.' She beamed at the dumb struck group, handing it to Sylvie who was put in charge of gathering signatures. Whilst she did this, Eddie and Bridget vanished to the small studio kitchen to chat.

'How are you getting on with the investigation websites?' asked Eddie in a hushed voice.

Opening her laptop, Bridget waved towards the screen. 'It's unbelievable. These armchair detectives seem to be on the website all day, every day. I don't know how they find the time.' She gestured to the comments section on one case, which had updated even as they spoke. 'And did I tell you about the email incident? I mean, who on earth thinks it's a good idea to send someone eighty-six emails in the space of a few hours?!'

'Yes, you did mention it,' Eddie tactfully said, deciding not to mention that this was the third time she'd told him. 'I think we need to choose some better search terms.'

'Whatever you do, don't type jam as a search term, you will get thousands of results,' she said quickly.

'Yes, you already mentioned that too.' Eddie sounded a little brisk.

Bridget ignored him and continued, 'However, I have now watched some tutorial videos about searches, I just haven't done anymore in the last couple of days as I had Verity and Anthea here on Monday to see the portrait. Oh, I haven't told you what happened, have I?' Bridget continued without drawing breath or waiting for Eddie to reply, 'I overhead them talking; I didn't hear any names, but they both seemed worried about the arrest of a League member up north. It might have been to do with that death in Bolton.' Bridget paused to breathe.

Eddie took the opportunity to jump into their so far one-sided, whispered conversation. 'Well, they would be upset, Bridget but that doesn't prove anything, does it?'

'I know but they then started talking about some illnesses at a workplace nearby. They were really concerned about it all and …'

Eddie interrupted her again, no longer bothering to whisper. 'Okay, okay, well we can probably find out more about that from the local news online or the local environmental health department – these things have to be reported you see.'

Bridget looked happier now Eddie seemed to be taking notice of what she'd heard.

'So I'll do that, and I'll see if I can find Verity's ex-husband. Bridget, you focus on some searches. Use the keywords *poisoning*, *women's league*, and *unexplained death* to start with and I'll email you with some other search terms that might help.'

'Did you just say that Verity used to be married?' Bridget was looking at him wide-eyed as she asked.

Eddie nodded and explained what Sylvie had told him, and that he would find a way to ask his auntie if she could remember anything else about that time. It was at this moment that the kitchen door flew open, followed by Sylvie holding the limp greeting card. She was on the brink of tears.

'What's going on? Why are you telling Bridget that stuff I told you about Verity. It makes me sound like an utter gossip and anyway, why is of any interest to you both and what's this about poisoning?'

Horrified to see gentle Sylvie so upset, Bridget beckoned to her to come and sit down and asked Eddie to make some fresh tea. He looked equally distraught and put the kettle on, leaving the two women to talk. Bridget decided not to tell Sylvie everything, but it was difficult to explain why they were talking about poison without letting it all out. She opted to say she had been trying to understand Verity better as it would help her with the portrait. She wove a story about Verity being secretive and having two mobile phones, but didn't say anything about the strange text messages. Bridget did admit they were talking about the suspected poisonings in Bolton and that a League member had been arrested and how shocking that must have been. And yes, Sylvie was right, it was none of their business and they were sorry.

Bridget apologised profusely and although Sylvie looked calmer, she knew this gentle lady was very shrewd and wasn't convinced. Although thoroughly kind-hearted, Sylvie always had her finger on the pulse and Bridget's explanations were weak and had been dismissed as soon as the words had left her mouth.

Eddie returned just as Sylvie stood up and was gathering her things, saying that Edgar was expecting her home. She left the room without looking at Eddie. She didn't collect her paintings or drink her tea, clear signs that Sylvie was far from happy.

SIXTY

William Grant dying in hospital, in the manner he had, automatically required a postmortem be carried out, which duly found deposits of arsenic in his liver and kidneys. The police had also found the child pornography on his laptop and although this gave her motive for murder, she dreaded people knowing about it as she felt it reflected badly on her. This rather incongruous thought was not lost on Glenda as she sat in Bolton police station, being charged with murder.

Her solicitor had quickly realised he was way out of his depth and arranged for an experienced criminal defence barrister to visit Glenda. Together they discussed options and Glenda admitted that she had killed William by lacing some home-made jam with arsenic. To the police and her barrister, she explained that her actions were not just in response to finding the child pornography and personal reports from family about his recent assault on her niece but was also due to years of financial abuse she had suffered at William's hand.

She made it clear that no one else knew about her plans and no one else was involved in the implementation of them. Glenda had researched how to obtain arsenic on her mobile phone, before she had disposed of her old SIM card. She explained clearly that she had made a large batch of poisoned jam but somehow William had taken a spare jar to work.

It didn't take long for her barrister to gather sufficient evidence and request an early court hearing. With her clear record and good standing in the community he had made it obvious that Glenda was no risk to anyone else and should be granted bail. The female judge agreed and unusually bail was granted on the condition that she surrender her passport, attend weekly appointments at the police station, and was available for any assessments needed before the trial.

The female judge who granted Glenda Grant's bail application, was a member of The Women's League. Glenda Grant, the fifty-five-year-old social care manager from Bolton, never told her family, the police or her legal team that it was The Women's League who supplied her with the jam.

No one ever found out how Glenda Grant, once released on bail, found an envelope in her home containing a fake passport and a plane ticket to Mexico leaving the next day. Glenda Grant vanished into thin air and was never heard of again.

No one knew anything, except perhaps, Verity Scanlan.

SIXTY-ONE

Eddie and Bridget knew they had upset Sylvie but also knew that what they were investigating went far beyond hurt feelings. They would make it up to her somehow and given time she would forgive them. They didn't contact each other for the next few days but quietly continued with their agreed plan.

Bridget decided to focus her efforts on two of the online investigation sites. One was Christie's Army, which she was now able to use more easily without getting hundreds of emails. The other website was 221b and was a little easier to use than Christie's Army. She signed up for one month's access to the site, hoping that her husband wouldn't notice the fee she had paid and was relieved that she noticed the small print that sneakily told her she would be charged a monthly fee if she didn't cancel.

I must remember to cancel this in a few weeks, she told herself, writing a reminder on a sticky note and then promptly losing it inside the sketch book that was open on her desk.

Armed with her much-improved search and filter skills, Bridget set about using the search terms Eddie had suggested. She didn't start by searching JAM, but rather Women's League UK and the search immediately came back with five hits.

The first three were old investigations going back at least ten years and mostly just mentioned that someone related to the case was in The Women's League. She ignored those and scrolled down to the most recent case which was called the Bolt-On Poisoner. As she read more, she became excited as it seemed to be something to do with the recent arrest that Sylvie had spoken about as Bolton was clearly *up north*. Bridget clicked on the button labelled *Investigation Map*. To her horror, this opened one of the most complicated screens of information that she had ever seen, and she had no idea what to do next. Reluctantly she clicked on the home button and went to find a tutorial.

'Why do they have to make things so difficult?' she grumbled to herself as she made a cup of tea and reluctantly clicked on the white triangle inviting her to play the video which was over twenty minutes long.

Eddie had decided to focus on finding Verity's husband, which was quite easy although he also had to pay a fee to display some records on an ancestry website. It appeared that Verity Scanlan had indeed been married to a Richard Sykes from 2001 until 2007. There was also a button next to this record which displayed two further records. The first record came as less of a surprise to Eddie than he imagined.

Richard Sykes had died in 2007, so Verity hadn't got divorced – her husband had just died.

Well probably not *just died*. The record gave no details of the death; he would have to find that out another way. However it was the second linked record, that made Eddie's heart miss a beat.

There had been a child. A child that had died.

Harry Arthur Sykes had died at just six months old, in 2007, mere months before Richard Sykes. No wonder Verity had changed so much. No one could go through two losses in such a short space of time and remain unchanged. Eddie turned off his laptop and found himself churning inside. He wanted to cry when he thought about the baby's death.

When Graham came up to the study to tell Eddie he was off to bed, he found his loving husband with his eyes damp and his face puffy. Eddie told Graham what had happened with Sylvie and about Verity's baby and Graham held him for a long time. In the past they had talked about having their own family, but both had decided it wasn't what they wanted, but now, looking at how the death of a baby had upset Eddie so much, Graham wondered if they needed to have that conversation again.

Not now, but someday soon.

SIXTY-TWO

In the fifteen years that Rob Clearwater had been making special preserves and jams for The Women's League, he estimated that he had dispatched around seventy parcels of jam, marmalade and other preserved substances to various places around the United Kingdom.

He had never kept records, that was too dangerous, and on the whole, he never heard about the results of his deliveries. In the early days he, Anthea and Verity had relied on letters and emails but these days they had a well-honed system of coded text messages, coordinated by Anthea and authorised by Verity. In previous years they had arranged discreet couriers to collect the parcels of jam, avoiding the standard postal services but now things were much easier with automated parcel collection points across the UK.

Whilst technology had made some parts of their service easier, it had somehow also increased the demand. These days they were getting a lot more requests for their bespoke service and it often felt to Rob like he was on the production end of a one-click husband murdering service.

He often reflected on why there had been such an increase in requests. Was it because of the internet and mobile phones? Perhaps adultery had been harder to detect before smart phones and apps that tracked people's whereabouts. And of course, there were so many messaging and social media platforms around which made it both easier to fuel elicit relationships but also easier to get caught out.

Other things were changing too. Rob was conscious that new post-mortem methods were being developed all the time and very soon it would be much harder to get away with poisoning someone without it being detected.

Before he became a professional Jam Maker or a professional poisoner or perhaps, professional hit man, Rob had been a forensic chemist, so he really knew what he was doing. Although he was now a retired member of the Royal Association of Forensic Chemists, he still received their professional journal and attended courses to help him keep up to date with new developments that might affect his *work*. He continued to write and publish papers related to his specialist field; confident it would head off any possible suspicions. Who would suspect a retired police officer who was also a published forensic chemist specialising in poison?

He was hiding in plain sight, but then no one was looking anyway.

With his specialist knowledge, Rob was still occasionally asked to be an Expert Witness in cases involving poison. So, when Rob saw an email in his inbox titled

Request for Expert Witness, he didn't think much of it until he opened it. As he scrolled down to the body of the email, Rob felt his stomach drop.

Bolton.

The email from the prosecution team stated clearly that the defendant in the case was a woman from Bolton. It explained that in preparation for the case against Glenda Grant, they were looking for an expert in toxicology, specifically arsenic poisoning. In the lightest of tones, the email said they knew of Rob's expertise and politely asked him if he would be an Expert Witness for the prosecution.

Rob stood up, quickly pushing his laptop away from him. For the first time in over fifteen years, he was utterly terrified. He scrambled for his mobile and frantically called Anthea who was working in the London office.

'Calm down, Rob, it's okay. Try and listen to me and just breathe.' Anthea quickly thought through all the options and possibilities and seemed to already have an answer. 'Rob it's fine, really it is. You don't have to accept this work. People turn down work all the time. It won't look at all odd, I promise.'

Rob was silent.

'Rob, I need to speak with Verity. I need you to stay put and not do anything, not call or speak to anyone. I'll call you back as soon as I can, okay?' Anthea spoke with a calm confidence which was in complete contrast to how she was really feeling.

As Rob put the phone down, he sat for a moment looking around him at his jam making equipment. He reached under the workbench and retrieved an unopened bottle of whisky he had been saving for a special occasion. Not this sort of occasion, but needs must. Pouring himself a large measure, he let the amber liquid slip down his throat, calming his thoughts and warming his stomach. He reminded himself of the reasons that he, Anthea and Verity had started their bespoke jam making operation all those years ago. All those women, and they were mostly women and their children, who had suffered abuse of all kinds. The people whose lives they had sought to improve, including the wider community, as they rid society of problems that the police and justice system seemed unable to tackle.

They had always known that one day it would end, and Rob felt that time was now here. As the whisky worked its magic, Rob decided he would talk with Anthea as soon as she got home – the Jam Maker was ready to hang up his sugar thermometer and his heavy bottomed jam pan, for good.

SIXTY-THREE

Verity put the phone down and sat back in her chair. She was smiling to herself when Anthea slammed into the office babbling ten to the dozen about Rob being an Expert Witness in a murder he had actually been an accessory to.

Verity continued smiling. Smiling because she knew that the case would never come to trial. She hadn't planned on telling Anthea but now she had no choice.

'Anthea, listen to me,' Verity interrupted with the swiftness and certainty she had spent years perfecting. 'I've just heard that Glenda Grant is out of the picture.'

Anthea took a sharp intake of breath, wondering for a brief second whether Verity had arranged an accident or something horrible to happen to Glenda whilst she was on remand.

Seeing her horrified face Verity said, 'Don't worry, she's out of the country. I made some arrangements.'

Anthea let out a cry of relief. Her friend of many years

wasn't a psychopath, she was all about protecting women in need; of course she was helping Glenda.

'Rob just needs to reply calmly saying something like he will get back to them in a week or so. Maybe saying he has been poorly and needs some recovery time before agreeing to new work.' She placed a strong, calm hand on Anthea's shoulder. 'She's due to sign in with the police on Tuesday, that's when they'll realise she won't be turning up. Rob won't even need to turn down the case. It will be postponed indefinitely and hopefully, abandoned altogether.'

Anthea hugged Verity and quickly left the room so she could call Rob and go home early to see him.

As the door closed Verity's calm dissolved.

This was all getting very messy.

Had they gone too far?

None of them actually knew how many successes they'd had, and they didn't keep records so it would be hard to prove a trace back to them.

But was it time to stop helping wronged women now?

SIXTY-FOUR

After attending the police conference and taking on board the suggestions made by his boss, Eddie was enjoying his job more. He had started to find more interesting ways to investigate cases and to top it off, there had been an actual murder in South Gloucestershire. Eddie had started to think that the place was so boring, there would never be a murder within the county, but he was wrong. The *real* murder, his team liked to call it, was not an open and shut case either, and Eddie was able to use some new skills and ideas he had brought back from the conference.

Everyone in the team suddenly had a spring in their step, well, everyone except the murder victim who had been found in a basement flat in the sleepy town of Thornbury. After some initial enquiries, a neighbour had shakily told Eddie that there had been another death in the same flat, ten years previously.

Eddie was tasked with finding out the cause of death of

this other person which meant he had to request details of the old post-mortem from the coroner's office. A colleague helped him search the linked database, something he had never done before. It didn't take long, and the results were clearly shown on screen. As he carried out this search, an idea flickered into Eddie's mind. It would be easy to find out Richard Sykes's cause of death, using the same database. All he needed to do was type the name, find the correct person, click on two boxes and he would have a vital piece of information that he and Bridget really needed.

His colleague had wandered off to get a coffee and without hesitation, Eddie carried out the new search, finding four other Richard Sykes. Thankfully the age at death made the correct one easy to find. He had to click an additional button as he was searching outside of his area, but with the final click, he found the details he was looking for:

'Richard Sykes died 4 May 2007. Cause of death: Unspecified natural causes.

Shit. That didn't help much. Natural causes could mean pretty much anything and if poisoning was involved, it could easily look like natural causes, he had learned that much from the seminar on poisoning. Shit. Eddie logged off his desktop computer and tried to refocus on the *real* murder.

Later that day, he returned home to the welcome sight of Graham at the stove, tea towel tucked in his pocket and a wooden spoon in hand. Graham loved cooking and a momentary thought flicked into and thankfully, straight out of Eddie's mind – it would be so easy for Graham to poison him.

'Goulash tonight.' Graham beamed. 'Although I have made it less spicy than last time.' He laughed a little. 'You okay, love? You look a little worried.'

'Yeah, I was just thinking about poisoning,' Eddie replied mindlessly.

'Christ, my cooking's not that bad. I always thought you liked it!' Graham's face showed fake shock and horror, followed by a wry smile.

'Sorry, I didn't mean that, I'm just a little stuck on this case that Bridget and I are exploring. I mean, I can't say we are investigating as such, but I managed to find out something today, which I thought would be important, but it didn't help and now I feel just as stuck. If this was a real case at work, I could talk to colleagues, bounce some ideas around and generally we would find a way forward, but I can't do that with this Women's League stuff.'

Graham turned the goulash down to a low simmer, put down his spoon, retrieved a pen and paper and sat Eddie down at the kitchen table. 'Okay, then I will be your sounding board, Eddie. Let's brainstorm this together, eh?'

As Eddie sat down he wasn't sure he wanted Graham to coach him like one of his people at work. Next he would say something like 'I'm not here to give advice – you have all the answers within you, Eddie.' But knowing how much Graham loved to feel he was helping, Eddie just smiled and prepared himself for the conversation, which actually turned out to be very useful.

After about fifteen minutes Graham said, 'There you go – here's the plan you made.' He pushed a piece of paper in Eddie's direction. 'Fuck, I forgot the goulash.

Quick, get some ready cooked rice out; that will have to do.'

They ate and after dinner Graham said he would wash up while Eddie made a start on the first action on his plan. This involved Eddie digging out his handouts from the policing conference and finding the session he had attended on poisoning. He was hoping there might be some information or signposts that would help him understand why poisonings were so difficult to detect, especially fifteen years ago when Verity's husband Richard Sykes had died. He found the handout and read through it and yes, one of the last bullet points clearly read that until 2018, poisoning cases were difficult to detect at post-mortem and a cause of unspecified natural causes would often be recorded.

Leaning over Eddie's shoulder, Graham added that the sentence was too large to have been a bullet point as there should be no more than four or five words.

'I think you just mansplained to another man, Graham, but yes, I get what you mean,' Eddie replied with a hint of irony in his voice.

Sheepishly, Graham said, 'Sorry, but can I just make one more tiny suggestion please?'

'Go on then.'

'Just make sure you look at the references. Sometimes there are useful hints in there,' he said before making the universal sign of pulling an imaginary zip across his lips, indicating he would now shut up.

Eddie flicked to the reference page and skimmed the entries. Immediately his eyes locked onto the second reference.

‘I recognise that name from somewhere,’ he said as he stared at a reference paper titled, *Classic poisons and their detectable side effects: from chemistry to fatal weapon*. The primary author was one Clearwater, R., Dr (2003) Durham University. Clearwater. Could this R. Clearwater be related somehow to Anthea Clearwater at The Women’s League?

A quick search indicated two things: Dr Robert Clearwater had left academia, joined the police force for a short period before retiring a couple of years ago but more interestingly he was, indeed, married to Anthea Clearwater, Verity Scanlan’s Personal Assistant.

Eddie immediately felt lightheaded and his entire body tingled with excitement.

SIXTY-FIVE

Bridget always questioned how she spent her days. She had done it for as long as she could remember and knew it was likely a symptom of her constantly needing to justify her existence as an artist. She laid the blame for this firmly at her husband's feet and his incessant need to know what she was doing and how much money she was earning. So having to watch a stream of tutorial videos showing her how to use the 221b website, was making her agitated. She wasn't painting, she wasn't teaching, and she wasn't earning money. She kept an eye on the studio door as she watched the videos, just in case the keeper of her time, decided to wander in and see what she was doing.

Thankfully, after watching the videos, Bridget felt more confident she could explore the investigation that someone had weirdly named The Bolt-on Poisoner. As she read that William Grant worked for a firm that made nuts and bolts, she realised that website administrator SherlokH clearly couldn't resist a pun.

The *Bolt-on Poisoner* webpage was like a sort of mind map, with links that expanded to include longer descriptions and links to further information. One of these was a section called: Basic facts of the case. This included information that had been verified, such as dates of death, name of victim, name of accused and place of work. Next to this was an expandable box where the administrator would add updates on the case, based on actual events, such as the arrest of Glenda and post-mortem results. The most recent addition to this section advised that Glenda had been released on bail, something which surprised Bridget, given the severity of the accusation. To the right of this was a general comments box which seemed to constantly update and mostly contained random comments or shouty opinions, to which several were added as Bridget watched. You could also sign you up to email updates for that specific section, which Bridget very cautiously did.

Around this core of general information was a maze-like structure which shifted and changed according to where Bridget hovered her mouse pointer. The sections that appeared had titles including: Cause of death, Possible motives, Physical evidence, Alibis and statements, Linked organisations, People linked to the victim, People linked to the suspects. It was an absolute minefield.

She decided to start with *Physical evidence* but when she clicked on the button, it opened a new tab on her browser and she was confronted with yet another huge mind map of floating buttons. These new buttons were labelled:

Fingerprints, DNA evidence, Victim's mobile phone, Victim's laptop contents, Kitchen items from home, Kitchen items from victim's workplace, Victim's personal hygiene items, (she shuddered to think what that meant).

'How on earth did they get hold of all this information?' Bridget muttered before deciding to click on *Kitchen items from home*. Here she read that an anonymous source had added that no traces of poison or suspicious substances were detected on any items from Glenda's kitchen at home. Next, she tried the button labelled *Kitchen items from workplace*, which contained some interesting comments.

'Forensics have found no food containing suspicious substances, but did find remnants of a substance on the refrigerator shelf that contained arsenic. Further testing found traces of arsenic on spoons, knives and plates in the kitchen suggesting that the substance of interest (that made Bridget chuckle) was probably spread or spooned and eaten from a plate,' which meant any food, didn't it?

A new comment had been added a day later, 'The substance on the shelf has now been analysed and found to contain high levels of sugar.' She expected there to be another comment making a guess at the food source, but nothing had been added yet. Slowly, the answer trickled into Bridget's mind. Weeks of ideas, guesswork, supposition, paranoia, imagination and random thoughts, all crystalised at once.

'Bloody hell,' she shouted out loud to the empty studio. 'It's definitely the bloody jam!'

She leapt to her feet and paced the room, trying to take in what she had just read. She immediately tried to call

Eddie, but his phone went straight to voicemail. Shit. She left a hurried message saying she needed to speak with him urgently but as she hung up, she noticed a new notification flash onto the case noticeboard. In bold letter it read:

'GLENDA GRANT GOES MISSING. After being bailed Glenda Grant has missed her first required meeting at the police station and cannot be found.'

The general comments section had instantly gone bananas.

'No one has seen her since the day after she was released from the remand unit and returned home', 'Police are concerned for her safety', 'Neighbours report seeing her leave the house with two suitcases.'

Someone had added, 'If she was planning to end her life, she would hardly take suitcases.'

Bridget watched as this comment thread unfurled with new comments added every few seconds.

'I reckon she's left the country,' to which someone else replied, 'How? They would have taken away her passport.'

Despite trying she couldn't get hold of Eddie, and she needed to take her mind off this ridiculous case; it was growing and taking up more and more time and even more of her precious headspace. She shutdown her laptop and stared around the studio, desperate for something to distract her. Instead of finding a distraction, Bridget felt someone's eyes watching her. She quickly turned around and her eyes immediately met the painted eyes of Verity Scanlan.

Verity's eyes were burning into hers and it was as if she had been in the room and watching Bridget all this time. Instead of waiting for Verity to speak, Bridget squared up to the portrait. 'I know what you've been doing, Verity. I know that you are somehow involved, and I know it's something to do with jam.' As the words left Bridget's mouth, she thought she could see Verity's mouth curl up. Picking up a palette knife, Bridget felt her temper rising again. Thankfully, before she did something stupid again, she heard someone call her name. She stopped in her tracks as the studio door opened.

'Bridget!' her husband called out as he entered the room. He rarely came into her studio space and he had a strange look on his face so she knew something was up.

'Bridget, I've just been going through our bank statements and…'

For fuck's sake! Was he monitoring every single time she used her bank card now? Her temper was rising again, and she noticed that her hand was still clenched around the palette knife. She looked away to avoid his questioning eyes.

'Bridget…Bridget are you listening to me, this is important. There seems to be an online payment made to something called 221b which I looked up because it seemed odd, but it says you authorised the payment a couple of days ago. What on earth are you doing paying for something like that?'

Bridget turned around and looked at his concerned face, which thankfully hadn't clocked the menacingly held palette knife. During their thirty years of marriage, Bridget had perfected the art of confusing her husband when she needed to cover things up. This time however, she changed her mind. Her immediate anger at being questioned over such a small payment of only £13.99, was softened by the slight anxiety over the unfolding situation she had embroiled herself in. Bridget was becoming aware that Verity may well be some sort of serial killer or at the very least, have access to a range of killers across the country and this knowledge could put both Bridget and her husband at risk. She sat her husband down, took a deep breath and started talking.

'Darling, let me get you a glass of wine and we can have a chat about this. There is a lot I need to tell you and to be honest, it's all got a bit out of hand.' Getting that sentence out so calmly and succinctly took a lot of effort and Bridget did it all whilst waving the palette knife about. Without waiting for an answer, she got up and reached for the already open wine. He gave her a withering look and reluctantly settled down.

Ten minutes later, Bridget had told him about the portrait, about the texts, about the deaths they knew about, the arrest of Glenda and Bridget's recent discovery on 221b.

'That's what the £13.99 was for, and it proved very helpful,' she blustered without giving him room to ask questions. She also told him about Eddie's involvement. 'He's a policeman, don't you know and once the portrait's been unveiled, he'll tell the police, and life will return to normal.' Bridget finished talking and to avoid looking at her husband, reached for her wine again.

Her husband was usually a man of few words, but in this instance, he had a lot to say. Most of them started with the words, 'How could you be so stupid…' or 'We can't afford for you to waste your time…' or 'How dare this boy

Eddie get you involved…' and her favourite which was, 'And it's ridiculous to think women are killing their husbands with poison jam. It's utter nonsense.'

She stifled her desired reply, 'Well right now I can fully understand the desire to be rid of your husband.'

The rather one-sided conversation ended abruptly. Bridget promised to be more focussed and agreed to start a second art group once the portrait had been unveiled, however her husband left the studio shaking his head, taking his untouched wine with him. Bridget was tempted to go after him but doubted this would achieve much.

The following morning as Bridget ran her art group, she doubted whether she even wanted to run any classes, ever again. Sylvie still didn't turn up and this time neither did Eddie, which made the group smaller and much quieter. To add to this, as the session started, Bridget received a call from Margaret's granddaughter to say she had passed away a few days before. The remaining members were devastated and spent most of the session, supporting each other and telling their own stories of loss.

Bridget made a lot of tea that day.

SIXTY-SIX

Sinking into her sofa at home, Verity imagined the soft cushions enveloping her completely and transporting her to a place far, far away from every aspect of her current life. Outside of the events around 2007, the past few weeks had been the most stressful she could remember. Back then, when it had all started, she was raw with rage which had propelled her forward in her career and helped justify the creation of the Jam Maker network. Revenge, in Verity's case, had been a dish best served hot, sweet and sticky, just like the special jams, marmalades, chutneys and relishes despatched around the country.

Over time Verity had become stronger, more determined, less trusting and accepted nothing other than exactly what she wanted. The rage had changed too, transforming into a deep, immovable, bitterness. It was no surprise that she had never entered into another relationship. Not only was she unable to trust anyone, but she also knew that it would be impossible to keep the Jam Maker a secret if someone got too close. Sometimes she felt lonely, and when she slept, her painful dreams of lovely baby Harry reminded her of what she had lost, and the fleeting moments of loneliness were quickly replaced with rage once more.

However, in recent weeks things had started to change again, and Verity had never felt so exhausted. What was happening to her? Her rational side told her that this was the first time anything had really gone wrong, but it had made her wonder whether the Jam Maker network should finish operations. It wasn't like their work was preventing new generations of rapists, murderers and paedophiles from crawling out of the woodwork, was it? Did she even want to stay involved with The Women's League? The Jam Maker and the League had both been lifelines for Verity for many years now, and whilst she would soon effectively retire from the League and become honorary president, perhaps now was the time for the Jam Maker to retire as well?

If she was completely honest with herself, she no longer got a buzz from hearing a batch of jam or chutney had been successful. It no longer eased the pain of losing Harry and didn't soften the hate she felt for Richard.

Yes, Verity decided it was time.

Without moving from her cocooned place on the sofa, Verity picked up the phone and called Anthea. The two old friends chatted at length and she was both pleased and surprised to hear that Anthea agreed with her decision. She was even more surprised that when she put the phone down, she felt a wave of deep sadness and relief wash over her.

Soft tears fell down Verity's cheeks and she realised that this was the first time since Harry's death, that she was crying tears of sadness, rather than tears of rage.

SIXTY-SEVEN

After three days and leaving at least five messages on his phone, Bridget finally received a short text message from an unknown number, explaining that Eddie had dropped his mobile down the toilet. Bridget replied with her usual okay, prompting Eddie to ring her and regale her with the whole saga. He explained at length that his mobile had spent two days in a bag of rice before he realised it was never going to revive. He then had to buy a completely new phone and found that the old SIM card didn't fit, so he had to get a new SIM and a new number. After what felt like forever, Bridget eventually interrupted.

'So, you haven't listened to my voicemails?'

'Nope, they all got lost when I had to get a new SIM card and phone number. How have things been going with the investigation sites, Bridge?'

Bridge? She didn't mind that – it was much better than Gitty.

'Eddie!' Bridget almost shouted in exasperation. 'Just listen for a moment. I have so much to tell you.'

Hearing his softly spoken and usually polite friend speak with such force, stopped Eddie in his tracks.

'The Bolton case. The poison was found in some jam, *some jam*, Eddie! I couldn't believe it at first, but forensics showed arsenic in what they described as a substance with a high sugar content. There were bits of it left on the shelf of the office fridge where William Grant worked. It's why his work colleagues were getting ill, they must have eaten some of the jam too.'

'Well, yes we already suspected this from what Tommo told me.' Eddie was struggling to see why she was so excited.

'Don't you see, Eddie? Well perhaps you don't know. Well, why would you, I suppose. You are too young. And I only just realised now.' Bridget tutted as she started to explain. 'When these sorts of women's groups were founded, jam making and baking were their thing. My old mum called the women the Jam and Jerusalem brigade because they were known for making jam and singing hymns, especially Jerusalem, which was a sort of anthem. Of course, they do different things these days, but jam is still an intrinsic part of their identity.'

Eddie was struggling to understand the relevance of the lesson in British social history that Bridget was giving him. He didn't know what the hymn Jerusalem was and didn't see why she was so excited about the fact that they made jam.

'Okay,' he said eventually, wondering if Bridget was

losing it ever so slightly. 'Let's put the jam thing to one side for a moment. Something else turned up which could be important, but again it might just be a coincidence.' Eddie explained about the seminar on poisoning he had attended and how the reference he had followed up was written by a leading forensic chemist, who was now married to Verity's PA.

'Are you saying that Anthea is married to a forensic chemist? And you think that's a coincidence, do you, Eddie?' Bridget couldn't quite believe what Eddie had just told her.

'Well, he left chemistry to become a police officer and is now retired, but basically, yes.' As he said the words out loud to Bridget, he realised this felt much less of a coincidence than it did before.

'So a chemist would know how to add poison to jam, I imagine?' Bridget said.

They both went quiet for a few moments, contemplating the information they had just told each other. Eventually Eddie broke the silence.

'And there's something else, Bridget. I found out that Verity was married and had a son, who died when he was a baby, about six months old according to the records. Her husband Richard died soon after from unspecified natural causes.'

'Eddie, do you think that she might have had something to do with her husband's death?'

Neither of them spoke for what felt like an eternity, but eventually recovering some calm, Eddie told Bridget that there was just too much speculation and whilst he himself had been shocked, it was unlikely they could find out exactly what had happened.

'Before we do anything else, we need to think carefully. We still don't have any real evidence, just a series of suspicions and information that is tenuous at best. We need something much firmer.'

The unlikely friends ended their conversation and agreed to meet in person the following evening.

Bridget woke after a fitful sleep. Her husband had slept in the spare bedroom, stating Bridget's snoring as the reason, but she knew otherwise. He was angry with her and experience told her that this would last at least three days. Bridget sighed and forced herself out of bed. There were decisions that had to be made today, and she had been putting them off since her last meeting with Verity and Anthea. Although the two women had thought they had seen the finished portrait, Bridget had some additions planned which were dependent on how the investigation into The Women's League panned out. Now, armed with the knowledge about the likely poisoning of William Grant, the choices about the final touches to the portrait became clear.

Bridget opened the studio window to freshen the air, turned on Classic FM and made a vast pot of fresh coffee. Setting up her chair, the easel, the portrait and choosing the required paints, she made a start. She knew she was possibly about to make one of the biggest mistakes of her professional art career, but she knew there were bigger things at stake.

As she dispensed some small quantities of paint onto her palette, it occurred to her that her actions were akin to laying a trap with some bait. It would likely alert Verity and Anthea to the fact that she suspected what they had been doing and might even provoke them into action of some kind, although she didn't know what. It would probably be wise to tell Eddie what she was doing. Yes, she would tell him about it when she saw him later that evening. She was slightly concerned that The Women's League might not pay the final instalment for the commission if they saw her additions, so she would ask for that payment prior to the unveiling – yes, that would work.

With her doubts put aside, Bridget dipped her brush in her turps, not into her coffee cup for a change, and set about making the finishing touches to the portrait.

SIXTY-EIGHT

Eddie's face gave nothing away. He had popped into Bridget's studio on the way home from work to talk about their investigation but was now sitting down, staring at the finished portrait of Verity. Bridget couldn't tell what he was thinking. Was that shock, dislike or maybe he hadn't noticed? She doubted the later.

'What do you think Eddie?' she asked with more than a little trepidation.

There was silence. A short but uncomfortable silence until Eddie spoke.

'Well, you've certainly captured her, but I'm a bit shocked to be honest. It really does capture the woman I saw at the ball,' he said, repeating himself as he grappled for some kinder words. 'You can see how powerful she is. Slightly scary but also beautiful, but I…I…' He stopped, trying to decide what to say next. 'But those,' he gestured to the last-minute additions Bridget had made. 'I mean it's genius really, but if we're right about our suspicions, Bridget, I doubt they will ever show this portrait to the public. I mean you are very brave, and this is one of the most stunning portraits I've ever seen, but…'

'I know, Eddie. I've lost a lot of sleep deciding whether I should do this, but I need to make a statement and if this ends my painting career, then so be it.' She paused but feeling she needed to justify her actions further she continued, 'And historically portraits do sometimes hide messages about their subject – it's not uncommon.'

Bridget's voice trailed off and she turned away from Eddie as she stifled a tear. For the first time since he had known her, Bridget looked scared, sad and more than a little vulnerable.

Putting his arm around her, he gently said, 'It's a superb painting, Bridget, it really is. I was just a little shocked that's all. Let's see what happens over the coming weeks and I'll help in any way I can.'

Bridget managed a small smile. It was good to have a friend, and a younger one at that. She knew Eddie would outgrow their little art group and move on to other things but right now she loved having him around.

Putting the portrait away, they now settled down around Bridget's laptop to discuss things so far. Bridget showed Eddie the *Bolt-On Poisoner* page, which had gained even more comments since she had last logged in.

'The bloody email notifications are still a nightmare,' she told him. 'I can't keep up with them, so I've unsubscribed again and I'll check the site every couple of days to see what's new.' Bridget scrolled down the comments as she spoke. 'That's interesting,' she said. 'Someone else has posted a comment about Glenda Grant's membership of The Women's League, look.' She gestured to the comment.

'What is The Women's League anyway, is it some kind of cult or an anti-male movement of some kind?'

This comment had received more thumbs down than thumbs up, suggesting that most people thought this was a ridiculous statement, with someone saying, 'Your paranoid mate,' to which someone else commented, 'Call the grammar police, it's you're, not your.'

Another person commented, 'I think the word you are looking for is misandrist,' which furthered the stream of unhelpful comments.

Eddie looked thoughtful. 'I think we need to add the knowledge we have to this investigation page. It's the only way to get people's feedback and find out if anyone knows of links to other deaths elsewhere. We just need to make sure your username and email are completely anonymous. Did you use a new email like I said?'

At this question, Bridget screwed up her face a little. 'I used an anonymous profile name, but no I forgot about a new email address. Sorry, Eddie'.

'It's fine, we can set one up now and change your username and email before we start participating in this website properly – it'll only take me a few minutes.'

Which it did, and before Bridget had even made a cuppa, he was finished. They then carefully added several pieces of information across the map, under Bridget's slightly strange username which was 'NinkyNonk78'.

Bridget screwed up her face. 'What on earth does NinkyNonk mean, Eddie?'

'I dunno,' he lied, knowing exactly what it meant. 'It was just the first thing that popped into my head and it's better if it doesn't make sense.' Bridget looked at him, wondering what other usernames he had.

'Should we ask for help with the text codes, Eddie, or perhaps wait until we have a better idea what they mean?' Bridget asked.

'I think we should wait a bit, but we could message the site administrator and see if they can help us find links to other cases. How did you get on with the other search terms?'

Bridget explained that searching 'Women's League' had identified a couple of old cases, but she hadn't looked into them any further.

'They were so old; I decided to not open them and then I got sucked into the Bolton one which took up so much time that I forgot about the others.'

'Thing is,' Eddie began, 'We don't know how many times they have done this, or for how long. If we assume for a moment that Dr Clearwater has something to do with this, he left his job as an academic about eighteen years ago to join the police force; this could all go back a long way.'

Bridget nodded but was trying to take in this possibility as Eddie continued, 'Anthea, as far as I can tell, has been working for Verity for about sixteen years, around the time Verity's baby and husband died, so I think we need to go back that far.'

Sixteen years! thought Bridget, that could include hundreds of unsolved cases or mysterious deaths.

Eddie opened a new window on the *221b* website and

typed, 'Women's League' in the search box again. The same five cases came up as Bridget had seen before, with the first three being over ten years old. They also extended the search to include similar organisations, in case the person who added the tags or information, used the wrong names. Amongst the many alternatives they tried were: Ladies club, Women's group and Ladies only, which resulted in all sorts of unexpected results.

Weeding out the decidedly dodgy and the highly irrelevant, the search finally proved fruitful. Between them, they now had twelve cases that mentioned The Women's League or something similar. Realising they had a lot of work to do, Eddie reluctantly raised another issue.

'We haven't found anything that mentions jam. Nothing at all. I don't know whether we've got it wrong, and I don't know what to do about it.'

Without hesitation, Bridget said, 'I'm not wrong Eddie. Trust me. It is the jam or something similar. I can feel it in my gut.'

Eddie stared at her for a while. Just as Bridget was developing the fledgling painter in him, Eddie wondered if he too was raising the fledgling detective in her. They sent a message to the administrator of *221b* to ask for help and were just about to close her laptop when a reply from SherlokH arrived. He was eager to help and suggested they start a thread on the home page, asking if anyone knew of any unsolved cases which used jam as a poison. He also said he would ask his colleagues who ran other sites, to see if they knew anything about jam, but admitted it was a long shot.

The unlikely pair of detectives felt that they were finally getting somewhere.

They parted company, agreeing that they urgently needed to solve the riddle of the text codes. As Bridget slumped into bed, she realised it was gone midnight. Her husband was snoring away in the room next door and although she was thoroughly exhausted, sleep did not come easily. The text codes were not going to be easy to solve and as she drifted off, she could see the numbers and letters dancing in front of her eyelids.

SIXTY-NINE

The next time the art group met, the mood was much lighter. Both Sylvie and Eddie had returned giving Bridget a much-needed break from helping people paint birds or cottages. Everyone had started to adjust to Margaret's absence and the chatter around her departing was slightly less upsetting. Sylvie had arrived early to talk to Bridget before the others turned up and apologised for her absence.

'I was just a little shocked at the time, Bridget and then embarrassed once I realised that I had overreacted – you know how it is sometimes.' She gave Bridget a little hug and both women were pleased the air was cleared. 'I'm going to send some of that nice fudge you like, Bridget, as an apology.'

'Oh, Sylvie there is no need,' Bridget replied unconvincingly. 'But if you insist,' she added with a cheeky grin. Both women laughed and then patted their waistlines.

'Well, look out for a little parcel in the post and don't

eat it all at once!' said Sylvie, completely misjudging Bridget who already intended to eat it all in one go to eliminate the risk of having to share it with anyone else.

After the session ended Sylvie hung around with Eddie and Bridget. In the end Eddie had to leave, encouraging Sylvie to follow, saying they should leave Bridget in peace. He then drove around the block before heading back.

'Sorry about that,' he said as he came back through the studio door about ten minutes later, 'I had to loop back round the Black Horse pub to lose her!'

'I feel so bad for not sharing all this with Sylvie,' said Bridget. 'She reacted so badly last time. I can't imagine how she will feel if, well, when she finds out the things we have uncovered.'

'I reckon that once we have sufficient proof, she'll understand. And at some point, I'll have to speak to the police formally and I imagine that will also change how she feels. She's a sensible lady and right now we just need to keep her out of it all.' Eddie said.

Bridget reflected how confident Eddie seemed which made her feel much better about the whole thing. 'You're right. I'm glad we have got some time to look at these codes – it's really playing on my mind. We need to solve them before the portrait unveiling next week.'

'So, we have two messages, one which we think is related to the death in Hertfordshire due to the partial postcode in the first message I saw - WD7,' Bridget said with so much confidence and clarity that for one moment, Eddie thought he was listening to one of his colleagues at work. 'The other has partial postcode of BS32 which is Almondsbury, where Sylvie's friend Sarah lived. Her husband died and he was called Frank Tisbury.' Bridget wrote the two text messages in full on a large sheet of paper:

'6lbsQMregular@BS32urgent' and '4lbsOspecial@WD7urgent'

'We have the partial postcode, and the last bits are obvious - clearly both are urgent, so what we have left are the first bits, 6lbs and 4lbs, which seem distinct from the second part which has a capital letter.

As Bridget wrote down 6lbs and 4lbs on the paper, a light bulb immediately lit up her mind.

'Jam!' she said quietly at first. Then with more certainty, 'It must be the weight of the jam. That's often measured in pounds or half pounds' she said. 'It makes complete sense.'

'Lubs?' Eddie said as his finger traced the words 6lbs and 4lbs on the paper. He quickly tried to suck back in the strange sound he had made, but Bridget had already heard it.

'No, lbs is shorthand for pounds, as in the measurement of weight, Eddie,' she said, trying not to giggle.

Eddie blushed slightly but vaguely remembered being taught about pounds and ounces at school during a history lesson. 'If we assume that's somehow a weight measurement, we just need to figure out what the middle bit means,' he quickly added.

They both became quiet, starring at the codes and notes they had made. Eddie picked up a pen and started doodling on the paper, his mind wandering as he traced the red felt tip pen into swirling patterns.

'It must relate to the jam somehow, Eddie, but I don't

have any idea what it might mean. If only we had the text relating to William Grant's death – that would really help.'

Eddie said nothing but continued to make his patterns which were now filling the corner of the paper. He was just about to reach for a different colour when he quietly said, 'Bridget, I'm not sure, but I think these text messages are some sort of ordering system.' The words fell out of his mouth effortlessly, as if he hadn't really thought about what he was saying.

Bridget's face looked as shocked as Eddie's did and they both sat in silence.

SEVENTY

Eddie pushed the remains of his ready meal around the plate. Graham was away for a few days, and he missed his cooking, just as much as he missed being able to talk things through with his husband. Although Eddie was pleased that he and Bridget were getting somewhere with the text message codes, had no idea what to do next.

He knew deep down that it was time to get some real help, some official help, but without firm evidence, he couldn't approach anyone at work. If he spoke to his boss with only the tenuous and circumstantial evidence he had, he would be a laughing stock. He could easily call one of his old colleagues in Hertfordshire, but as they were mostly traffic cops, it wouldn't help much. Eddie also knew that his boss disliked the type of online forums that he and Bridget had been exploring. More than that, he would probably be accused of jeopardising any formal investigation.

And yet there seemed to be no formal investigations

happening anyway. Apart from Glenda Grant's husband, was anyone looking into these deaths? Of course not. Outwardly they seemed completely unconnected. Eddie was not only getting frustrated; he was also getting worried too. The portrait unveiling was less than a week away and they needed to find some hard evidence and they needed it now. If Bridget unveiled the portrait, with its not-so-subtle additions, who knew what could happen.

Picking up his mobile, Eddie decided to call his mum. Perhaps if he could talk to her friend Clara, about her husband's death, it might provide new information. He was sure he could come up with some excuse as to why he needed to speak with her. He rang his mum straight away and casually asked Clara's surname telling his mum that there was a new service that police were involved with, which supported the families of victims of sudden death. His mum seemed to accept this explanation easily, which worried Eddie a little.

'It's 'Cheeting', Clara Cheeting,' she replied without question. 'She is such a strong woman and seems to have adjusted incredibly well, given all that has happened to her. She is back at The Women's League now and everyone is so pleased to see her.'

Eddie quickly changed the subject, so that his mum couldn't ask more about his so called support service.

'Mum, did I tell you that I went to a Women's League ball with my friend Sylvie? We had such a good time.'

Eddie's mum helpfully latched on to this new thread of conversation, and they chatted about the ball at length.

Finishing the call, Eddie promised he would visit his mum soon.

During his lunch break, Eddie Googled Clara Cheeting and easily found her address online. Striking while the iron was hot, Eddie decided to take the afternoon off, saying there was an emergency at home. He drove to Oxley in Hertfordshire and sat outside Clara Cheeting's home, working on his back story which explained why he was knocking on the door of this recently widowed woman. He decided to go with the same story he had told his mother and just flesh it out a bit. Although he knew he could get into big trouble, he and Bridget needed some new leads and fast.

He knocked on Clara's front door and flashed his police ID badge briefly, holding his thumb over the words South Gloucestershire. He told her that he worked for the Loss and Support Service, a new scheme to support people who had suffered from a sudden or unexplained death in the family, so she invited Eddie in.

After making a pot of tea and pouring them both a cup, Clara sat down opposite Eddie. He asked how she had been since the loss of her husband and she talked openly about how it had been a shock but so much else had happened at the same time, that she had not really had time to process his death or grieve properly. Eddie asked what else had happened and she told him about Aaron's other family in London.

'It's okay, I should have suspected as much. He used to spend so much time at his London flat. In fact, I have made friends with Sasha now. She came to the funeral with her little boy, and it seemed to be the right thing to do.' Clara brightened slightly as she spoke about the little boy and the new baby. 'In some ways, she's suffered as much as me and she now has a young family to raise alone. I couldn't find it in my heart to hate her and we have spent quite a lot of time together in recent weeks.'

Eddie struggled to hide his surprise. He was having so many conflicting feelings and thoughts and was trying to keep his face from showing any shock or surprise, so he gently asked, 'What's Sasha's surname, Clara? I just wonder whether she might need some support from us as well?'

Not only did kind, forgiving Clara give Eddie Sasha's full name, she even gave him her mobile number too. After finishing his tea, Eddie asked if Clara would like to have an appointment with an online counsellor. She said she would think about it and took the hurriedly invented contact number Eddie wrote out for her. With a great deal of discomfort at misleading this lovely lady, Eddie left Clara, saying she could call anytime.

Eddie quickly drove away but stopped just a few blocks from Clara's house. He needed some thinking space. He found himself so moved by what he had just heard that he almost forgot that kind, caring Clara may well have orchestrated her husband's death. Finding out about her husband's second family would certainly be a motive for murder, but how strange that both women had come together like this. Was Sasha somehow involved? Did Clara know about her before her husband's death, rather than finding out afterwards? Eddie wished he still smoked. He had given up when he moved in with Graham, but it was times like this that he really missed it. Right now a cigarette would have calmed his nerves and sorted his head out. He had tried vaping but sucking on what looked like a highlighter pen which blew out wafts of cherry flavoured smoke, just didn't feel the same.

Using the details Clara had given him, Eddie searched Facebook, found Sasha's details and looked at the last few posts. His attention was drawn to a post about how poorly her young son had been just after the death of Aaron. Something made the hairs on the back of his neck prickle, and he made a mental note to ask her about it.

Eddie used the same story when he called Sasha, telling her that Clara was concerned how she was coping on her own. As she lived in London, Eddie asked if he could video call her. She agreed and once they could see each other, he flashed his police ID in front of the camera briefly. The young woman on the screen looked exhausted and Eddie could hear the cries of a small baby in the background.

Sasha said she could only talk briefly as she had to pick her son up from pre-school and she would need to feed the baby while they spoke. She didn't turn off the camera as she positioned the baby to feed. Eddie was aware he was blushing, so he quickly asked Sasha how she was coping. He told her that he knew about the double life Aaron had been leading. The poor young woman started to cry, and big tears fell onto the face of the baby breastfeeding below. For the second time that day, Eddie felt like a complete shit and hoped this was all worth it.

'I'm slowly getting there although I can't wait for Juno

to sleep through the night. I'm just so tired. When Henry was a baby, I had Aaron staying with me occasionally. The hope that he would eventually be here all the time, kept me going. Now, all I can do is go from day to day.' Sasha sighed, and her eyes filled with tears again as she continued, 'At least Henry is better now. Those couple of weeks were dreadful. Aaron had just died and suddenly Henry was in hospital.' She blew her nose loudly, so Eddie took the opportunity to ask what had happened to the little boy.

'The hospital said it was inconclusive, but I think he had food poisoning. I'm not sure, but Aaron had a jar of olives that he used in his Martinis, and I gave Henry some. Not long after, he started to become ill. Perhaps they were out of date and once we were home from the hospital, I went to throw them away, but I couldn't find them which was strange. I emptied the rest of the fridge though, just in case it was something else.'

Eddie stared at her and felt his draw drop. Did she say olives? Surely not. He was half expecting her to say the kid had eaten some raspberry jam or perhaps some marmalade, but not olives. Eddie knew his mouth was still open and for some reason that he never quite understood, he decided to pretend that his picture had frozen. Keeping his mouth open, he now kept his eyes still and just for a few seconds, he also stopped breathing.

'Hello? Are you still there?' said Sasha's voice. 'You've frozen.'

'Erm, yes, still here. I think the signal dropped out for a bit, sorry,' he said, springing his face to life again. He also made a mental note to work on his interview skills, especially his poker face as he wouldn't be able to do this in a real interview.

'Anyway,' Sasha had resumed speaking, 'It doesn't really matter now. I don't think we'll know for sure what made Henry ill. I have let go of all that and just need to focus on this bundle of joy.' She held Juno up to the camera. Juno burped and spluttered a little dribble of milk down her chin.

Seeing the baby's face brought Eddie's focus back and he asked Sasha what she thought had caused Aaron's death. Sasha blushed at this question. Eddie already knew the answer as he had spent weeks trying to forget hearing his mum saying shagging.

'He'd been feeling poorly for a couple of weeks but didn't want to see a doctor. He put it down to stress and that night he had a big meal followed by quite a few Dirty Martinis.' Sasha smiled fondly and continued to tell Eddie that they had been having sex later that evening, when Aaron just rolled off her, vomited and stopped breathing. Without asking, Sasha told him that the official cause of death had been natural causes. 'A mix of an undetected heart condition combined with the stress of recent weeks, the alcohol, a heavy meal and a little bit too much exertion.' Sasha had clearly told this story quite a few times now and it just rolled off her tongue with little emotion, as if she were reciting a recipe.

She told Eddie she needed to collect Henry from school and the strange conversation ended. Feeling guilty about misleading her and feeling so very sorry for the young woman, Eddie had texted her a thank you message and included the details of some local low-cost counsellors.

Sitting in the quiet car now, he felt exhausted. Eddie had been shocked to hear the stories of both women. Did either of them really have it in them to kill someone? He was too distracted to drive back down the M4 and called Bridget instead.

'I just need to tell you where I've been,' Eddie said assuming Bridget was always available; she didn't have a real job, did she? He chastised himself for that assumption.

'Only got a few minutes, Eddie, make it quick,' snapped Bridget, which brought him up short. 'I'm in the middle of using a fast-drying varnish and it will ruin if I leave it too long,' she explained.

'Oh, okay,' he said, knowing his unspoken assumption had indeed been wrong. 'I just visited Clara, the wife of Aaron who died in Hertfordshire, and he had a second family. Clara claims she found out about it after he died but I'm not convinced. It all seems very odd.'

Bridget immediately put down her brush. 'How on earth did you get to speak to her? Don't answer that, I don't have time. What else did you find out?'

'She gave me the other woman's name. Apparently, they are quite friendly now, which is also odd. I video called her and we had an interesting chat too.' Eddie drew a quick breath but was desperate to tell Bridget as much as he could. 'She has a toddler and get this Bridget, the boy was very poorly around at the same time Aaron died and she thinks it was food poisoning, perhaps it was the same stuff that killed Aaron?' Eddie was speaking so quickly now, that he didn't let Bridget interrupt. 'I know we don't know for sure, Bridget, but those colleagues at William Grant's work also got ill, so it's kind of possible, isn't it?'

'Did she say what she thought had made the boy poorly?' Bridget managed to interject at last.

'She thinks it was some olives that Aaron had brought from home, which is disappointing as I was hoping it was jam or marmalade, so it doesn't really fit what we've been thinking. When she went to throw the olives away, she couldn't find them. It's all a bit odd, isn't it? I mean kids don't even eat olives, do they? Bridge…Bridget? Are you still there?'

There was an eery silence on the other end of the phone and eventually Bridget said, 'Eddie, the text code, the one with the Hertfordshire postcode. It said 'Ospecial' Eddie. What if the O stood for olives, but what a strange thing to choose.'

'Oh my God. Sasha said he loved Dirty Martinis – that was his special drink.'

'Dirty Martini?

'The olives are the dirty bit,' Eddie said.

'I have to get back to my varnish, so I'm going to put you on speaker phone, alright?' She was already raising her voice before she pressed the speaker icon and Eddie had to hold the phone away from his ear.

'Okay. Let's assume O is olives,' Bridget bellowed across the studio. 'Perhaps it was Ospecial, because it was something different to the usual jams, I mean, if the olives were in brine, they would be preserved just like other preserves, like pickles and chutneys.'

Eddie was acutely aware that he didn't understand anything about preserves or pickles. Jam he had started to understand but not preserves.

Bridget continued to bellow, 'If we assume that second part of the code is the actual substance, that might make it easier to figure out the other jams or preserves. I must go now – the varnish is turning. Please come to the unveiling. I really need you to be there in case something happens. Bye.'

With slightly tingling ears, Eddie drove back to Wiltshire. As he stepped out of his car, a text message arrived from his boss requesting he come in early the next day for an urgent meeting. Eddie briefly wondered what it was about but was too tired to give it anymore thought. A glass of wine and a Prawn Bhuna were waiting for him.

Graham was back and the ready meals were all but a distant memory.

SEVENTY-ONE

As requested, Eddie arrived at work early the following day but was surprised to see the stern face greeting him as he entered the Detective Chief Inspector's office.

'Come in and sit-down,' said DCI Janine Ferrell.

Eddie sat down and realised something was wrong.

'I am not going to assume anything until I hear your side of the story, but our computer monitoring system shows you made an unauthorized search. Our records show that you searched for a Richard Sykes including his cause of death back in 2007. Can you confirm that it was you who made this unauthorised search?'

Eddie felt his mouth dry up. He knew he couldn't deny it unless he pretended someone else had used his login, but that was pointless.

'Yes, it was me,' he replied feebly.

'This is a serious breach of information access, privacy laws and service protocol. Well in fact, it's also a bit stupid as you could have found out that information elsewhere in the public domain which makes it even more upsetting that I have to reprimand you.' DCI Ferrell did indeed look upset but continued, 'Please tell me why you searched for this person and their cause of death? As far as I can tell it has nothing to do with any cases you are working on.'

Eddie decided that this was a good opportunity to tell someone senior the truth. At some point he would need to ask for help and although he wasn't ready, he now had no choice. With more than a little trepidation, he asked politely if he could explain without being interrupted. She bristled at this but agreed and listened as Eddie told her everything. He hoped there was enough information for DCI Ferrell to see that these two deaths were linked and there were probably more.

But she didn't. She thought he had completely lost the plot.

The meeting ended with Eddie being sent home for the day whilst DCI Ferrell decided what to do about his misconduct, but not before she told him to immediately stop any further investigations into what she called, 'A ridiculous mess of half-baked theories, limited evidence, vague coincidences and misguided imaginings.'

On reflection Eddie had been surprised that she hadn't said more as there seemed to a host of other words on her lips. He slunk out of her office, avoiding his colleagues and as he got into his car, he received a phone call from DCI Ferrell saying she had decided to suspend him for a week and review the situation on his return.

Eddie was too numb to even cry and drove home in a haze.

SEVENTY-TWO

There was a slight chill in the air on the sunny May afternoon as Bridget arrived in London for the unveiling of the portrait. She had opted to bring the painting to London herself.

'It will reduce the risk of damage,' she had told Anthea but in reality, she needed to make sure that no one unwrapped the painting and saw her secret additions before she was ready.

Sylvie had almost begged her to let her come along, but Bridget knew that when she saw the painting, she would be very upset. Although Sylvie would eventually find out and Bridget didn't have a clue what she would say to her once that had happened.

The train journey from Swindon to Paddington only took an hour and Bridget hailed a cab to take her straight to The Women's League headquarters. Standing outside the lovely Georgian building just over four months since her first visit there, Bridget reflected on everything that had happened since she first met Verity Scanlan. Even more so, Bridget wondered what on earth would happen after today. She knew that her career might suffer, but there was so much more at stake.

Somehow, they needed to force Verity's hand and hope that if she was confronted with their suspicions, she would cave in and admit the truth.

That part would be Eddie's responsibility but as Bridget thought about it more, she realized this was a stupid, half-baked plan. They should have told the police beforehand, got them on side and then unveiled the portrait. It was ridiculous to think that this woman who had so much to lose, would just give in. Realising she had made a big mistake, Bridget was just about to turn around and take the portrait home, when Anthea appeared at the door and beckoned her in. Shit.

She was starting to sweat now, despite the chilly May weather and as she entered the headquarters, she knew she had no choice. The portrait would be unveiled and what would be would be.

Anthea showed Bridget to the main lobby where the drinks reception and unveiling would take place. People were already arriving and hovering around the table where serving staff were trying to put out the wine glasses and nibbles. Anthea brought out a small table which she stood against a wall. Covering it with a dark orange cloth.

'This should go nicely with the portrait, don't you think? And there's another one here to cover the portrait,' she said, pointing to the cloth.

Bridget just nodded frantically. She couldn't speak.

What the hell had she been thinking? Her anxiety levels were rocketing, and her body responded unhelpfully by demanding an immediate visit to the toilet, but she couldn't leave the portrait alone. She tried to breathe but could feel her guts doing somersaults. Eventually Anthea wandered off to chat to the arriving guests and Bridget quickly asked one of the waitresses to watch the portrait.

'Don't let anyone unwrap this. I'll be really quick.' She darted off to the toilet and ran slap bang into Verity.

'Bridget.' Verity smiled a hurriedly stuck on smile. 'Are you excited to show the world your work?'

'Yes, yes but I'm nervous as well,' Bridget spluttered. 'And I'm just desperate for the loo. I think the coffee I had on the train has gone straight through me.' Bridget tried to manoeuvre past her, but Verity blocked her path.

'Perhaps we can have a little chat after the unveiling, Bridget. There's something I must talk to you about.' Verity looked her in the eye.

Bridget nodded and Verity moved aside to let her through.

Locking the toilet door, Bridget held her breath until she heard the outer door close and promptly burst into tears. This was all too much. She wasn't cut out for this. Rummaging through her handbag, she found some Rescue Remedy and instead of dropping a couple of drops in her mouth, she drank the whole vial. She had to get through the unveiling and then leave straight away, without anyone noticing. Managing to compose herself, she left the cubicle and saw her face in the mirror as she washed her hands. She looked ghastly but thankfully had thought to bring some makeup with her, which she now applied thickly, trying to cover her red-ringed eyes and blotchy skin.

When she arrived back to collect the painting, the waitress was grumpy and complained about having to wait so long. Bridget apologised and set about unwrapping the painting, taking care not to let anyone see it before she had covered it back up with the orange cloth. As she pulled the cloth over, Verity's left eye seemed to look at her from underneath, as if it she was spying on her. Bridget took a slow breath and then checked her phone.

Where on earth was Eddie? She hurriedly sent him a text message. Eddie had promised to be early but now lots of people were turning up and heading toward Bridget to chat. She just wanted the earth to swallow her up, but now she was trapped. The usual questions came quick and fast.

'How did the portrait go?'

'How long have you been an artist?'

'My granddaughter is good at art; can I show you the painting she did of my dog?'

Bridget wanted to scream and run away, but the stream of people kept coming. Thankfully a kind young woman gave Bridget a glass of wine discreetly saying, 'You must be fed up with all these questions. Pretend you're talking to me and no one will bother you for a while.'

It worked but there was still no sign of Eddie. Neither had he replied to her texts or answered her calls. She would have been more worried had she not been so busy talking to the guests but suddenly she heard a *chink chink* as Anthea tapped a wine glass to get people's attention.

Bridget swallowed hard.

Anthea stepped forward and the room fell quiet. She thanked everyone for coming and invited Verity to come forward.

'As you all know, today is a very special day. Today we celebrate twenty-five years of Verity Scanlan leading and indeed growing, this worldwide organisation into what it is today. We gather to thank Verity for her dedication, vision and hard work which has seen The Women's League flourish, with more women than ever getting support to build their hopes and dreams, be it at work, a new business or support at home.'

It was at this point that Bridget felt a numb feeling travelling up her arms, the sort of feeling that often precedes fainting.

'To mark her retirement,' Anthea made imaginary speech marks in the air, suggesting that little retiring would take place. 'We were delighted to commission Bridget Sullivan to paint a portrait of Verity and are very excited to unveil it today.'

Everyone clapped as Anthea gestured towards Bridget who was turning pale and gripping the table next to her.

'Sadly, Verity won't be speaking today as she has a very sore throat and has lost her voice.'

At this there were noises of disappointment from the crowd but not from Bridget who felt immense relief. This would shorten the time until she could leave.

'But Verity wants to extend her thanks to Bridget for the portrait and The Women's League for all their support over the past quarter of a century!'

Everyone clapped again and then the room fell silent.

'And so, without further ado, Verity, will you please unveil your portrait.'

Verity strode over to the painting, catching Bridget's eye as she gently, but purposefully, pulled down the cloth to reveal the portrait. Bridget gulped and looked away as rousing applause went around the room. Verity stepped back, her face surveying the portrait she had seen in Bridget's studio just a couple of weeks ago.

But it wasn't exactly the same as the portrait that she and Anthea had seen and approved. Instead of an unidentifiable book on the table, Bridget had added the author's name clearly.

Lucretia Borgia.

Also on the table, two mobile phones could now be clearly seen, with several jam jars behind. Although she had stopped short of labelling them as jam, Bridget had also hidden little pots of jam and chutney in Verity's hair, disguised amongst the curly locks. The vase on the table now contained wildflowers of indigo and pale yellow. If you knew your wildflowers, which very few people do, you would know that these were Wolf's Bane and Monkshood, two varieties of highly poisonous Aconite.

Verity's face gave nothing away, but as Anthea stepped up to see the portrait, she gasped and every ounce of colour left her face. Their reactions or in Verity's case, lack of reaction, were hidden amongst the crowds of people clamouring to get a look at the portrait. People were pumping Bridget's hand in congratulations, masking the crisis that was unfolding for Verity, Anthea and of course Bridget.

As soon as she could, Bridget grabbed her handbag and

quickly sidled out of the crowd, making sure that Verity and Anthea couldn't see her. She made for the side door, telling people she was feeling faint and needed some air. She hailed a cab and thankfully one pulled over straight away. As she clambered into the cab, she turned back to look at the League headquarters and saw Verity, standing at the doorway, cigarette in hand, her eyes locked on Bridget. Those cold eyes followed the cab as it sped away and there was no mistaking her mood.

As the cab rounded the corner out of sight, Verity reached into her pocket and opened the old mobile phone. She typed a text, one final text to The Jam Maker which read:

'1lbFstrong@SN34vurgent'

The Jam Maker replied straight away with, 'F?' to which Verity made a swift reply and closed the phone shut.

SEVENTY-THREE

When he received the strange text from Verity, Rob Clearwater had been in the middle of dismantling his jam making shed. He had been enjoying a glass of red wine, or two and was feeling quite nostalgic. This shed, his man shed, was very different to most men's sheds and he would miss it. He had always felt a sense of purpose when he was here, boiling away, pouring jam into clean jars, adding pretty labels and packaging them up. As he looked around his shed, which was starting to look a little bare, he wasn't sure what he would now do with all his spare time. Men of his age often took up golf or bowls but neither grabbed him. For a fleeting second, he thought of joining an art class, but considering recent events, he dumped that idea. He and Anthea had often talked about moving abroad and now might be the right time.

Refilling his glass, Rob's eyes landed on the bottle of red wine he'd been drinking and he started chuckling to himself. How had he not noticed it before? His favourite red wine, named after his very own jam making shed. It was as he took a sip and savoured the jammy red flavours in his mouth, that Verity's text message arrived.

'1lbFstrong@SN34vurgent.'

Well, that was strange. Firstly, he had agreed with Anthea and Verity that they were finishing their jam making activities and secondly, what on earth was F? Rob punched in a quick reply and his question was answered straight away.

'Oh, now that's different,' Rob muttered, as he started to unpack his large stainless-steel pan and jam thermometer. 'Might take some practice but I reckon I just need to stop boiling at a different temperature.'

SEVENTY-FOUR

Once back at Paddington, Bridget threw herself out of the taxi, ran to the concourse toilets and promptly vomited. Staring down at the toilet bowl, she realised she had never felt so terrified. She vomited a second time, this time her throat rasping as she had nothing left to bring up. She really needed to speak to Eddie and had tried to call him during the cab ride, but he still hadn't answered. It had been a mistake to add the hidden images into the portrait. It had been a mistake to go to the unveiling on her own. It had also been a mistake not to involve the police earlier, but she would remedy that as soon as she had spoken with Eddie.

Splashing her face with water, Bridget made for the platform and took the first train back to Swindon. Unfortunately, the train was packed with commuters and she couldn't find a seat. Not having the strength to stand, she sat on the grubby train floor and tried to call Eddie again. His phone was switched off, she was sure of that now. Why had he let her down so badly? She had risked everything by changing the portrait and facing Verity and Anthea today. Without realising, she had started to cry. Seeing how distressed she was, an elderly woman offered Bridget her seat. On any other day, Bridget would have declined but today was different. She struggled to stand from the floor and flopped into the seat, thanking the woman profusely. The woman offered her a tissue. She mopped the tears and tried to compose herself. She hadn't eaten or drunk anything since breakfast and now even that was in the toilet at Paddington.

Bridget closed her eyes and tried to think how she could get hold of Eddie. She only had his mobile number and had never needed to visit him at home, so she didn't even know his address. The tiredness of the day began washing over her and she started to drift off to sleep but suddenly remembered she had a next of kin contact number for him. Jolting awake she quickly called her husband and asked him to look in folder in the studio, marked Group Admin. In there, he found Eddie's next of kin contact details. Jotting the number down, Bridget sighed with relief and called Graham.

Answering Bridget's call, Graham told her what had happened to Eddie at work and she was horrified. Graham had spent several days supporting Eddie who had been so distraught at being suspended, that he had switched off his mobile phone, gone to bed and refused to speak to anyone.

'The poor boy, he must be so upset,' she said with sincerity. 'It's all my fault, Graham, I must speak with him. Please put him on.'

Bridget could hear Graham stomping up some stairs, but it went quiet as he put his hand over the phone while he spoke to Eddie. He had just woken from a fitful nap after drinking a whole bottle of wine at lunch. He knew that Bridget would have been alone in London for the portrait unveiling but couldn't face calling her to tell her why he couldn't be there. Now, hearing she was on the phone and asking to speak with him, Eddie felt even more ashamed.

'You need to speak to her, love. I know you are struggling but it's not fair for her to face this on her own. Just speak to her for a little bit. It'll make you both feel better.' Graham held out the phone and at the same time, he squeezed his husband's hand. Reluctantly Eddie took the phone.

'Bridget, I'm so sorry about today, I have been in such a state over my suspension. I just couldn't face it, and I would have probably got into even more trouble. Are you okay? How did it go?' He breathed out and started to relax as he heard Bridget's friendly voice.

'Oh, I'm so sorry. I can't believe you have been suspended. I'm sorry I ever started all of this.' She didn't wait for a reply, reckoning he would be happy to just listen for now. 'But I won't lie, today was awful, but I managed to get through it. I left as soon as I could and saw Verity staring at me as I got into my taxi. I don't think I have ever seen anyone so angry but contained. She had over a hundred guests there, so she couldn't do anything, but if I had been left alone with her, God knows what she would have done.' Bridget shuddered at the thought but continued, 'I know you're already in a lot of trouble and I know you can't do anything else, but I have to talk to the police. I am so scared and can't let this go on anymore. I'll make an appointment and speak to your boss. I'll try and make them understand. They can't just ignore me, can they?' Bridget stopped talking.

'I'm worried that Ferrell won't listen to you, any more than she did to me. She was so angry when I spoke with her. You might be able to reason with her or maybe there were things that I forgot to tell her. I just don't know. I know you need to do this, Bridget and I'm sorry I wasn't there for you today. To be honest, I might have to leave and get another job, I'm not sure I can go back.'

Bridget heard his voice crack as she replied. 'I know but try not to think too far ahead. Nobody knows how things work out. I might have just ended my painting career as well, so you and I can figure it out together, eh?' She was trying not to cry again.

'I just wish we had something else, something more concrete like another text message that we could link to a death. If we had that, I think she would have to listen,' Eddie said.

SEVENTY-FIVE

Graham wrapped his arms around Eddie and felt his body sink into him.

'You need to stop giving yourself such a hard time, Eddie. It was a small incident – you only accessed some information that was already available in the public domain. I reckon if you hadn't told Ferrell about the poisoning and The Women's League, she wouldn't have been as bothered as she was.' He sighed, renewing his hold on Eddie. 'It's not worth throwing away your career over this. Other police officers, senior officers, will have done much worse than this, trust me.'

Eddie didn't reply straight away, instead nestling into Graham's hug further before saying, 'Thank you. Some part of me knows you're right. I do feel a little better now I have spoken to Bridget, but I have let her down badly as well. I should probably ease off the wine too.' He eased a half smile from his lips.

'Excellent, that's more wine for me then!' Graham laughed and dug Eddie in the ribs. 'Why don't you go for a walk and clear your head a bit. I'll make you a coffee when you get back.'

Stepping out into the fresh spring evening, he took a deep, calming breath and set off for a walk. He walked into the village and sat on his and Graham's favourite bench by the pond.

He steeled himself to turn his phone back on, clicking the on button. It came to life and spent a frustrating few minutes pinging and vibrating as it updated all the text messages, voice mails, emails and various social media notifications. 'I should unsubscribe to all those pointless sites,' he muttered as he realised that the online detective sites had been sending him numerous emails.

Checking his texts, he saw that there were several from Bridget, one from his mum and the last one was from Tommo, the officer he had met in Birmingham.

He swiped to open it and saw that Tommo had sent him a photo from their night out. The laughing faces of his new friends made him smile and he realised how much he loved being part of the police community. As he looked at the photo, it occurred to him that Tommo was from Bolton, the same place where Glenda and William Grant had lived. He tried to dismiss this thought but the more he tried to ignore it, the more an idea grew in his mind.

What if Tommo could find details of Glenda's text messages in the weeks before William's death?

If there was a text on her phone that pointed to the jam

somehow, this could provide a clear link between Glenda and Verity. Could he really ask Tommo to look into this? Even asking him was a risk to them both but if he found something useful and proved that he and Bridget were right, it might exonerate him in the eyes of DCI Ferrell. Deciding it was worth the risk and because he owed it to Bridget, Eddie sent a text to Tommo asking if he could call him.

Eddie's phone trilled straight away.

'Hey, lightweight,' Tommo said, referring to Eddie being the first to go home from their night out in Manchester. 'How's life?'

Eddie wondered whether he should tell Tommo everything or just casually ask whether he was involved in the Grant murder case. He opted for the first option. Tommo had seemed like the sort of person who would want to be told everything especially if he was going to become involved somehow. Eddie steadied himself and told Tommo every detail from Bridget's first suspicions all the way through to suspecting that William Grant's murder was related to his wife being part of The Women's League. Eddie decided not to tell him that he was currently suspended, as it might spook him.

'Tommo, are you involved in the Grant investigation at all?'

'Yes, I was working on evidence for the prosecution, which has been an eye opener, I can tell you. She is such a normal lady, it's so hard getting my head round the fact that she poisoned her husband, but we are finding more and more evidence.' Tommo seemed happy to talk about the case, so Eddie decided to ask him for his help.

'Tommo, I really need your help. If we are correct there could be other men that have been murdered in a similar way to William.' As the words left Eddie's mouth, he felt renewed confidence build inside of him. 'I have tried to speak to my DCI, but she dismissed everything. I think the only way I can make her listen is if we can find something on Glenda's mobile that links her to The Women's League or maybe a similar message to the ones we already have. Tommo will you help me?' Eddie tried not to sound desperate, but he knew he was failing.

When Tommo replied, Eddie knew he had nothing to worry about. 'Of course, I'll help if I can, Eddie, but we already have a problem. Glenda's phone record only goes back to the day after her husband death. We think she changed SIM card and if what you say is true, that would explain why. If she was receiving some sort of help or information via text, she would want to get rid of those messages. We have applied to her old network to gain access to the old messages, but we are still waiting to hear back from them.'

'Tommo this could really prove a link and might show who sent the texts to Glenda.' Eddie was feeling his spirits lift. 'Would you let me know when you hear back from the network?'

'Of course, but can you give me everything you've got so far. That way I can justify my line of enquiry if people start asking questions. Our main job now is trying to find her, she's disappeared.'

'I heard,' Eddie said, as he sent Tommo a photograph of the sheet of text messages and what they had figured out so far about the postcodes, the weights and what the substances might be. Tommo replied with a thumbs up and said he would keep in touch.

SEVENTY-SIX

If Bridget had checked her emails, she would have seen several from SherlokH alongside numerous automatic notifications from the various threads she was following. SherlokH had spoken to other armchair detective site admins, and he had lots of new information.

If Bridget had opened the emails from SherlokH, she would have seen that across four other sites, they had identified at least eleven or twelve cases which looked like they followed a similar pattern. This pattern involved an abusive husband with a partner or wife belonging to The Women's League, dying suddenly with the cause of death always listed as unspecified natural causes.

If Bridget hadn't been so busy varnishing and preparing the portrait and had looked at the message threads she was following, she would have seen comments such as, 'poisoning is often the murder method chosen by women', 'many poisonings go undetected, and are often put down to natural causes', 'very sweet or strong tasting food and drink are ideal carriers of poisoning as they disguise any bitter or strange tastes', 'poisonings were on an increase due to increased availability on the dark web'.

If Bridget and Eddie had been able to delve into these other cases that seemed linked to The Women's League, it's likely they would have been able to persuade the police to investigate further.

So many ifs and there was only so much that a suspended police constable and his artist friend could do.

SEVENTY-SEVEN

After the unveiling, Bridget stayed in bed for the whole of the following day. She managed to eat a little but mostly slept and watched television. She tried to avoid the murder mystery programmes which seemed to proliferate daytime TV, but the alternatives were meaningless quiz shows and programmes about people trying to escape their lives and move to the seaside.

She was roused from her TV stupor in the early afternoon by her husband bearing a fresh cup of tea, a small scone with jam – well, he wasn't to know, was he? He sat gently on the edge of the bed and for a moment she remembered how kind and warm he could be. He handed her a piece of paper.

'What's this?' she asked, pointing to the folded paper as she discreetly scraped off the jam.

'I opened one of your letters by mistake Bridget, sorry. But I am kind of glad in a way. It's the remittance advice from The Women's League.' He avoided making eye contact with her. 'I know you're feeling poorly Bridget, but we really need to talk about this,' He pointed at the paper with all the previous payments clearly listed.

Bridget's stomach dropped again, this time unrelated to the jam she had scraped off and what it reminded her of. 'Okay, what do you want to know?' she asked, but already knew.

'Well, I'm feeling a bit confused, surprised but also a bit angry if I'm honest. I don't really know what to think. I had no idea that your portrait commissions were so lucrative. I thought you earned about half of this.' He gestured to the total amount on the paper. 'I am impressed but I also don't understand where the rest of the money has gone? And why you don't focus on portraits more if this is what you can earn?' All of the questions tumbled out of his mouth in one go and Bridget knew there were more lurking, so she leapt in before he carried on.

'Well, firstly, I have a lot of overheads, which I don't think you realise. Outside of materials, framing costs a fortune and of course I have travel costs and insurance and things like that. It all adds up you know.'

He didn't seem convinced.

'I might only have one or two commissions a year, so the money has to last me for the months in between.' She hated how, once again, she was having to justify this all to him. This was the exact reason why she kept these things to herself.

'So, you pretend to earn less than you really do?' He

didn't wait for her to answer and carried on talking. 'I sort of understand that, but what I don't get is why you don't focus on painting portraits all the time and earn more money, rather than bothering with landscapes that no one wants to buy – it seems pointless to me.'

And there it was. That statement summed up everything he had said and felt about her work, for over thirty years: she should earn as much as she could, even if it meant doing something she didn't enjoy. And there was sub-text too, the unsaid words that lurked behind his eyes.

She knew this well and it went something like, 'I have to do things I don't like doing to earn money, so why shouldn't you?'

She hated this all so much. She hated that he saw her work as a commodity – something to be used to make as much money as possible, regardless of her happiness. Thirty years of pushing down her feelings, hiding what she earnt and doing things she didn't like, started to build up inside her and were threatening to explode, when the doorbell rang.

As her husband left the room and went downstairs, she felt the feelings sink back down. Now was not the time to be tackling this long-standing issue between them – she was too weak, too tired and didn't have the words to argue her case. She would wait until she felt better. They could talk again in a few days, and she would announce that the last few months had been torture and she was never taking another portrait commission. She would rather mop floors than go through that again.

Hoping he wouldn't notice her reddened eyes, Bridget finally looked up to see him standing at the end of the bed, holding a hamper.

'Look Bridget. Another bonus of portrait painting. A thank you gift from The Women's League!' As he placed the hamper on the table and started to unwrap it, she could see that the hamper included a selection of jams, chutneys and preserves.

'What the actual fuck,' she muttered under her breath, shaking her head as her husband gleefully examined all the contents. 'Not only do they murder people, but they do it with a sense of humour.'

He didn't hear her as he took out the jars and read the labels to Bridget. 'Oh nice. Ruby Raspberry Jam, Much Merrier Marmalade with added gin, Quirky Quince Jelly. Hmm not sure about that one.'

Bridget reached for the card attached to the hamper, it read:

'Thank you so much for the beautiful and truly unique portrait, Bridget. Love from Verity, Anthea and everyone at The Women's League.'

Bridget couldn't believe what she was reading. The audacity of the woman. She had expected Verity to do something, but this was unbelievable. There was not a chance in hell that she would touch any of this.

'I'll just pop and get some crackers and cheese,' her husband said brightly as he left the studio. Just for a moment, just one little moment, Bridget wondered if she should let her husband tuck into the jams and chutney. Just for a tiny, passing moment, but by the time he returned bearing crackers and some nice Brie, she had hidden the hamper and pretended to be asleep.

He left disappointed but Bridget had probably just saved his life.

SEVENTY-EIGHT

Having cancelled the last art group as she was in London unveiling the portrait, Bridget was pleased when her friendly group turned up the following week. Ralph announced he had finished his painting of the robin and was planning to get some prints made and use them as Christmas cards. He then started work on a new painting. This time he was painting a pigeon, so all was well with the world.

It had been a lovely afternoon and as everyone was leaving, Sylvie gave Bridget a big hug and told her to expect a little surprise pressie from her in the next day few days. Bridget knew this would likely be the fudge Sylvie had mentioned.

Tidying up the studio, Bridget turned to the wall where a few studies and drawings of Verity remained, including the sketch with the text code written down the side. Had Verity noticed this when she visited? Is that how she realised that Bridget suspected something? Is that why the references to jam and poison in the portrait had not seemed to shock Verity during the unveiling? If that was the case, it really was no surprise she had sent her a hamper of jam and chutney. On reflection Bridget doubted that any of it was poisonous, Verity wouldn't be that stupid. No, Verity had been sending a clear message with the hamper contents, in the same way that Bridget had sent a clear message to Verity in the portrait.

She sighed. She had spent the previous evening writing a letter to Detective Chief Inspector Ferrell, explaining everything including her suspicions and all the hard evidence she had, which turned out to be a lot less than she originally thought. She would show the letter to Eddie before sending it as she didn't want to get him into more trouble, but somehow, they needed to draw a line under it all.

'Draw a line under it all!' she said chuckling to herself as she ripped up the sketches of Verity. 'Stick to drawing lines and making paintings, Bridget!' she told herself firmly.

The next day she rose early and lit a fire in the fire pit outside the studio. As she watched the flames burn through the sketches and studies of Verity's face, she hoped that the whole saga was truly over. It was nearly June and half of this precious year had been consumed by this horrible portrait and the stress and worry that went with it.

Back in the studio, Bridget dug out the drawings she had made during her visit to Severn Non-Beach. It had been such a brilliant day and for weeks she had longed to create a series of paintings based on the mud and the natural patterns the tide produced. Squeezing some lovely browns and greens onto her palette, she mixed them a little and applied them thickly to some primed board she had found. This felt so, so good. The painted mud flowed and twisted and turned on the board making her feel so relaxed. The imagined faces and people she often saw in paint, were absent. She couldn't see any eyebrows, hair, noses or ears. There were no sickly, smiling faces whispering secrets to her. There was just mud. Bloody hell she had hated working on the portrait; this was so much better.

Grabbing a second board, Bridget squeezed out more paint and this time used the paint thinly, using lots of turpentine to make the paint run into rivulets, just like mud when the tide goes out. This wonderful flow state was broken by the studio doorbell ringing. Answering it reluctantly, a small parcel was placed into her hand, and she immediately knew what it was. As she unwrapped the little parcel, the smell of sweet, buttery fudge hit her nose, and she breathed it in.

The card attached to the parcel just read 'Bridget, I'm sorry, thank you for everything,' followed by three kisses. Sylvie had found the exact fudge that Bridget loved. In fact, it was a selection box which included several different flavours all of which Bridget sampled, noting that she enjoyed the salted caramel much more than she had expected. Perhaps she would buy that next time instead of plain clotted cream fudge. For the first time in what felt like months, Bridget felt happy and relaxed. She returned to her mud paintings and sensibly folded the fudge box shut, promising she would try and make the fudge last at least one more day.

SEVENTY-NINE

As he waited to hear from Tommo, Eddie tried to keep himself busy. In the three days since they had spoken, Eddie had cleaned the whole house, mowed the law and baked three cakes. He was due to return to work tomorrow and hoped he would be able to tell DCI Ferrell that he had some new evidence about the poisonings. Graham, who was now on his second piece of lemon drizzle cake that day, was also ready for Eddie to return to work. Any longer and he would need to dig out his post-Christmas clothes to create trouser space for all the cake related weight he was rapidly gaining.

When the text from Tommo finally came, Eddie found himself praying for the first time since Sunday school when he was nine. He opened the text.

Results in, call me asap.

Eddie fumbled with his phone nervously and called Tommo who answered straight away.

'What did you find, Tommo? I've been on a knife edge

for days.' Eddie did little to hide the desperation in his voice.

'We got it, Eddie. You were right. We analysed Glenda Grant's old phone records and there was a text which appeared to be a code, similar to the ones you sent me. She was also sent a QR code to collect a parcel from an automatic collection box which we think contained the jam. Oh yes, and we do think it was the jam.' Without seeming to need to breathe, he continued, 'The text said '4lbsSJamregular@BN1 confirmed, collection details to follow. Following your reasoning, we think it means four pounds of strawberry jam to be delivered to somewhere in Bolton. Our forensic team are running further tests now to confirm it was strawberry jam in the fridge at William Grant's workplace, but it's looking good. I think this has clinched it, Eddie, well done.'

Eddie was speechless.

He tried to form a sentence 'Wha…do…next…?'

Tommo jumped 'I'm sending a colleague down with this new evidence, so they can speak with your DCI.'

'Whose phone number did the text come from? Do we know?'

'Indeed we do, Eddie.'

EIGHTY

It was not unusual for Bridget to be awake at three am. Her overactive brain often kept her awake for hours, but tonight it was her stomach that woke her up. She had fallen asleep quickly and deeply but woken up and only just made it to the toilet. She hadn't thought much of it as she'd suffered from irritable bowel syndrome for many years. It flared up during stressful times and recent events most certainly constituted a stressful time. Having IBS was horrid, but she knew what to do about it. In the morning she would take some Slippery Elm and an anti-spasmodic tablet. She would avoid spicy food for a week or two and it would settle down, especially now the events surrounding Verity's portrait were a thing of the past. She settled back to sleep and slept soundly until late the following morning.

When she finally awoke, her husband had already left for work. She didn't bother getting dressed and went over to the studio in her dressing gown, taking a Ginger and Lemon

Tea to settle her stomach which was still gurgling and sore. Settling down with her new mud paintings, she sipped on the tea which helped her nausea. Chastising herself for not getting dressed, she took care to not get brown paint on her pink fluffy dressing gown and set about working on the two new paintings.

Bridget had treated herself to some new oil paints – expensive ones for a change as she'd read how much denser the pigments were. Squeezing small amounts of the new paint out, she realised this was true. Not only were the colours stronger but they felt smoother and softer as she moved the paint around the primed board. She worked back into the surfaces she had painted yesterday and was struck by how the new paints seemed to glow, even though they were muted, muddy tones.

Feeling a little better, Bridget spied the box of fudge on the studio worktop. It didn't take much to convince her that it wouldn't inflame her IBS; fudge wasn't spicy. As she tucked into the remaining pieces, the sun streamed in through the studio window warming the room nicely. Popping the last piece of fudge into her mouth, she decided to have a nap, savouring the sweet taste as she snuggled down and nodded off.

It was less than an hour later when Sylvie turned up at the studio to pay Bridget a surprise visit. She knocked on the door, but when she didn't get a reply, she tried the door handle which opened. Seeing Bridget asleep on the sofa, she tiptoed around the studio having a little tidy up of the fudge wrappers that littered the floor.

'Bugger,' she said, someone else had already given Bridget some nice fudge, and a posh selection box at that, judging by the empty fudge box.

Sylvie decided to wait and see if her friend woke up, so she sat and thumbed through one of Bridget's sketch books. She glanced at her every now and then to see if she was waking up and it was then that she noticed that Bridget wasn't breathing normally. Come to think of it, she also looked a little sweaty and grey.

Worried now, she shook Bridget, gently at first and then more vigorously, starting to realise that she was more than just asleep. She carried on shaking her and was just about to slap her face out of panic, when Bridget started to stir. She tried to sit up by herself but needed help from Sylvie. Sylvie now knew something was very wrong.

'Wa you doin here, Sandra?' Bridget mumbled, slurring her words and dribbling slightly.

'Huh?' said Sylvie 'It's me…Sylvie, are you okay?' She looked around for a glass of water to give her.

Taking a sip, Bridget said, 'No thank you, good night,' and immediately tried to lie back down and go back to sleep.

'No, I don't think that's a good idea, and it's Sylvie, not Sandra,' Sylvie said raising her voice and trying to help Bridget to stand. 'Christ you're heavy,' she said quietly.

'Let's have a little walk around the studio, shall we? I don't think you're very well and I think you should try and stay awake.' Propping her up the best she could, Sylvie tried to help Bridget stand but quickly realised she was too heavy and sleepy.

'Okay, let's sit down. Look Bridget, I brought you a little pressie,' Sylvie said, trying to get her to focus, in the hope that it might help wake her up. She reached for the box and said in a chirpy voice, 'I'm sorry I couldn't remember the exact place your favourite fudge came from, but I hope this is as nice.'

Blearily Bridget stared at the box of fudge and seemed confused. Why had Sandra given her another box of fudge? She tried to form a sentence but instead of words, all that came out of Bridget's mouth was projectile vomit, which covered her lovely friend. Sylvie let out a little scream but now realised that Bridget really wasn't at all well. Extracting herself from Bridget's sticky body, she found her mobile phone. Wiping vomit from the screen, she tried to call Eddie, but his phone was engaged so she dialled 999 instead.

The woman at the end of the 999 line didn't seem to think it was an urgent call and said that an ambulance would be with them in between two and four hours. Sylvie didn't know what do, so she tried Eddie again. This time he answered with a light and happy tone in his voice, which quickly changed when Sylvie told him what had happening.

'Okay Sylvie, I will call the ambulance service back because unless they think she is in real danger or at risk of dying, they won't hurry themselves. Try and keep her awake and tell me about the fudge again.'

Sylvie explained that Bridget had eaten a whole box of fudge and then looked confused when Sylvie had also given her box. 'She said something like, why have you given me another box of fudge, Sandra? Then she vomited all over me.'

'I'm coming,' he said, suspecting what had happened.

Praying he was wrong, he jumped in his car and headed for Swindon.

EIGHTY-ONE

Detective Inspector Thomas Posner, known to his friends as Tommo, arrived in London later that same day and met with three officers from The Met. They parked on a side road near The Women's League headquarters and Tommo checked that everyone understood the plan. They were here to arrest Verity Scanlan, quickly and quietly. They also needed to secure her mobile phone, or phones, as they suspected she had more than one. They would also arrest the staff who worked closely with Verity, including Anthea Clearwater.

As the team from Bolton entered the building it was quietly busy with everyone going about their usual business. Tommo asked to see Verity Scanlan who happened to be standing at the reception desk, checking her diary against the reception diary, something she did every day. She looked up to see Tommo brandishing his badge and two other officers already making their way to her office.

She didn't resist arrest; she didn't speak as they escorted

her out of the beautiful Georgian building that she had loved and considered her second home for the last twenty-five years. As the second officer secured her in the rear of the car, Tommo's phone rang – it was Eddie. He reluctantly answered.

'Thank God you're there. I'm on my way to Bridget's studio, she is the artist who painted Verity's portrait. Tommo, I think she has been poisoned. An ambulance is on its way to her, but I am so worried. Have you arrested Verity Scanlan yet? Can you see if she knows anything about Bridget and some fudge, please?'

Tommo responded with a simple, 'Hmm okay,' and hung up. He turned to Verity in the rear of the car, who looked as if nothing could shake her and said, 'Know anything about some fudge? Fudge that was sent to Bridget Sullivan who is now on her way to hospital with suspected poisoning?'

A flicker of something passed over Verity's face, he was sure of it, but she said nothing.

'Sir,' said one of the other officers. 'We have her phones, two of them.' He handed two evidence bags to Tommo and Verity stiffened. Donning a glove Tommo looked at them both, choosing to open the old phone. It was so old that it didn't need a code to unlock, and he immediately skimmed through the sent messages. The last text message contained only one word, fudge, with the previous text giving Bridget's postcode. Tommo knew better than to say anything to Verity, but he just got out of the car shaking his head.

EIGHTY-TWO

As he frantically pulled into Bridget's driveway, Eddie received a text message from Sylvie telling him they were already at the hospital. Punching Swindon District Hospital into his Satnav, Eddie noticed Bridget's husband arriving home. Shit. He wouldn't know what had happened. After a quick conversation, they got back into Eddie's car and sped away from the studio.

The sat nav gave twenty-five minutes to the hospital and whilst the speed limit was thirty, Eddie felt justified in putting his foot down a little, although it did cross his mind that he was already in trouble at work and a speeding ticket wouldn't help matters. He reluctantly slowed and noticed that the sat nav didn't change its opinion regarding his arrival time, still saying twenty-five minutes.

'That's so odd, isn't it. You'd think the travelling time would increase at least a little if you slowed down. Why do you think it doesn't?' Eddie said, trying to get Bridget's husband to speak as he hadn't said a word since they started driving.

'No idea.' As the words left Bridget's husband's mouth, it was clear that he wasn't interested in making conversation and he turned his head to look out of the window. Eddie wondered if he was crying.

They hit the Swindon rush hour traffic and there was nothing they could do but be patient. Bridget's husband vaguely asked if Eddie had one of those magnetic blue lights he could put on the car roof, to clear the traffic. Eddie explained he didn't, clarifying that it wasn't like it was on the TV and his fifteen-year-old, one litre Hyundai would look rather silly with a blue light on top. The sat nav thankfully decided to prove its worth and gave an alternative route, avoiding the traffic and cutting two minutes off the journey time. Eddie accepted the new route and in within seconds they were navigating the back streets of Swindon to the dulcet tones of the American woman who lived inside the sat nav. Eventually they arrived at the Accident and Emergency department.

Swindon District Hospital was known locally as The Bunker as its appearance reminded people of a nuclear bunker. It was indeed a grim building. Built in the 1960s, it had received the full force of post-war Brutalist design, with none of the added features that could have redeemed it slightly. Places like The Barbican in London at least had those repeating patterns, well-kept ponds, flower borders and interesting walkways. But Swindon District Hospital was grey, square and unwelcoming. Once you stepped inside though, it was like any other large Accident and

Emergency department – ordered chaos, orchestrated by brilliant, caring, professional staff seemingly conducted by an invisible god.

After a fraught journey to the hospital, Eddie and Bridget's husband found themselves sitting and waiting for what felt like an eternity. Eventually Eddie called Sylvie who was in the League of Friends café.

'Do you know where that is?' she asked Eddie, who had only tuned into the word league. Fortunately Bridget's husband seemed to know his way round the hospital. He led them to the café where Sylvie threw her arms around Eddie and then, despite not really knowing Bridget's husband, gave the weary looking man a hug too.

'Bridget's still being assessed, and they say we can't see her yet.' Sylvie could feel tears forming in her eyes but was determined not to cry.

'We'll see about that,' said Bridget's husband, marching off in a surprising burst of assertiveness to tackle a poor health care assistant who led him off to see the nurse in charge.

Alone with Eddie now, Sylvie told him that because of their quick actions, Bridget had been given some charcoal in the ambulance and because they knew it was poison the emergency doctor was able to act quickly once she arrived at hospital. Eddie felt as shaken as Sylvie looked but gently filled her in about the phone call from Tommo: it was about time she knew the truth about what had been happening.

'Verity Scanlan has been arrested in relation to the death of William Grant, and it looks like she also arranged for poisoned fudge to be sent to Bridget,' he explained to a horrified Sylvie. 'They are arresting other senior staff at the League as others must have been involved. I'm sorry Sylvie, this must all be such a shock.'

At that moment Eddie's phone pinged and he read the text message, 'Actually, it looks like Anthea is missing.'

Looking at Sylvie's face, Eddie thought how much had changed in the space of a few short weeks. The rosy-faced, dressed-up Sylvie that he had escorted to the Gala Ball had vanished, and been replaced with vulnerable Sylvie who had aged beyond her years and was completely exhausted. He hugged her.

'I don't know about you, Sylvie, but I'm starving.'

Sylvie agreed but looking at the food on offer in the hospital café, they decided they would both rather have a McDonald's. To Sylvie's amazement, Eddie took his phone out and ordered a McDonald's to be delivered to them at the hospital.

'Well, I never knew you could do that. I must tell Edgar when I get home. Do they do food other than McDonald's? I'm not sure it's his kind of thing.'

Eddie spent the next half an hour showing Sylvie all the different food delivery apps that he knew of and installing them on her phone. Once they had eaten their burgers, chips and something yummy called a McFlurry, the odd duo set off to see if there was any news on Bridget. They were relieved to find out that she had been moved to a ward and they could now visit her.

After navigating the endless, grey corridors of Swindon District Hospital, Eddie and Sylvie finally found their friend. Bridget was in a separate room that Sylvie said looked good enough to be a hotel room, except for the lino floor.

'It had an ensuite shower, TV and everything,' she told Edgar later that day.

Bridget's husband stood and gestured for them to come in, saying he would go and find some coffee. Looking towards the hospital bed, Sylvie and Eddie hardly recognised the hollow-faced, pale woman, who was dozing quietly. The person in the hospital bed looked nothing like their friend. Sylvie seemed to know what to do, so Eddie followed her lead. She sat down next to the bed and took Bridget's hand, so Eddie pulled up a chair and took the other one.

'Bridget,' Sylvie said softly. 'Bridget, are you awake? Can you hear me?' She squeezed Bridget's motionless hand as she spoke.

Bridget murmured and opened her eyes. A smile appeared on her lips as she quietly said, 'Hello, Sandra, it's so good to see you,' smiling a little more as she said the name Sandra.

At first Sylvie was horrified, Eddie was just confused, but then Bridget's smile broke into a little chuckle. 'Got you there, Sylvie, didn't I?'

Sylvie breathed a sigh of relief and laughed back.

'How are you feeling?' Eddie ventured, already knowing the likely answer.

'Bloody awful,' she said, louder than he was expecting, 'It was the fudge, Eddie. The fudge I thought Sylvie had sent me, but then she arrived with another box of fudge.'

Bridget needed to retell the story, but it was exhausting for her.

'I know. When they arrested Verity, they found her phone and saw a text message thread arranging the fudge. Just as we thought, it was how they arranged all the poisonous jams and other foods.'

'The League sent me a hamper a few days ago, which I didn't touch of course, so when the fudge arrived, I thought it was from you, Sylvie.'

Sylvie gasped as Bridget continued, 'I had no reason to suspect otherwise. That Verity, is very clever you know, more than we ever imagined. She's been arrested you say?'

Eddie wasn't sure he should keep talking, but Bridget waved her hand for him to continue.

'Yes, and they planned to arrest Anthea too, but they can't find her or her husband. I think they realised that you were onto them and Verity arranged Anthea's escape somehow.' Eddie stopped. 'Perhaps I should shut up for a bit and let *Sandra* speak.'

Sylvie pulled a face which made the three of them laugh and any remaining tension slipped from the room.

EIGHTY-THREE

After three frustrating days in hospital, Bridget was finally discharged. Driving home, her husband chatted gently, gauging her mood and consciously not bringing up subjects that might stress her out. Bridget appreciated this unusual level of self-awareness, something her husband rarely showed, and she planted a kiss on his cheek as they entered their home.

The kitchen table heaved under the weight of flowers from various family members and friends including a pretty bouquet from her art class. Ralph had made a card with a bird on the front and Bridget noted with a chuckle, that the bird's feet were hidden behind a leaf, to avoid him having to paint its claws. There was also a tasteful card from The Women's League, signed by the new acting Chief Executive, who simply wrote, 'We cannot apologise enough for what has happened – this doesn't reflect who The Women's League really are.'

Pouring a cup of Earl Grey tea, her husband asked her if

she wanted some lunch. She declined as her appetite had not fully recovered, although she was feeling better each day. They sat together quietly for a while, sipping their tea and making small talk. Eventually Bridget took a breath and spoke with a little more intention, 'I'm sorry about everything that's happened, my love. I never intended for it to get so out of control. I had my suspicions, but Eddie and I knew we needed real evidence.'

'I know. Eddie filled me in, love.'

'His boss just laughed at the suggestion of a nationwide, poisoning network – well you would, wouldn't you? It's ridiculous that something like that operated for years without detection. I just got caught in the crossfire so to speak.' Bridget took a breath and sighed. She was clearly fatigued but wanted to continue. 'I have started to accept that without our interfering, many more lives would have been lost and although it seems like the men killed were not nice people, no one deserves to die in that way.'

Her husband nodded. He had spent the last few days trying to figure out how on earth Bridget had become caught up in this awful situation, but now he wanted to forget about it all.

'You don't have to do portraits if you don't want to – you do know that.' He looked like he wanted to say something else, but his voice started to crack. 'I don't know what I would do without you, Bridget. I was so scared I was going to lose you.' He turned away from her as he struggled to finish his words.

Bridget knew this was as close as he ever got to demonstrating any kind of emotion, even after more than thirty years of marriage. Walking over to him, she made him face her. His face spoke a thousand words.

'Thank you. Yes. I'd already decided not to accept any portrait commissions for a while. But you are always so worried about money, and I always feel guilty about not earning more.' She struggled to get the words out so perhaps she found it just as difficult to talk as he did.

'Okay. It's all okay. We won't starve. Let's see how the rest of the year pans out. We need to get you better and try and get things back on an even keel. I could do with a break – why don't we plan some time away once you are fully recovered, eh?' He gently kissed her and for the first time in ages, Bridget remembered just how much she loved him.

'That's a great idea. I'm going to pop over to the studio for a while – I could do with tidying up and need to remember what I was doing before all of this happened.' Bridget squeezed her husband's shoulder as she stood to leave the room, saying, 'I do love you, sweetie'.

As she opened the door to the studio, she breathed in the familiar smell of oil paint and turpentine.

'Hello, old friend,' she said to the room, taking in the surroundings which felt different somehow. Although her husband had tried to clear up a little, there were tell-tale signs of what had happened a few days before. A few things were out of place and there was what looked like dried vomit on the sofa leg, which someone had missed. She also found a blue, plastic glove which she guessed was used by the paramedics.

Slowly she ran some warm, soapy water and sponged the sofa fabric, removing the poisoned-laced fudge vomit.

'Well, old sofa, that's a new one for you, isn't it!' Poisoned vomit removed, she found a Sharpie and drew a line around the stain that was forming, saying to no one in particular, 'One day someone will ask about that stain – what a great story.'

Sitting on the now vomit free sofa, with the walls bare, her studio was starting to feel a lot better. The memories of Verity Scanlan would take a while to fade but this at least was a start.

Bridget found the sketches and muddy drawings she had made at Severn Non-Beach and stuck them up on the wall instead. Gosh, it felt like a lifetime ago since she had that lovely day drawing and painting at that strange place. As she looked at the images she noticed the familiar stirring in her mind's eye. The muddy rivulets and beautiful colours of the swirling muddy river started to dance before her eyes. She could see interesting patterns and shapes emerging, things she could explore. Yes, she was ready to paint the landscape again.

EPILOGUE

Following the arrest of Verity Scanlan, the police discovered the full extent of the Jam Maker programme but admitted they may never unearth the full truth or the actual number of people who had been murdered over the years.

Detective Sargent Eddie Best was seconded to the Metropolitan Police in London for six weeks to help with the continued investigation into the Jam Maker murders. On his return to South Gloucestershire, he received a commendation for his work, alongside a discreet bollocking.

Six months after her arrest, the National Portrait Gallery asked permission to borrow the portrait of Verity Scanlan for an upcoming exhibition titled, *The Darker Side of Portraiture*. The CPS was initially reluctant but agreed to the request given that the weight of evidence was so large against Verity and the investigation was likely to last for many, many years.

Given that Bridget Sullivan now has a portrait in one of the most famous national galleries in the world, she is currently reconsidering her pledge never to paint portraits again.

ALREADY MISSING BRIDGET?

Her next adventure 'The Final Drop' is now available. You'll find it on Amazon…

To keep up with Bridget's future adventures and Jen's new book releases, sign up to her email newsletter and you'll get the first chapters of 'The Final Drop' FREE.

Sign up here:
https://bit.ly/455ad6o

…and follow Jen Gash on her socials here:
Jen Gash Author on Facebook: **https://bit.ly/4k3dJ5K**
Jen Gash on Tik Tok : **@jengashauthor**

And if you want to see Jen Gash's real life paintings, you can also follow her on Facebook:
https://bit.ly/4kwAkIb
Or on Instagram @jengash
https://www.instagram.com/jengash

www.ingramcontent.com/pod-product-compliance
Ingram Content Group UK Ltd.
Pitfield, Milton Keynes, MK11 3LW, UK
UKHW041943200725
461008UK00002B/80

9 781068 441905